DANGEROUS Witness

BOOK SEVEN

O'CONNOR BROTHERS

RHONDA BREWER

Dedication

This book is dedicated to my uncle, the late Hugh Westcott. My family lost him suddenly shortly before the release of this book. Uncle Hugh was a kind man, and when I would visit him, he would always say how proud he was that I took the chance and fulfilled my dream of being an author. Thank you, Uncle Hugh, for all your support and heaven certainly has gained another angel.

Acknowledgments

There are so many people to thank for making this book possible; I could almost write another book on that alone. A simple thank you never seems enough to convey my gratitude, but I will try to do that the best I can.

The first thank you goes to the ladies who help with editing and errors. Michelle Eriksen, Abbie Zanders, and Amabel Daniels are amazing women and dear friends. I want to thank them for their constant support and a keen eye. To my dedicated betas and dear friends, Jackie Dawe Ford, Nancy Arnold-Holloway, and Karie Deegan thank you so much for the support and encouragement. Also, a special thanks to the many authors who have become both friends and mentors. Last but certainly not least, to my readers. You are the reason that I can continue to do this.

A very special thank you to my husband, Danny who gives me the inspiration for the romantic heroes I write and encourages me every day. To my two children Laura and Colin, both of you show me every day how proud you are and how much you love me. To my beautiful granddaughter, Emma. You may not be old enough to read yet, but your smile inspires me to keep going. To my dad, James, I thank you for loving and supporting me every day.

I love all of you.

Prologue

September thirteen years ago….

Aaron O'Connor slumped against the lockers and listened to one of his best friends give a play by play of his date with one of the girls in grade twelve. Cory Fleming didn't have a player reputation but certainly wasn't a virgin. The fact he'd gone out with Raquel wasn't a huge leap. Raquel Evans was popular but not for her perky personality.

Holy Cross had gone from an all-boys school to a co-ed three years earlier. It was strange in the beginning, but the boys adjusted to it pretty quickly. Especially with girls like Raquel offering things that the boys only dreamed about. She was anything but the virginal Catholic girl.

"We drove up to Greeley's Peak around midnight," Cory whispered in a hushed tone. "Her idea. When I turned off the car, she was all over me. I swear at one point I thought she had ten hands."

Greeley's Peak was where teenagers hung out to do things that their parents would otherwise frown upon. It stood between Hopedale and the highway, and over the years a path had worn down that brought everyone to the top where it overlooked the harbor.

Sean and Kathleen O'Connor knew what went on up there and made it known to Aaron and his brothers they didn't fool them.

"Did she, you know, give you head?" Joey Mayo, the other friend in their trio, almost seemed as if he'd been the one getting his dick sucked.

He was the youngest of their group even though he was in the same grade. Joey, as they called him, was a little on the immature side but it didn't matter to Aaron or Cory. He was their friend.

"Not only did she mouth fuck me, but she swallowed." Cory wiggled his eyebrows.

"You two are the biggest perverts I've ever met." Aaron chuckled as he shoved his hands into his grey school pants pockets.

His friends might be perverts, but Aaron got hard hearing Cory's story. Not that he was interested in Raquel putting her mouth anywhere near his junk, but he was an eighteen-year-old red-

blooded guy. Aaron was the only one of his group who hadn't gotten past first base with a girl. Not because he couldn't, he didn't want to be that guy.

The very open about sex talks with his parents made Aaron and his brothers cringe. They were open about everything sometimes to a fault, but they wanted their sons to be sure they were ready before they went that far. Aaron tried to abide by that. As difficult as it was at times.

Aaron was the youngest of seven brothers and the only one left in high school. The two oldest John and James were fraternal twins and started their second year as police officers in St. John's. Ian was in the middle of medical school and only came home to Hopedale on weekends or holidays.

Keith was ready to move to Yellowknife to find out what he wanted to do with the rest of his life. He'd finished university with a Business Degree in less than three years and seemed to be a little lost. He was considered something of a genius because of his eidetic memory which was why he wanted to find his own way.

Mike was in his third year of university and headed to law school in Ontario the following fall. Then there was Nick who started his first year of university and was preparing to be a lawyer as well.

"Jealous, O'Connor?" Cory gave Aaron a playful punch in the shoulder.

"That you let Raquel fucking Evans suck you off? Not a chance. I wouldn't touch her with a ten-foot pole." Aaron snorted.

Stories circulated in school, Hopedale, and the other small communities about Raquel sleeping with guys all over the place. Rumors were not something Aaron liked to spread, but she didn't seem the least bit ashamed of her reputation. In fact, she bragged about what she was willing to do.

"A.J, can I get a ride home with you today?" his cousin, Kristy shouted as she hurried toward him.

"Why can't you take the bus home?" Aaron didn't mind driving her home, but he also didn't want to get in shit if she was supposed to go home on the school bus.

"I've got choir after school, and since you have basketball, I don't have to bother Isabelle to come get me." Kristy was one of four female cousins that were like sisters to him and his brothers.

"Sure, just make sure you're done by five because Uncle Kurt will kick my ass if I'm not at Karate by six." Kurt was his father's younger brother and Kristy's father.

Kurt O'Connor was a police officer, and he'd heard it said more than once that his uncle would be Chief of Police someday. Aaron didn't doubt it. Kurt was highly decorated and spent a lot of his free time volunteering with kids from all over the province. He was a Shihan in Karate which meant a senior instructor with a fourth dan black belt and taught Aaron, his brothers and cousins Karate.

"I will. Thanks, cuz." Kristy continued down the corridor, giggling with a couple of her friends.

"Your cousin gets hotter every day." Joey leered at Kristy as she disappeared into one of the classrooms.

"Hands off, Mayo. One, Uncle Kurt will kick your ass if you even think about touching her and two, she would kick your ass." Aaron shoved Joey.

"Hi, A.J." Aaron's head turned to the right as Raquel stepped behind Cory.

She winked the way she always did, and as usual, her school blouse was unbuttoned down to where her ample cleavage was visible to anyone who wanted a peek. She'd been warned numerous times about keeping her uniform buttoned, but she'd make a point of popping a button or two when she was around the guys.

"No hi for me?" Cory wrapped his arm around the girl he'd been bragging about not ten minutes earlier.

"Of course." She leaned in and practically shoved her tongue down Cory's throat.

Aaron rolled his eyes. He knew what she was doing. Raquel tried everything to get him to go out with her since grade ten, but he wasn't interested. Not in a girl like her.

Nick was eleven months older than Aaron and graduated the year before. The month Nick graduated she cornered him on Greeley's Peak and told him she could rock his world. Knowing her reputation, Nick declined, and now Raquel had her sights set on Aaron. It was no secret she wanted to bag an O'Connor.

"Excuse me." A quiet female voice interrupted his thoughts.

Aaron turned his head, and his breath caught as his eyes met the prettiest green eyes he'd ever seen. The glasses she wore brightened her eyes, and faint freckles appeared across her tiny nose. Her light-brown hair was pulled back into a high ponytail, and small tendrils framed her pretty face.

"I need to get into my locker." She motioned toward the locker behind Aaron.

"God, Beatrice. Can't you wait until our conversation is finished?" Raquel snapped at the pretty girl.

"My name's Bethany, and I've got to get my chemistry book for class." Bethany's voice trembled as she responded to Raquel.

"Nobody cares what your name is, Butterball." Raquel snarled.

"You weren't actually talking to anyone, Raquel. I'm pretty sure your tongue was down Cory's throat," Aaron snapped.

"Jealous, A.J?" she purred.

Aaron bit his tongue as he stepped out of Bethany's way. He disliked Raquel, but he was quickly on the way to hating the bitch. Since she wasn't in his circle of friends, Aaron didn't have to put up with her very often. Except when she hit on him, but he'd witnessed her bully other girls and guys frequently.

The one time he saw her get what she deserved was when she set her eyes on Kristy. During lunch the previous year, she told Kristy she needed to stuff her bra a little because the boys were going to think she wasn't a girl. Kristy smiled sweetly as she stood over Raquel.

"I'm going to tell you this once, Raquel. I'm not easily intimidated by you or anyone. I may not have your overinflated balloons, but it's because I work out every day with my dad, you know, the police officer who teaches me how to defend myself, taught me to have respect for myself. The next time you try to make me feel bad, I may show you how much I can hurt someone with one hand." Kristy stood up, smiled, and sauntered away, leaving Raquel wide-eyed.

She never picked on his cousin again or any of Kristy's friends. Raquel knew better than to push his cousin. Kristy really could hurt someone with one hand.

Aaron glanced back behind at Bethany fumbling in her locker as if she wanted to get away quickly. Aaron sometimes wished that someone else would stand up to Raquel and stop her reign of terror on other students. It was pointless for him to do it because she always twisted it around as him fighting his attraction to her.

Bethany retrieved her book, closed her locker, and started down the hall as if she couldn't get away fast enough. As she tried to make her way around them, Raquel stuck out her foot so it wouldn't be noticeable but still sufficient to trip Bethany. Aaron winced as the poor girl fell onto her hands and knees.

"Oops," Raquel pressed her fingers against her lips as Bethany struggled to get up and gather her things.

"What the hell is wrong with you?" Aaron snarled at Raquel as he crouched to help Bethany retrieve her things.

"Seriously, you're going to defend her? She should be more careful where she's walking. I'm not surprised. It's probably hard to hold up all that fat." Raquel laughed as well as a couple of other girls that everyone referred to as her shadows.

"Are you okay?" Aaron ignored Raquel as he moved his attention back to Bethany.

"I'm fine." Bethany's voice cracked as she scrambled to pick up her things.

Aaron grabbed a calculator and book that slid across the corridor when she fell. When he glanced in her direction, she was ready to burst into tears. It broke his heart.

"Come on." Aaron held out his hand to her. "We're in the same class."

He nodded to the name of the teacher on the cover of her book. Aaron had the same class himself and was suddenly happy to be heading to chemistry class. She stared at him without moving, and he glanced up at his friends behind her. He didn't want to scare her or make her think he was friends with Raquel. Thank God, his friends picked up on his silent plea to help him.

"You don't want to be late for Mr. Grant's class." Aaron smiled.

"A.J.'s right, Grant is a hard ass." Joey stepped behind Aaron and gave the girl a friendly smile.

Bethany tentatively put her hand in Aaron's, and he helped her to her feet. When she stood, she snatched her hand back as Aaron returned her things.

"I'm Aaron O'Connor, but everyone calls me A.J. This is Joseph Mayo, but we call him Joey, and that guy there is Cory Fleming, and we call him lots of things but none I would say in front of a lady. We're all in Mr. Grant's chem class." Aaron shoved his hands into his pockets.

"It's my second day at this school." She smiled, but it didn't meet her eyes as she glanced at Raquel and her shadows.

"The first week in a new school is the worst, but you only missed a few days of classes. It'll be easy to catch up. Welcome to Holy Cross Senior High." Aaron bowed with a flourish and finally got a giggle out of her.

"Beatrice, don't get used to them being nice to you. He only wants to get in your pants. Well, maybe not yours. I mean look at you." Raquel's eyes traveled up and down Bethany with disgust in her expression.

Anger bubbled inside him, and he opened his mouth to defend the pretty girl next to him. Before he had a chance to say a word, Cory yanked his arm away from Raquel and stepped next to Bethany.

"I'm pretty sure she said her name was Bethany," Cory growled. "And there is nothing wrong with how she looks. You're such a bitch."

"And I've seen bigger dicks on a guinea pig," Raquel spat at Cory.

"You don't have to worry about that anymore because you won't see this one again." Cory pointed to his crotch.

Raquel spun on their heels and stomped down the corridor in the opposite direction with her shadows right behind her. When Aaron turned back to Bethany, she was already halfway down the hall toward the classroom.

"Hey, don't mind her. She's probably the biggest bitch in the school," Aaron said when he'd caught up with Bethany.

"It's fine. I'm used to her. She's lived next door to me for over a year." Bethany sighed as she hurried down the hall.

Aaron didn't like the sound of that and was about to say as much, but Mr. Grant called out from the entrance to his class. The one thing you didn't do at Holy Cross High school was, be late for Oliver Grant's classes.

"Sorry, Mr. Grant, we were just getting to know our new student." Cory walked by the teacher with a grin.

"Ms. Donnelly, are these boys bothering you?" the teacher asked Bethany.

"No, sir." She shook her head as she made her way to the desk closest to the door.

"That's not nice, Mr. Grant. Why would you assume the worst of us?" Joey stood next to the teacher as more students hurried into the classroom.

"Because I've known you boys since grade ten, Mr. Mayo." Mr. Grant pointed his finger into the classroom.

Aaron was a little confused as to why Mr. Grant knew Bethany since she'd said it was her second day. It wasn't his business, but it was apparent they knew each other.

Bethany took the first seat in the first row as soon as she entered the classroom. Aaron usually headed right to the back of the room but decided he wanted to get to know this girl. For the first time in his life, he sat in the desk at the front of the classroom right next to her.

"Planning on actually doing some work this year, Mr. O'Connor?" Mr. Grant closed the door to the classroom and locked it.

The teacher would always lock the classroom door at the start of class. If anyone was not on time for the class, they couldn't sneak in without a lecture.

"Just because I sit in the back usually doesn't mean I don't work hard, sir." Aaron grinned.

Mr. Grant rolled his eyes, but Aaron didn't miss the twitch of his lips. He'd had the teacher for the last two years for chemistry, and although he was a hard ass, Mr. Grant was one of his favorite teachers.

Aaron glanced toward Bethany and winked. A slight blush turned her pale skin a beautiful shade of pink. She was cute and a girl he wanted to get to know.

Chapter 1

Bethany waved to her sister and nephew as they disappeared through the door. Allyson and Cameron were going back to Newfoundland and leaving her alone in Ontario. It was her choice of course, but Bethany would miss the only family she had in Toronto.

Thirteen years ago, Bethany left her hometown in Hopedale, Newfoundland, because her high school sweetheart shattered her heart. He'd asked her out a month after arriving at the high school, and for the rest of the year, they were together almost every day.

They'd even gone to the senior prom together, and it was that night they both lost their virginity. At first, it was awkward, but he'd been so sweet and gentle. The night was magical, but the next day when they returned to school to retrieve their report cards, her heart broke.

June, thirteen years ago….

Bethany stared at herself in the mirror of the girl's bathroom. She didn't look any different, but she was. Aaron had been so gentle with her and made sure she was completely ready before he pushed inside her.

She closed her eyes as she thought about the way her heart raced and how strange it felt at first. It was obvious neither of them had experience, but somehow, he made her body tremble as he brought her to orgasm just before he did himself.

She hadn't seen him since the prom the previous night. His grandfather fell ill and ended up in the hospital. Aaron called her that morning and said he'd be in school by lunchtime to get his report card and he'd tell her all about his Grandda.

Bethany's thoughts were interrupted when she heard a voice that made her stomach churn. She ran into the nearest stall and pulled her legs up so nobody could see if they looked under the stall.

"Come on, Raquel, you never told us how it happened," one voice whined.

"Yeah, all you said it was the best you've ever had." The other voice giggled.

Bethany knew both voices well, as well as the one they were begging for information. Celine Hearn and Denise Rowan, otherwise known as the shadows of Raquel Evans. She disliked all three girls since they bullied her constantly. When they found out Bethany and Aaron were dating, things got worse.

They called her fat, tubby, and their favorite was Butterball. Raquel would blatantly flirt with Aaron and make sure her assets *were on display for him to see. Bethany did her best to avoid them unless she was with Aaron's cousin Kristy. They kept their distance from his feisty cousin.*

"You girls are so desperate." Raquel giggled.

"Of course, we are. You've been saying all year you'd get him in bed and when you do you keep your mouth shut." Celine's voice was a little louder than it probably should have been inside the hollow sounding room.

"Jesus, Celine. Keep your voice down," Raquel whispered.

"Sorry, I'm just itching to find out if what they say about him and his brothers is true."

"What do they say?" Denise asked.

"They're all hung like horses, and they know what they are doing in bed." Celine sighed.

"I don't kiss and tell. Or in this case, fuck and tell." Raquel sighed, but Bethany could hear the hint of arrogance.

"Since when don't you brag?" Denise snickered.

"You finally fuck A.J. O'Connor, and you keep it from us." Celine sounded in awe, but all Bethany felt was devastation and sick to her stomach.

"He made me promise to keep it quiet until he can dump the Butterball. He said fucking her was like fucking a fat cow. When he dropped her off last night, he met me at Greeley's Peak." Raquel

giggled. "But I will say this, A.J. knows how to use what he got, and he's got plenty."

"When are you seeing him again?" Celine asked.

"Well, since he won the bet with Cory about getting into Butterball's pants, he should be dropping her like a hot rock sooner rather than later." Raquel snickered. "Then we can fuck whenever we want."

With that statement, the three girls left the bathroom giggling. Bethany jumped to her feet just in time to throw up into the toilet as tears poured from her eyes.

Bethany had to find out for sure if it was true. Aaron asked her to meet him at his locker after lunch, and she wiped the tears from her face as she made her way out of the bathroom.

Bethany saw him with Cory and Joey right where he told her to meet him. It was hard to believe he could do what Raquel said and she'd almost convinced herself it wasn't true, but it was what Cory said that had her stop in her tracks.

"I can't believe you won the fucking bet." Cory slapped an envelope into Aaron's hand.

"I told you I don't lose. When I want something, I get it." Aaron shoved the envelope into his backpack.

"I have to say I'm impressed that you pulled it off." Joey handed another envelope to Aaron.

"It was a piece of cake, and I've got big plans for these four hundred dollars from you two losers and the two hundred I have tucked away." Aaron laughed.

Raquel didn't make up the story. No. Aaron used her to win a bet. He'd strung her along until he got into her pants so that he could win four hundred dollars. He took her virginity and her heart all to win a bet.

Bethany kept her head down as she spun around and made her way to the exit. She didn't care that she didn't have her report card yet. They could mail it to her. She needed to get home. She had to get as far away from school before she ran into Aaron. If anyone was going to end their relationship, it wasn't going to be him.

As she rode her bike home, she made the decision. She was going to Ontario with her sister and father. There, she'd forget all about Aaron O'Connor and his cheating ways.

Bethany shook her head and gulped down the lump in her throat at the painful memory. Allyson begged her to move back to Newfoundland with her and Bethany wanted to go back to be with her father, and she would have, had he not decided to move back to Hopedale once Allyson returned.

She did miss the small town and definitely missed all her old friends. Aaron's cousins Kristy and Jess were two of her best friends, and it was one of her few regrets in life that she didn't tell them the real reason she left Newfoundland.

17

Her excuse had been believable since her sister and father decided to move because Allyson's fiancé was posted in Ontario. Bethany told them she wanted to be with her family and although they were surprised at the sudden decision, they understood. Aaron didn't.

Bethany shook the memories from her head as she made her way out of the airport and headed to her office. She was going to be over an hour early but going back to her empty apartment was not something she wanted to do at that moment.

Bethany was a pharmaceutical sales rep for National Pharmaceuticals based in Ontario. Her boss, Craig Molloy, was also from Newfoundland and it was one of the reasons he'd hired her eight years earlier right out of university.

Craig pushed a lot lately for her to take over the Newfoundland district. She would laugh and ask if he was trying to get rid of her, but the truth was she hadn't been back to Newfoundland in thirteen years. Her excuse was her family lived in Ontario, but with her dad and sister moved back home, that excuse would no longer fly.

The sun was up by the time she made it to the building where she worked. Since it was a little after six in the morning, she knew nobody would be in the office, and she would need to use her key card to enter the building.

Her heels clicked along the pavement as she made her way to the entrance, and she struggled with her briefcase and supply case as she searched for her entry card. Before she made it to the front step, the door to the main entrance opened, and a smiling security guard greeted her.

"Morning, Ms. Donnelly." Harrison Chapman, the building security guard, gave her a friendly smile.

"Morning, Harrison." Bethany stepped inside the door as he closed and locked it behind her.

"You're here early today." He made his way behind his desk.

"I had to drop my sister and nephew off at the airport. I figured it was easier to come to the office instead of going back to my apartment at this time of day. It saves me the aggravation of fighting traffic later on this morning." Bethany hit the up button on the elevator.

"Smart lady." He sat back in his chair and chuckled.

The door to the elevator opened and she stepped inside. As the elevator moved smoothly up to the tenth floor, Bethany scrolled through the emails on her phone.

There was one from her sister, telling her they were getting ready to take off and several from her boss. There were also a few from local drug stores. By the look of her email, it would be a long day.

The doors of the elevator opened, and she stepped out and turned right to head to the office. It wasn't the first time she'd come to work early which was why she was surprised to see Craig standing in the doorway to his office. A concerned look on his face.

"Craig, you're an early bird today." Bethany turned the knob to her office.

"I didn't go home last night. Beth, I need to talk to you." His serious expression concerned her.

"Let me drop this on my desk, and I'll come to see you." Bethany pushed open the door to her corner office.

"Okay." Craig turned and disappeared as he closed his door.

She trembled as she dropped her things on her desk. Bethany had a feeling that what Craig was about to say was terrible news, but she couldn't think of anything she'd done that would get her fired. He'd always told her she was the best sales rep he had which was why he wanted her to take over the Newfoundland district.

She took a deep breath, squared her shoulders, and walked confidently toward her boss's door. Before she could knock, he pulled open the door and motioned for her to come inside. He hurried around his desk and plopped down in his seat.

"Craig, what's wrong?" Bethany couldn't take it anymore.

"I know I've asked you this, and you've declined several times, but you're the only one I can trust to do this." Craig held out a thick folder to her. "I need you to take over the Newfoundland district. This isn't a request."

Bethany's heart practically flipped over in her chest. She'd never seen him so tense or concerned. She placed the folder on her lap and slowly opened it. Nothing out of the ordinary seemed to be inside as she flipped through page after page of invoices for orders.

"Why would you want to take this away from Randy? From the look of this, he's doing great." Bethany was impressed with the number of sales the current district rep had completed.

"You would think he was, wouldn't you? That is until I made a call to one of the pharmacies he's sold several cases of opioids. I wanted to see if they were happy with him. I know it's not my job, but I do it from time to time, and before you ask, all your clients love you." Craig smiled.

"Good to know." Bethany looked through the invoices.

"There are two things I found out when I called Larry." Craig handed her another piece of paper.

"What?" Bethany glanced down at the paper.

"They didn't buy anything from him. They didn't even know him." Craig sighed.

"He's sending in false orders?" Bethany stared at the paper that he gave her.

"Yes, I know this is not your job, but I need you to go to Newfoundland and check out all these invoices. I can't confront Randy until I know everything." Craig plowed his hands through his greying hair. "I know your family moved back to Newfoundland for good and I don't know what your aversion to going back there is, and it's frankly none of my business, but you are the only one I trust with this."

Bethany stared at her boss for a moment. Was he serious? He should be calling the police about all this, not using one of his sales reps to do an investigation. The thought of going home gave her a multitude of emotions, but she loved her job, and the idea that one of her co-workers could do something like this angered her.

"Maybe you should contact the police," Bethany suggested.

"I need to have an internal investigation done first." He sighed.

"Craig, I don't know if I'm qualified to do this." Bethany held up the folder.

"You are the best one to do it. You are good with clients and Randy wouldn't think twice about you dropping into the Newfoundland office since I've told him I'm trying to get you to take over a portion of the district." Craig smiled.

"That's not what you wanted me to do, Craig." Bethany shook her head because he wanted her to take the whole section over.

"I know, but he doesn't need to know that. Please, Beth." Craig folded his hands in front of him on the desk.

Bethany stared at her for a moment. Craig was in his late fifties and still quite handsome with the grey flecks streaking his dark-brown hair. He'd lost his wife a few years back and recently started seeing a woman from back home. Her boss took several trips home during the year since his kids and brother still lived there. With his new girlfriend, he had more reasons to travel back and forth.

"So, you want me to go back and get the proof you need to have him arrested and take over that position." Bethany raised an eyebrow because she knew that was what he wanted.

"I need to know where these drugs are going. I got a sick feeling that Randy's selling them to people that shouldn't have them and yes, I want you there to take over, but mostly I don't want my company to be known for selling drugs to criminals," Craig admitted with a slight grin.

As much as it scared Bethany to think what kind of people Randy could be dealing with, she was pissed enough that he would be using a reputable company to do it.

"I'll do it." Bethany held out her hand and nodded.

What the fuck am I doing?

Chapter 2

Aaron jumped down off the small stage at *Jack's Place* where his cover band just finished for the night. His Aunt Alice divided the building into two businesses. She turned one side into a diner, and the other an Irish pub. They'd opened it when Aaron was in high school, and it had become a meeting place for not only his family but all the residents of Hopedale.

His grandfather had been so proud to have his name on the business, but unfortunately, he passed away not long after it opened. That year Aaron lost two people he loved. Grandda and Bethany Donnelly.

He saw the group of men around the three tables pulled together and glanced toward the bar. The new bartender was Nick's soon to be brother-in-law and was loading a tray with several shots. Aaron sauntered over to the bar and leaned over the bar to turn off the switch for the stage lights.

"Why is it I always end up shutting all that shit down?" Aaron grumbled as he nodded his head toward where the other members of his band were laughing and tossing back drinks.

"Come on, how often do all your brothers get away from the ball and chains at the same time?" Ethan Norris poured another ten shots and carefully placed them on the almost full tray.

"Good point. Now Nick is joining their merry band of collared men." Aaron grabbed the tray and motioned for Ethan to join them.

Ethan's younger sister was engaged to Nick and Lora wasn't the only one to wrap Nick around her finger. Lora's daughter could have his older brother jumping with just a flick of her finger. Aaron was happy for Nick and all his brothers for that matter, but part of him envied them.

Aaron lost the woman he'd thought he was meant to be with the last day of high school. She ended their relationship the day after their prom and moved to the mainland. With his heart shattered, he started on a path that turned him into what his brothers called a player.

"So this is what happens when a bunch of old married men gets together." Aaron placed the tray of filled shot glasses in the center of the tables.

"Hey, I'm not married." Cory grabbed a glass from the tray.

"Neither am I." Jason Brenton a school friend of Aaron's other brother Mike and also played in the band.

"I'm not married either." Joey winked at his life partner Braden Payne.

"Just because you're here with a bunch of hot men doesn't mean you're not taken. You remember that, hot buns." Braden narrowed his eyes at Joey.

Aaron and Cory had been shocked when Joey came out after high school. It didn't change their friendship at all; in fact, it probably made it stronger. When Joey met Braden eight years earlier, he'd introduced his new partner to Aaron and Cory first.

Braden was funny and kind of reminded Aaron of a gay male version of Sandy. He didn't care what he said to anyone and spoke like a sailor who'd been out to sea for too long.

"Time to put a ring on that, Joey." One of Aaron's brothers, James, chuckled.

"We're already married in the true sense of the word." Braden wiggled his eyebrows and Joey blushed.

"I'm not married either, but I envy you bunch of bastards." Aaron glanced toward one of the large men sat on the other side of the table.

Brent 'Crash' Adams worked for Keith and Kristy's husband Dean 'Bull' Nash. They ran a high-end security firm called Newfoundland Security Services or NSS for short. They'd moved it from Yellowknife to Hopedale almost ten years earlier, and since then, all the men that worked for the company had become like part of the family.

"Me too, having something warm and soft to go home and crawl in next to. You're a bunch of lucky assholes." Ben 'Trunk' Murphy, another of the guys that worked for Keith, raised the shot glass and then tossed it back.

"I don't envy them. One woman. Every day for the rest of your life." Aaron feigned a shudder. "I like variety."

"Little brother, just because you have one woman for the rest of your life doesn't mean you can't have variety in the bedroom." Keith wiggled his eyebrows.

"There's a lot to be said for being married to a woman willing to try anything once." Ian winked.

"You're wasting your breath on him, bro. A.J. likes the ones who follow him around like a lost puppy," Mike teased, and Aaron wanted to punch him.

Aaron had been seeing a woman on and off for a few months. More off than on and it was more for sex than anything else. The problem started when he told her he wanted to end things. Jocelyn Rees didn't take rejection easily and from that point on seemed to show up everywhere Aaron did.

Luckily, she couldn't get to his residence. Aaron lived on Keith's secure property that most people referred to as *The*

Compound. A seven-foot fence surrounded the entire three acres of land, and the only entrance was an iron gate. Nobody could get on the property unless they were allowed in or had a code.

"How is your stalker these days?" James taunted.

"She was front and center when we were on stage," John teased.

"Come on, guys. We've all had women like her." Nick handed Aaron a shot glass.

"She stood outside the gate for two hours last week and tried to convince Hulk to let her onto the property. She wanted to surprise A.J." Keith nodded toward another of his employees.

"Offered to make my world rock if I let her in." Bruce 'Hulk' Steel snorted.

"Okay, A.J., I can't even help with that level of crazy." Nick laughed.

"Sweet Jesus, even I wouldn't be that crazy." Braden snatched a shot glass off the table.

"Maybe we can get Abbie to pretend she's your girlfriend and scare her off," Mike snickered, referring to his wife's best friend.

The light growl from Trunk told Aaron that the man was still pining over the spunky woman. Why Trunk wasn't making a move on her was beyond Aaron but then again what did he know. He was currently trying to avoid all women for a while.

"Great set tonight, guys." Ethan held up a shot glass, and each of the men did the same. "Long may yer big jib draw."

After the group helped Ethan clean the pub and lock up, they all headed to their homes. Since everyone lived within a fifteen-minute walk of the pub, nobody had to worry about driving after they'd been drinking. They'd get their asses kicked by their father and uncle if they even tried it.

The slight nip in the April air was typical for the time of year, but after being behind the heat of the stage lights all night, the chilly wind was a blessing. Aaron waved at each of the men as they broke off and went to their homes. He and Keith lived the farthest from the pub. By the time they got to the end of Harbour Street, it was just him and Keith.

Keith strolled next to him in silence, a look of contentment on his face. It was an expression all his brothers had since they met the loves of their lives. Again, Aaron felt that twinge of jealousy.

"She'll get the hint eventually." Keith dropped his big hand on Aaron's shoulder as they turned on to Main Road.

"I'm not worried about it." Aaron laughed.

"I heard you were helping Father Wallace with the one-hundred-year anniversary of Holy Cross." Keith dropped his hand and shoved them into the pocket of his ever-present leather jacket.

"Yeah, I'm there practically every week anyway." Aaron had been coaching the baseball team and basketball team for the last couple of years.

"Still coaching the boys?" Keith asked.

"Yep, it's a lot of fun. Reminds me of when we were kids, and Uncle Kurt used to coach us." Aaron smiled.

"I'm proud of you, A.J." Keith stopped as they walked in front of his property.

"Thanks?" Aaron stared at his brother with a raised eyebrow.

"Don't look at me like that. Sure, you're a, what is it Sandy calls you? Oh yeah, whore boy." Keith chuckled as he punched the code into the panel next to the gate.

"Fuck off." Aaron shoved him as they walked through the large iron gate.

"Seriously, you're a damn good cop." Keith stopped at the path to his own house.

"How much did you have to drink tonight?" Aaron laughed.

"Not too much that I couldn't kick your ass if I wanted to." Keith held up his fists in a boxing stance.

"I don't fight with senior citizens." Aaron snickered as he bounced back to avoid a playful swing of a fist from his brother.

"Okay, boys. It's time for Keith to come in and go to bed." Aaron and Keith glanced up at the open door.

Emily smiled at them as she crooked her finger at Keith. Like a lap dog, his brother's tongue practically hung out, and he gave Aaron a wink as he dropped his hands.

"Sorry, bro, I got someone else to play with." Keith wiggled his eyebrows as he practically ran up the steps to his house and pushed his blushing wife into the house.

"Lucky bastard," Aaron grumbled as he trudged his way to the small bunkhouse at the back of the property.

Aaron pushed open the door, kicked off his boots and headed for the small kitchen. Even after a fun night of playing music and tossing back a few with his brothers and friends, he still felt empty.

Over the last couple of months, he'd been drifting back to the last time he'd been in a serious relationship and the only one he could remember was high school. Bethany was the only steady girlfriend he'd ever had in his life, and he could never get her out of his mind.

Aaron had been head over heels in love with the girl, and the night of their prom, he'd shown her just how much he did. Then the next day, as if it meant nothing, she met him on the beach and dumped him. The same night he had planned to propose to her.

The beginning of grade twelve, Aaron, Cory, and Joey had made a bet on who would graduate with the highest average. Each month they put twenty dollars into a jar in their rooms and on the day report cards went out, the highest grade average got the money.

It turned out to be six hundred dollars, and Aaron won by three marks. He'd gone out the week before and put an engagement ring on hold and paid when he won the bet. He'd planned to propose to Bethany at the end-of-the-year bonfire the high school students had on the beach.

He'd been so nervous as he watched her walking across the beach but when she stopped in front of him, and she pulled away when he reached for her, his heart had dropped. Two minutes later, she tore his heart out when she said she was moving to the mainland with her father and sister. Since Aaron was in shock, Bethany was halfway up the beach before he thought to run and stop her. It didn't change her mind because she told him to leave her alone and left him with a crushed heart.

"Yep, that's why you're not stupid enough to fall in love again." Aaron chugged a bottle of water and then headed to his bedroom.

The buzzing next to him made him want to take out his weapon and shoot whatever was causing it. He lifted his aching head off the pillow and glanced at his cell phone vibrating on the nightstand. He snatched it off the night table and cursed when he saw the number on the screen.

"You've got to be fucking kidding me." Aaron hit ignore and groaned at the time.

It had been almost three in the morning by the time he got home and then a little after four by the time he finally passed out. He didn't think he was that drunk, but his pounding head told him otherwise. His headache only intensified as he saw Jocelyn's number on his phone at seven in the morning.

He tossed the phone on the table again and flopped back on the bed. When the phone vibrated again, he flung his arm over his eyes and groaned a string of curses that would make a sailor blush.

"What the fuck do you want?" Aaron didn't bother to look at the number on the phone as he answered.

"Aaron Jacob, is that any way to talk to your mother?" Aaron cringed as he pulled the phone away and glanced at the time.

It was after eleven, and he hadn't even realized he'd fallen asleep after the first phone call. Now he had to explain his nasty attitude toward his mother of all people.

"I'm so sorry, Mom. I didn't know it was you." He kicked off the heavy quilt and sat up on the side of the bed.

"A.J., that's not the way to answer the phone for anyone." Kathleen O'Connor always had a way of making him feel as if he was eight years old and chastised for being a naughty boy.

"I know, and I'm sorry." Aaron knew no explanation was going to make his mother understand how he'd answered the phone.

"I just wanted to let you know we have some old friends over for our Sunday family supper." His mother began.

Aaron squeezed his eyes shut as he held in the curse that threatened to escape. Kathleen O'Connor's famous family supper had become much more than the family gathering. It had become more of a community potluck with the number of people she continually invited for gathering.

"Mom, in all the years you've had Sunday family supper when did you ever call to tell me who you were inviting?" Aaron teased her all the time about needing to build a bigger house all the time.

"Well, these are probably going to be a little uncomfortable for you," his mother confessed.

"Mom, please tell me you didn't invite Jocelyn and her friend Kylie?" Aaron groaned.

"Heavens, no. Those two are … I'm not going to say what I think of those two but the guests coming today… well, they…" His mother stopped.

"Mom, who is it?" Aaron couldn't understand why his mother acted so evasive.

"It's Lewis Donnelly and Allyson." His mother's tone was apologetic.

"Okay." Aaron's heart felt as if it stopped in his chest.

"Bethany's not here. Lewis moved back with Allyson and her son. The poor girl lost her husband. Poor man got killed overseas." His mother, always the soft heart.

"That's terrible." Aaron forced out the words but what he wanted to say was, 'Where is Bethany? Is she back in Newfoundland? Is she married?'

Fuck! What is wrong with me?

"You're still coming to supper, right?" The tone said it wasn't a request, it was an order.

"Yes, Mom. I'll be there. Why would you think I wouldn't?" Aaron sighed.

"You were so crushed when Bethany left. I thought it might be too hard to see her family." His mom always knew how to get to the point.

"Mom, that was thirteen years ago," Aaron replied, but it still stung like it was yesterday.

"Yes, and you still haven't been able to settle down and find the right girl because she was it for you. Cora said that years ago." His mother returned with a roll of his eyes.

Cora the cupid. His father's younger sister was supposed to have some weird gift and knew when couples were meant to be together. He remembered her telling him Bethany was the one for him back then, and he believed it. Then she left and as far as he knew, it was the only time she was ever wrong.

"Yeah, I know I'm the only strike on her perfect cupid record." Aaron chuckled.

"It's not a strike yet." His mom singsonged before she told him she loved him and reminded him to be there on time.

Aaron tossed his phone on the bed and scuffed his way to the shower. If he was going to see Bethany's family, he was going to look his best. He had no idea why, but they weren't going to be able to go back and tell Bethany that she made a good choice in dumping him all those years ago.

"That's not the least bit pathetic." Aaron groaned to himself.

Chapter 3

Bethany felt guilty for not telling her sister and dad she was back in Newfoundland. She'd call them when she finished with the job Craig had sent her to do.

She arrived the night before, but exhaustion kept her from doing anything productive. Bethany went straight to the hotel and plopped down on the bed, but she couldn't put it off anymore. She needed to make her way to the small office where Randy Knight worked.

It was a little after nine by the time she made her way to downtown St. John's and got to the sixth floor of the office building on the end of Water Street. It was a new building, and Craig said the rent was cheap because they were trying to fill the building fast. He'd given her the code to the office and told her Randy was aware she was dropping in to meet with him, but Craig didn't tell him how soon.

Of course, he didn't know the real reason she'd been sent to meet with him. She pushed open the door and entered the tiny reception area that didn't appear used. She took a couple of steps toward the closed office door but stopped when she heard angry voices coming from inside.

Bethany moved to hear the voices and see if it was possible to eavesdrop on the argument. As she got closer, it became easier to distinguish the conversation between two men and a woman. She saw an open bathroom door next to the office and stepped inside in case they came out.

"I told you I couldn't send any more orders. I've explained all this to your other guy. My boss is getting suspicious and is already asking questions about my invoices. Your boss needs to back off." Bethany recognized Randy's voice.

"You won't be dealing with the boss anymore. You're dealing with me, and I need more, and you're gonna fuckin' get it." The tone of the other man's voice made Bethany shudder.

"Give it a couple of months, and I'll place another order. I assure you." Randy's voice quivered.

"Melvin, baby, calm down." A female voice cooed.

"Go down to the car, and I'll deal with this. You did your job already, now go." The other man roared.

"You're such a prick. I'm out of here. Good luck with this dicktard, Randy." The woman snapped.

Bethany pressed her body against the bathroom wall as the door opened and slammed shut again as she heard the unmistakable sound of spiked heels clicking against the hard floor as the woman stomped out of the office. Bethany held her breath until she heard the click of the other door closing. She probably should have tried to get a glimpse of the woman, but she was afraid of being seen.

"Now, place the fuckin' order or you know what comes next." The man's voice sounded sinister.

Bethany closed the door to the bathroom, leaving it open a crack. It was enough to see out, but nobody would notice at a glance. At least that was what she hoped.

"Be reasonable. If I order too many of these drugs and supplies, we're going to get caught. Then we're both up-shit creek." Randy sounded a little braver with that statement.

"Place. The. Order." The man didn't even seem to be hearing Randy.

"I'm not doing it. Not now." The sound of a chair scraping the floor startled her.

"I said order it now," the man shouted.

"Jesus Christ, put the fucking gun away." Randy's voice squeaked, and Bethany sucked in a breath.

"I don't have time for you or this shit," the man snapped.

The next sound was two loud pops and a thud. Bethany covered her mouth to contain her gasp as the door to the office opened, and a man sauntered by the opening of the bathroom door. Bethany wanted to close her eyes to ensure he didn't see her but she had to see the man who might have possibly just ended the life of her co-worker.

At first, all she saw was the back of his head. Dark, thin hair pulled back into a short ponytail. He was wearing what looked to be a tailored business suit with black shoes. Almost as if he sensed her, he turned. Bethany pressed her lips together and eased back enough so she could still see him and hoped he didn't see her. When his dark eyes scanned the bathroom door, she held her breath and prayed harder than she ever had in her life.

Her heart pounded so hard in her chest that she was sure the man would hear it. For some reason, he stood in the middle of the reception area staring at the bathroom entrance. When he took a step toward the door, Bethany was sure he saw her.

Thankfully his phone jingled, and it distracted him. He put it to his ear and turned away, but Bethany had memorized every feature of his face and the scar across his forehead. She had an excellent memory for faces.

"I'm on the way down now. Stop being a bitch," he snapped as he opened the door and left the office.

Bethany pressed her back against the bathroom door and slid down the wall until she sat on the floor. She tried to slow her heart rate and prayed that she didn't just hear what she thought.

After what seemed like hours but was probably only a couple of minutes, she stood up on shaky legs and slowly opened the bathroom door. She peeked out to make sure nobody was there and stepped toward the office where she'd heard Randy and the man.

The door was open, and it was quiet. Eerily quiet. Bethany held her hand to her chest as if it would slow her heartbeat to a normal rhythm. Slowly, she stepped into the office and scanned the room.

At first, she didn't see Randy and exhaled in relief. She stepped further into the office and turned. All the air whooshed out of her. Randy lay in a pool of blood on the floor behind his desk. His eyes were vacant, and Bethany didn't need to check to know he was dead.

"Oh, God." Bethany stepped back until she was outside the room and with trembling hands pulled her phone from her purse.

Ten minutes after she'd called nine-one-one, the reception area filled with first responders. Bethany sat next to the reception desk with her hands curled around a cup one of the officers handed her. She couldn't lift it to her lips with her trembling hand without spilling it over herself.

"Ms. Donnelly, I'm Constable Blake Harris. If you feel up to it, can you tell me what happened?" Blake eased into the chair next to her.

"I came from the head office to meet with Randy. My boss. Oh… I need to call my boss. He needs to know about this. The guy just shot him. Right there in that room. He didn't seem fazed over it." Bethany glanced up at the officer.

"We can call your boss, but I need you…" His phone rang and cut Blake off.

Bethany placed the cup of water on the table next to her chair and rested her elbows on her knees. She covered her face with her hands and tried to calm her frayed nerves.

"She can describe the guy, so we need Melinda Fox on this," Blake spoke into the phone. "How close are you?"

The rest of the conversation faded as she tried to tune out the sounds around her. She heard someone take another man's life. Never in her wildest dreams did Bethany expect to be able to say that. Nor did she ever want to. It wasn't comfortable to know she was the only one that could identify the murderer.

"Ms. Donnelly, my sergeant is in the building and wants to be the one to question you." Blake crouched in front of her, and she lifted her head.

"That's fine." Bethany nodded and dropped her head into her hands again.

Bethany didn't bother to lift it again when she heard the hushed voices of the officers around her. She listened to a couple of female officers as well as another male. She only looked up when someone touched her shoulder.

"Bethany?" She stared into the face of one of her old friends.

"Jess?" Bethany couldn't believe she was looking at Jess O'Connor.

"I didn't know you were back." Jess sat next to her and wrapped her arms around Bethany.

"I came back yesterday for work and had come to meet with …" Bethany stopped and pulled back from Jess. "You're a police officer?"

"Yep, and I'm not the only one." Jess nodded her head toward Blake and another man with his back to her.

"I don't know Blake." Bethany glanced back at Jess.

"Not Blake." Jess nodded. "Him."

Bethany turned her head to where the other man turned. The recognition on his face probably mirrored her own, and she completely forgot how to breathe as he stepped slowly toward her.

Aaron O'Connor stood in front of her larger than life. His hair was a little longer than he wore it in high school but still thick, light-brown waves that she loved running her fingers through back then. His features matured and the five o'clock shadow looked sexy as hell. Then there were those blue eyes that always held a glint of mischievousness and the dimples that not only showed when he smiled but when he pressed his lips together. For a moment she forgot what she was doing there and just stared at the man who broke her heart.

"Ms. Donnelly, I understand you saw the shooter." Aaron's face didn't show any emotion as he pulled a notepad from his jacket pocket.

"Ms. Donnelly? Really, A.J.?" Jess grumbled.

"I think they need you outside, Constable O'Connor." He glared at Jess.

"Asshole." Jess shot to her feet and stomped out of the office.

Aaron cleared his throat as he pulled a chair in front of her and eased down into it. As a teenager, he was breathtaking, but as a grown man, he was heart stopping. Broad shoulders, full muscular chest covered by a black t-shirt with *POLICE* written across the front. His jeans hung just right on his hips and clung to his muscular thighs.

Jesus, stop ogling him.

"Ms. Donnelly?" Aaron repeated, and she raised her eyes to meet his.

"Bethany." She didn't recognize her own voice as it cracked when she spoke.

"Bethany," She loved the sound of her name coming from his lips.

"Aaron," She whispered his name, and he smiled.

"Still refuse to call me A.J." A slight smile made his dimples more defined.

"It's how you introduced yourself to me," she reminded him.

"True. Okay, Bethany, can you tell me what happened?" The smile disappeared, and his jaw clenched.

Bethany didn't tell him why her boss had sent her to meet with Randy, but she did tell him everything else. Guilt made her stomach turn. Keeping what she knew from the police probably was illegal, but she needed to talk to Craig before she said anything else.

"There's something you're not saying." Aaron narrowed his eyes as he studied her.

Bethany jumped to her feet, and the sudden movement made her head spin. As she turned to steady herself, she saw a gurney being wheeled out and it was as if all the air in the room disappeared. She tried to breathe but the room blurred and then everything faded into black.

Chapter 4

Aaron caught her just as her knees started to buckle. He shouted for someone to grab one of the paramedics and lifted her into his arms so that he could carry her to the small sofa in the second office across from the reception area.

He couldn't believe he was looking down at the only woman he'd ever loved. The only woman to mean more to him than a quick fuck. The only girl to break his heart. Who was he kidding? His heart shattered into pieces when she broke up with him.

"Fuck." Aaron plowed his hands through his hair as he stepped back as the paramedic took over.

"You know her?" Blake whispered next to him a few minutes later.

"Yeah, we went to high school together." It wasn't a lie.

Blake didn't say anything else as Bethany's eyes fluttered and opened slowly. She glanced around for a moment and then her eyes met his.

"I wasn't dreaming," she murmured.

"You fainted." The paramedic Bobby Tucker, an old friend of Aaron's brother Mike smiled..

"This isn't a good day." Bethany sighed as Bobby helped her sit up slowly.

"We all have those days. Are you feeling dizzy or lightheaded?" Aaron didn't like the way Bobby held Bethany's hand, and he certainly didn't like the way the asshole smiled at her.

"I'm fine. Thanks." Bethany gave him a weak smile.

"I'll keep an eye on her. You can go, Bobby," Aaron snapped at the guy.

"I should stay and make sure her pressure doesn't drop." He glared at Aaron.

"I need to ask her some questions, and I'm sorry you're not a police officer. It's a murder investigation. You can wait outside, and if I need you, I'll send for you." Aaron hated to sound like an ass, but Bobby could be a huge flirt.

"Fine." Bobby grabbed his equipment and left the room.

"I never knew you to be so rude." Bethany smoothed her hair back from her face.

"I never knew you to faint," Aaron returned.

"It's been a stressful day, Aaron." Bethany glared at him.

"I understand. I need to know what you aren't telling me." Aaron tried not to sound like the jerk he had with Bobby.

She shook her head and scanned the room as if she wanted to look anywhere but at him. It gave him a glimpse of the Bethany he'd met in the school corridor that first day and his heart felt as if it would flip in his chest.

"Bethany, what are you not telling me?" Aaron crouched in front of her.

"I sent her here to investigate Randy because I suspected him of selling medications but not to pharmacies." Aaron turned around at the sound of a man's voice.

"And you are?" Aaron stood and stared at the man in the doorway.

"Craig Molloy, I own National Pharmaceuticals." He held his hand out to Aaron and then quickly made his way to Bethany's side.

"Craig, when did you get here?" Bethany asked the older man.

"I flew in this morning. I was coming to meet you here in case Randy gave you any trouble." Craig wrapped his arm around Bethany and gave her a side hug.

"Mr. Molloy, why didn't you call the police to investigate this?" Aaron asked.

"I wanted to have proof first. I know it was stupid, but I didn't want to believe one of my employees would do this." Craig sounded crushed.

"You put Bethany in danger," Aaron told the man.

"I'm sorry, Beth." Craig kissed her temple. "You're like my daughter, and I should never have put you in this situation."

"You did," Aaron snapped.

"Aaron, he gets it. Do you have to keep needling him?" Bethany glared at him.

"It's okay, dear. He's right. Whatever you need to get this guy, ask." Craig stood up and held his hand out to Aaron. "Beth will give you everything she has and if there's anything else just ask me."

"Bethany." Aaron felt the need to correct the man on her name.

Aaron didn't know what else to say to the man, but he didn't like the fact that Bethany was in danger. If the killer found out that she could identify him, he'd come for her. They also needed to find out who the woman was.

"Your sister is on the way." Jess stepped into the room and glared at Aaron.

"You called her?" Bethany groaned.

"Yeah, she was a little surprised to know you were here." Jess raised an eyebrow.

"Why didn't your family know you were here?" Aaron blurted the question before he thought about it.

"I got here late and was going to see them after the meeting but...well ..." Bethany dropped her head and sighed.

"I got the impression at supper yesterday that you had no intentions of coming back to Newfoundland." Aaron crossed his arms over his chest.

"I didn't, but my boss asked me to do this and... well... I didn't want them to get their hopes up about me moving back here." Bethany flopped back on the small sofa and looked past him.

It was as if she didn't want to meet his eyes, and the questions that had plagued him through the years swirled around his brain, threatening to spill out. He managed to keep them from doing just that by clenching his teeth together.

"You haven't been home in what? Twelve years?" Jess sat next to her.

"Thirteen." It spilled out before he could stop it.

"Thirteen years. Wow. You didn't want to come and see your old friends? Your family? I mean, Hopedale used to be your home." Jess seemed hurt.

"I know, but the memories I have from there are not all pleasant and there were some people I just didn't want to see." Bethany glanced at him and then back to Jess.

"You know Raquel doesn't live there anymore, right?" Jess smiled.

"Good to know." Bethany finally smiled.

It was the beautiful genuine smile he remembered. The one that always made his heart skip a beat, and it pissed him off because it still did and she didn't even direct it at him.

"Beth." Aaron turned when Allyson pushed into the office and almost knocked Blake over in the process.

"Ally," Bethany grunted as Allyson wrapped her arms around her sister.

"I'm so pissed with you right now." Allyson released the hug and then slapped Bethany gently on her arm.

"I'm sorry. I was going to call you after my meeting but... that didn't go really well." Bethany's eyes filled with tears and she gulped in a breath.

"Jess said you saw the killer." Allyson glanced at Jess and then at Aaron.

"We're going to put her in protective custody until we can find this guy." Aaron was finding it harder to keep his professional demeanor.

"What? No way. The guy didn't see me. He doesn't know I saw him." Bethany shot to her feet, and she swayed again but caught herself before she made a complete fool of herself again. "He didn't even know I was here."

"You don't know that. You also don't know if this guy is close by." Aaron was stubborn about this, and he wasn't sure why.

"Are you saying her life could be in danger?" Allyson stood next to her sister and wrapped her arm around Bethany's shoulder.

"Until we're sure, she's going to have to come with me." Aaron pulled out his phone but froze when she snatched it from his hand.

"I'm not going anywhere with you," Bethany snapped.

"You don't have a choice." Aaron met her defiant gaze.

"I have plenty of choices. None of them includes you, Aaron." Bethany stepped around him and stomped out of the room.

"Is she in that much danger?" Allyson touched Aaron's arm.

"Look, Ally, we don't know what we're dealing with here. We have no idea what happened. This guy Randy, we don't have a clue what he was involved in or who he pissed off." Aaron was sincere.

"Would you tell this officer to let me leave?" Bethany grumbled from the doorway of the office.

"Beth, you really should listen to A.J." Allyson moved next to her sister.

Aaron clenched his jaw at the shortened name again, but he didn't correct her sister. He had to admit, Bethany wasn't the same timid girl he knew all those years ago. She had spunk, but her body still did him in. Bethany was curvy in all the right places, and although she'd slimmed a little, those curves only got sexier. He prayed nobody could see the erection he was trying to hide with the file folder he held in front of him.

"What about Jess? Can't she stay with me? What about Officer Harris?" Bethany didn't seem against protection, just as long as it wasn't Aaron.

"Could I speak with Bethany alone please?" Aaron tried to keep his voice monotone as he locked his eyes with her pissed-off gaze.

The room cleared quickly, and Bethany stood just inside the door with her arms folded across her chest, pushing up her full breasts. The phrase *if looks could kill* came to mind as Jess closed the door, leaving him alone with Bethany.

"Just what is your problem with me?" Aaron snapped.

"I don't have a problem with you," she returned.

"Is it the fact that I'm your ex-boyfriend and you dumped me." Aaron couldn't help the childish comment, but it came tumbling out.

"I'm sure you got over it pretty fast." Bethany rolled her eyes.

"That's where you'd be wrong, but I don't understand why you hate me so much." Aaron wanted an answer to at least that question

"I don't hate you. I don't hate anyone. I would rather deal with someone else." Bethany reached for the knob, but Aaron was in front of her in an instant, crowding her against the closed door.

He didn't miss the catch in her breath or the way the pulse in her neck beat faster. What got him was the way her eyes widened when he trapped her. The scent of some kind of flowers filled his nose, but he wasn't sure if it was from her skin or her hair.

"Aaron, what are you doing?" Her voice came out in barely a whisper.

"I'm making something very clear. This is my case, and I'll be the one to make sure you're safe until we catch this guy. I'm also going to find out what the hell I did to make you look at me like I'm the worst person in the world." Aaron stared at her for a moment and then stepped back. "I'll be bringing you to The Compound to set up security before taking you home."

"The Compound?" Bethany braced herself against the wall.

"Keith has property in Hopedale where he lives but he also uses it when he has clients that need a secure location, and if I feel you need to stay there to be safe, you will stay there." Aaron couldn't tear his eyes away from her beautiful face.

"What does Keith do?" Bethany eased away from the wall and smoothed her skirt and blouse.

"He runs a high-end security firm." Aaron pushed down the overwhelming feeling to grab her and kiss the life out of her.

"Not what I ever saw Keith doing." Bethany's eyes scanned the room, avoiding eye contact, again.

Aaron pulled open the door of the office to the shocked expressions of Jess, Allyson, and Blake. If they were trying to make it look as if they weren't listening, they were doing a shitty job, and in any other situation, Aaron probably would have laughed, but at that moment, he didn't find it the least bit funny.

"I'll be taking Bethany to Keith's place." Aaron stalked out of the office.

"I've already called him." Jess stepped back as Aaron practically pushed his way between the three eavesdroppers.

Aaron didn't turn around to see if Bethany was behind him because he had a feeling she was still fuming in the office. He pulled out his phone and stood next to the entrance of the reception area. Everything in his body roared at him to find out why she broke up with him all those years ago, but until she was out of danger, it was strictly business. He was going to keep this professional if it killed him.

Chapter 5

Bethany sat in the back seat of his car with her sister next to her. Aaron had arranged for someone to drive both Allyson's and Bethany's cars back to Hopedale. Since she'd already checked out of the hotel and had her luggage in her trunk, she didn't have to go anywhere but where Aaron dictated she go.

She was pissed, but it was hard to remember that when he'd crowded her against the wall. His scent of sandalwood and some sort of citrus she couldn't distinguish because her mind was too muddled with being within inches of Aaron. No matter what happened all those years ago, he still played havoc with her libido.

"A.J., does the building have any video surveillance?" Allyson held Bethany's hand and seemed to be uncomfortable with the tense silence in the car.

"It's a new office building. A lot of the offices are empty. According to Blake, the owner said he is in the process of setting it up, but it's not working yet." Aaron glanced at Bethany through the rearview mirror.

"You think that is why Randy picked that building to set up his office?" Allyson asked.

"If he's involved in criminal activity, yeah. Blake said he only had a four-month lease on the office." Bethany pulled her gaze away from the back of his head and watched the scenery of the highway back to Hopedale.

"I want to stay with my dad and sister," Bethany grumbled as Aaron dropped Allyson to their old house.

"I want to win the lottery, but if the guys think it's safe, then you can, if not, you'll have to stay at The Compound." Aaron snorted when she called him an asshole under her breath.

Bethany wanted to stay at her old house. Once, she thought her father was crazy for not selling it. He'd been renting it out ever since they'd left the island. Her Uncle Oliver, her mom's brother, had been the property manager for her father.

She smiled to herself, remembering the first time everyone found out that the hard-ass chemistry teacher was her mother's brother. Bethany didn't get any special treatment from him though. No. Uncle Oliver made her work her ass off to pass the course.

"Wow, you do still smile." Aaron pulled up to a large iron gate and opened his window.

"When I have something to smile about," Bethany replied with enough snarky attitude that she cringed at her response.

After he'd pushed numbers into the panel next to the gate, there was a click, and the gates slowly opened. Bethany couldn't help but stare at the impressive iron entrance. Keith was obviously doing well for himself.

"We'll stop at Keith's house and see who he's putting on your detail. They're at your dad's house and will let me know if it's safe to stay there." Aaron pulled through the gate and waited for it to close before he continued down the long, paved driveway.

"This is all Keith's property?" Bethany spun around in her seat as they drove by two large buildings where she saw two large men jogging around what looked like a running track.

"Yep. Those two buildings are the gym and offices for both N.S.S and his construction company. He's a bit of an overachiever." Aaron chuckled, but she could hear the sense of pride in his voice.

Seconds later, Aaron pulled up next to a large house with a covered deck on the front of the house. An orange cat sat on the rail cleaning its face, and he only lifted its head once when the car stopped.

"Come on." Aaron startled her as he pulled open her door.

She'd been so focused on the cat she hadn't heard Aaron get out of the car. Bethany stepped out, carefully making sure she didn't step too close to Aaron. He must have noticed because he shook his head as he slammed the car door.

"Hey, Burlap. Keeping the house safe from mice and birds?" Aaron gave the cat a head rub, procuring a purr from the large cat.

"Burlap?" Bethany snickered at the name.

"Keith found him as a kitten tangled in the burlap he puts around his bushes during the winter. Hence the name." Aaron knocked once and then pushed open the front door. "Everyone decent in here?"

"Keith goes around his house naked?" Bethany didn't move inside the house.

"I'm sure he does when his wife wants him to." Aaron chuckled and motioned for her to come in.

"Keith's married?" Bethany stepped inside but didn't go any further into the house.

"Yes, everyone except Nick and me is married, but he's getting married in July." Aaron walked further into the house and shouted out again.

"A.J., if you wake Patrick I will rip off your balls and give them to the cat." A pretty auburn-haired woman came into view and poked Aaron in the chest.

"You know how to scare a man." Aaron bent down and kissed the woman's cheek.

"Yes, yes I do." The woman smiled, and Bethany instantly liked her.

"Bethany, this is Keith's beautiful wife, Emily." Aaron wrapped his arm around his sister-in-law. "Em, this is Bethany Donnelly, she's the woman we need the security for."

"I'm so sorry you had to deal with something like that. Come on in. I'm sure you must still be in a state of shock. Let me get you something to drink. What would you like, tea? Coffee? Or something stronger?" Emily linked her arm into Bethany's and guided her into a large kitchen.

"Coffee would be great." Bethany sat on one of the stools next to the island.

"Where's Keith?" Aaron stood behind her, and she had trouble containing the shiver as his breath blew across her neck.

"He's in his office." Emily didn't turn around as she poured two cups of coffee.

"Hey, I don't get a cup?" Aaron tossed his hands in the air.

"You can get your own." Emily sat next to Bethany and slid a cup in front of her.

"And here I thought you loved me," Aaron grumbled as he grabbed a cup himself.

"I do." Emily winked as Aaron disappeared down the hallway.

"You're safe here. Nobody can get on this property and A.J. will make sure your home is secure." Emily covered Bethany's hand.

"Thank you, but I honestly don't think all this is necessary. I mean, the man who shot my co-worker didn't even know I was there." Bethany sighed.

"Honey, I know exactly what you're going through. Keith and I didn't exactly have the typical start to a relationship." Emily gazed out the window, lost in a memory that made her smile like a woman in love.

"It obviously worked out, but what does that have to do with me?" Bethany shifted on the stool.

"Keith was hired by my dad to protect me because of a threat against my life. I didn't know about it until the last minute, and I was not happy about it. I didn't exactly make it easy for Keith in the beginning." Emily rested her cheek on her fist and laughed.

"That's the understatement of the decade. This beautiful woman nearly got me killed." Bethany turned to the deep grumbly voice from behind them.

"I am a dangerous beauty, or so he says, but he loved every minute of it." Emily's face lit up like a light bulb when she turned to face her husband.

"Not every minute. Getting shot wasn't fun." Keith stepped next to Emily and kissed the top of her head. "It's nice to see you again, Bethany."

"You too, Keith. It's been a long time." Bethany smiled, but she couldn't keep her gaze from looking over Keith's shoulder to where Aaron stood lazily against the door jamb.

"How is it you haven't aged, and the rest of us look ten years older?" Keith winked.

"Speak for yourself, asshole." Aaron made his way to the sink and placed his cup in the sink.

"Oh, I don't know. You've matured in the last four years I've known you. You don't hit on every woman you meet anymore." Emily laughed.

"No, just every second one." Keith chuckled.

"You know, you two used to be my favorite. I'm leaning more toward Ian and Sandy now." Aaron rested his ass against the counter and crossed his arms over his chest.

"Did I hear my name?" Bethany turned at the female voice coming into the room.

"Yeah, A.J. doesn't like us anymore." Emily laughed.

"What's wrong, manwhore?" the woman teased.

"Manwhore? Really, Sandy?" Aaron shook his head, obviously frustrated with the teasing.

"I call it as I see it." The woman rested her arms on the island and smiled at Bethany. "I'm Sandy O'Connor, and you must be Bethany."

The pretty woman with short dark curls held out her hand, and Bethany shook it. She was trying to remember if she'd ever met the woman.

"It's nice to meet you." Bethany shook Sandy's hand.

"Sandy's married to Ian and they have four kids." Aaron wrapped his arm around Sandy's shoulder.

"Wow, you don't look like you've had one child." Bethany waved her hand up and down at the woman's tiny figure.

"Ian and I work out. A lot." Sandy wiggled her eyebrows, making Aaron and Keith gag.

"Yeah, Bethany doesn't need to know about any of that, Sandy." Keith shook his head. "Sandy's going to look into Randy."

"Our company does a full investigation on employees. All the information came back clear," Bethany explained.

"I look for the things that aren't so obvious." Sandy winked.

"Sandy's the Penelope Garcia of Newfoundland Security Services." Emily grinned at her referral to one of the characters on the television show *Criminal Minds*.

"Do you have a Derrick Morgan as well?" Bethany chuckled.

"No Derrick but we have tons of hot, sexy, muscled men." Emily sighed.

"Princess, you do remember you're married to me, right?" Keith growled.

"Don't worry big boy; you're the only one that rocks my world." Emily stood up and pressed her lips against Keith's cheek.

"You're damn right." Keith grinned.

"When we've finished discussing my brother's sexual prowess, could we discuss his newest client?" Aaron rolled his eyes.

"Awww, are you feeling a little lacking in that department? Maybe you should stop running around with all those airheads and find a woman with brains." Sandy nudged Aaron with her shoulder, and the way his eyes went immediately to her caused her stomach to flutter.

"Yeah, that's what I need, a woman who makes me feel like a piece of shit," Aaron snapped at Sandy and stomped out of the house.

The surprised expressions on Sandy, Emily, and Keith told her they were shocked by his behavior. She was as well. His brothers and cousins teased him all the time when they were teenagers, and she hadn't seen him get upset once.

"Wow, who pissed in his cornflakes?" Keith stood up and glanced at Bethany. "I'm going to go talk to him."

Sandy and Emily glanced at each other, and when Bethany heard the sound of the front door, they turned to her.

"What happened between you and A.J.?" both women said at the same time.

"Nothing, he was one of the police to show up when I called for help." Bethany shrugged her shoulders and prayed they would leave it at that.

"No, why did you two break up? From what Ian told me before I came here, you and Aaron dated in high school." Sandy smiled.

"Yeah, and as far as we know, he hasn't had a serious girlfriend since then," Emily continued.

"Kristy said A.J. changed after you left." Sandy tilted her head. "Why did you break up, anyway?"

Did she want to discuss ancient history? No, but it was hard to believe Aaron hadn't had a serious girlfriend since high school. She remembered the rumors about the O'Connor brothers floating around Hopedale back then. Her sister even warned her about dating one of the O'Connor boys, but in the eight months she and Aaron were together, Bethany never saw anything but a devoted and loving boyfriend.

"I moved away," she said, but the truth was she left because she didn't want to see the smirk on Raquel's face when Aaron came clean.

"Bethany, are you okay?" Emily covered Bethany's hand with her own.

"Yeah, I'm fine," Bethany lied.

The truth was, feelings she'd thought were long gone were resurfacing again. Humiliation, anger, and devastation. Bethany felt them all when she realized the truth. Now that she thought about it, she was no different than Aaron because she hadn't been in a long-term relationship since him. No man ever lasted more than a month in her life. She'd never found anyone that made her feel the way Aaron did. Even if it was all a ruse to win a bet, it hadn't been for her because she loved him with her whole heart.

Now those feelings were resurfacing, and it terrified her. Had she ever stopped loving him? The only question bouncing around in her brain was, why hadn't Aaron ever had a serious relationship in the last thirteen years?

Chapter 6

Aaron slammed the door behind him and stomped to the end of the front deck. Sandy and Emily teased him all the time, and he'd laugh it off. Why did all of a sudden their little jokes piss him off? He knew the answer, but he didn't want to admit it.

"Fuck." Aaron punched the side of the house in frustration.

"If you want to punch something, there's a heavy bag in the gym." Aaron didn't look up at the sound of Keith's voice.

Aaron turned and braced his back against the side of the house. He stared at the line of trees that surrounded the sides and back of Keith's house. It didn't calm him as he'd hoped. The only place he could go that would help him relax was the beach. It was always the place he went when he needed to calm himself or forget everything.

"Are you going to be able to deal with this?" Keith leaned against the house next to Aaron.

"Don't be stupid," Aaron replied.

"A.J., all of us know." Keith turned so that he was facing Aaron and crossed his arms over his chest.

"What the fuck are you talking about?" Aaron turned his head and looked into his brother's blue eyes.

"You never got over her," Keith spoke the truth, but he'd be damned if he'd let his brother know it.

"You're out of your mind." Aaron scoffed.

"Maybe, but I remember how you were after she dumped you. I also remember how you changed and turned into the love em'and leave em' guy." Keith raised an eyebrow.

"Oh, because you were such a virgin up until you met Emily." Aaron rolled his eyes.

"I admit I slept around before Emily but not for the same reason you started doing it. You were doing it to kill the pain of losing her." Aaron hated that his brother was so observant.

"That was thirteen years ago. Jesus, I've moved on." Aaron turned away from Keith and hoped his brother would drop it.

"No, you haven't," Keith continued

"Look, Dr. Phil, drop it. I can do my job without losing focus. Bethany is just a witness to a murder, and I'll make sure she's safe until we find the killer. End of story." Aaron pushed off the house and started to head back into the house.

"So, you're okay with me putting Crash and Crunch on this?" Keith asked.

Brent 'Crash' Adams and Hunter 'Crunch' Crawford were two of the men that worked for Keith and his business partner Dean 'Bull' Nash. They ran NSS together and were one of the best security firms in the country. Aaron thought of the men as brothers but something about having them look after Bethany had his teeth clenching.

"That's what I thought." Keith stepped in front of Aaron.

"What? Crunch and Crash are good at their jobs." Aaron tried to step around his brother.

"But your jaw clenched, and your shoulders tensed at the thought of anyone else protecting Bethany." Keith was getting on his last nerve.

"I'm a cop, not a bodyguard. My only job is to make sure she makes it to court once we find the fucker that killed her co-worker. Nothing more." Aaron hadn't meant to shout, but the sound of the slight gasp behind Keith had his gaze darting to the left.

Bethany, Sandy, and Emily stood next to the open door, and the look on Bethany's face made him want to ask Keith to punch him. She turned and headed down the steps toward his car without a word.

"You're such a fucking idiot. You need to stop catching your dick in your zipper. Crash texted and said the house is secure." Sandy glared at him.

"I'll get her home." Aaron hurried around Keith and down to his car where Bethany was already sitting in the passenger seat staring out the front window.

Aaron got into his Dodge Charger and closed the door. For a few seconds, he sat with his hands on the steering wheel. He felt like he needed to apologize for what he said but nothing he said was a lie. Bethany was a witness. He was doing the same thing that he did with anyone that could be in possible danger. Right?

"How long will I need security?" Her voice cracked.

"Until we can find this guy." Aaron started the car.

"What if you don't find him?" Bethany replied.

"We'll find him." Aaron pulled away from Keith's house and turned toward the exit of the property.

Aaron would rather she stay at the secure bunkhouse, but he knew Bethany would never go for it. Keith built them for his staff to stay when they were in Newfoundland. As the years went on, many of the employees bought houses around Hopedale, leaving most of the bunkhouses vacant. Aaron and Nick had taken over one of them when they were assigned to the Hopedale Division of the Newfoundland Police Department.

Nick no longer lived with Aaron. His brother and his fiancée, Lora, bought the house on Sunset Street in Hopedale because it was close to the station. It also helped that Lora's little girl enjoyed her backyard right next to John's little girl. His brothers had to put a gate in the fence that separated their property, so the two little girls could play.

"People get away with things that hurt people all the time." Bethany's voice was barely above a whisper.

She was right, but as Aaron stopped the car in front of the gate, he turned to her. Tears threatened to fall from her eyes; she was scared. The whole reality of the situation had to be hitting her like a ton of bricks.

"They do, but I'm not going to let this guy hurt you." Aaron studied her profile.

"I can't have someone follow me forever." Bethany sighed.

"I'm aware of that, but for now, we're just cautious." Aaron covered her hand with his and realized he'd made a colossal mistake by touching her.

Her hand was cool, but she didn't pull away. Bethany turned her gaze and met his eyes. Her green eyes always took his breath away, and that hadn't changed. When a tear slipped from the corner of her eye and trailed down her cheek, Aaron instinctively reached to wipe it away.

"Don't." She pulled back before he could touch her. "Take me home, Aaron."

With that statement, Aaron opened the gate and made his way to the street where he saw her for the last time. He'd left a box on her doorstep with the ring and the letter he'd written to her because she'd told him once that handwritten notes were romantic. It didn't mean anything to her because she never even sent it back to him. She probably tossed it without opening it.

Aaron pulled into the driveway of her house and jumped out of the car. He glanced at the door as he made his way around the car to get her things. Her father stood at the top of the steps as a young boy ran down the steps and wrapped his arms around Bethany.

Does she have a kid?

"Holy crap, are you okay?" The boy looked to be about twelve years old and was a little taller than Bethany.

"I'm fine, Cameron." Bethany hugged the kid, and a sudden realization hit Aaron like a punch in the gut.

Was it possible the kid was his? If he was the age Aaron thought, then it was possible, but how was he supposed to ask that question? He carried her bags up the front steps and nodded at Lewis Donnelly. Bethany's father looked the same as he had the first time Aaron met him. Aaron didn't understand the scowl he got from the man.

"Mr. Donnelly, nice to see you again." Aaron held out his hand, but Lewis just continued to glare.

"So, you're a cop. Didn't think someone so dishonest would make it in the police force." With that statement, Lewis stomped down the steps and wrapped his arms around Bethany.

Aaron was dumbfounded. He didn't understand why Bethany's dad would say something like that, but when he thought about it, he hadn't spoken to Aaron at the family supper either.

Before he had a chance to ask what the man's problem was, the young boy came running up the steps. Aaron almost passed out at the blue eyes staring at him.

"Hey, I'm Cameron." He held out his hand to Aaron.

"A.J. O'Connor." Aaron shook the boy's hand and was impressed with his firm handshake.

"I want to be a cop, too." He grinned at Aaron.

"First, you need to start bringing your grades up." Aaron turned around as Ally came out of the house.

"Yeah, yeah." Cameron groaned, and Aaron couldn't help but laugh.

"You need to have good grades to get into the academy." Aaron glanced at Bethany as she stepped next to the boy.

"That's what we keep telling him." Bethany tussled Cameron's light-brown hair.

"Aunt Beth, give me a break." Cameron rolled his eyes.

Aaron felt a wave of relief fall over him. It wasn't that he didn't want children, but if Cameron had been his son, then it meant Bethany kept him from his child all those years.

"A.J." Aaron turned to where Crash and Crunch stood at the bottom of the steps.

"Holy mother of God." Allyson gasped.

"That's Crunch and Crash; they'll be doing security for Bethany." Aaron nodded toward the two men.

"Ummm, Crunch and Crash?" Bethany wrinkled her brow, and Cameron laughed.

"Cool names." The kid nodded.

"They're nicknames. All Keith's guys go by them. Crunch's name is Hunter Crawford, and Crash is Brent Adams." Aaron chuckled but lost the humor when he glanced at Bethany's dad.

Why was the man staring daggers at him? Aaron had always thought Lewis liked him. He'd even taken Aaron fishing a couple of times before they left Newfoundland.

"Since they're here, you no longer have to be, right?" Lewis snapped.

"Dad," Bethany and Allyson said together.

Lewis grunted and made his way back inside the house. Bethany looked embarrassed at her father's behavior, but Allyson looked confused.

"What is wrong with him?" Allyson shook her head. "I'm sorry about that, A.J."

"It's fine. I'm just going to talk to the guys, and I'll be on my way." Aaron started down the steps.

"You're leaving?" Bethany touched his arm but pulled back her hand so fast that he almost didn't see it.

"They're your security, and I trust them completely. I'll keep in touch with updates on the case." Aaron forced himself to turn and put some distance between her and him.

It was harder to walk away from her house this time than it had been thirteen years ago. He still had a dozen questions and a million emotions swirling around him. He wasn't used to feeling so out of control. Aaron didn't like it one bit.

Chapter 7

Bethany watched him pull out of the driveway, and it was like someone plunged a knife into her stomach. Her father's reaction to Aaron didn't surprise her. He'd been the only one she'd told why she ended the relationship. Her father had wanted to kick the shit out of him, but Bethany had begged him to let it go.

"Dad was pretty rude to A.J.," Allyson said later that evening as they sat on the back deck of the house.

"Yeah." Bethany sipped the glass of wine her sister had given her.

"I wonder why." Allyson sighed.

"I never realized how much I missed this view." Bethany changed the subject, but it was the truth.

"Me too. I'm so glad you came home. You are staying, right?" Allyson curled her feet under her in the large deck chair.

"I'm pretty sure. Craig wants me to take over this region. If he still has a company after all this." Bethany rested her head back on the chair and watched the waves crash against the beach.

The house was on the corner of Sandcastle Road and Beach Street. From the edge of the deck, they had a partial view of the beach. She'd spent many a day and evening and some nights walking across the rocks by herself and with Aaron. There was a jut of land that separated part of the beach from a small cove behind Aaron's parents' house. She and Aaron would go there to be alone.

"Those security guys are so damn hot." Allyson sighed.

"Yeah, they are." Bethany snickered

"Not that I'm ready for dating again, but they are nice to look at." Bethany glanced at her sister and saw Allyson playing with the wedding ring she still wore.

Corporal Trent Sullivan died while he was on peacekeeping duty overseas six months earlier. Her sister was devastated by the loss of her husband, and it was probably the main reason Allyson decided to move back home. It had been hard on Cameron as well, but thankfully he was doing well.

"It will take some time, Ally." Bethany took her sister's hand and gave it a comforting squeeze.

"I know. I still miss him so much." Allyson's voice cracked.

"I know you do, but if you ever need to talk, I'm here." Bethany pulled her chair closer to Allyson.

"So, A.J.? Any old feelings come back?" Allyson raised an eyebrow and Bethany knew her sister was trying to keep from bursting into tears at the thought of her late husband.

"No," Bethany lied.

"You are such a liar." Allyson pushed Bethany's arm and laughed.

"Your sister doesn't need that louse back in her life." Bethany turned around at the sound of her father's voice.

"Dad, what is your problem with A.J.?" Allyson sat up in the chair.

"I never liked him." Her father lied because he thought Aaron was a great guy until she'd told him what happened.

"That is such bull." Allyson glanced at Bethany and then back to their dad.

"Drop it, Ally," Bethany warned.

"No, I want to know," Allyson pushed.

"I'm going to bed." Bethany stood up and made her way inside.

The last thing she wanted was to rehash the most painful time of her life next to losing her mother. It had taken her years to start dating again and seeing him again was like opening an old wound.

"Goodnight, Beth." Her father kissed her cheek as she passed him and made her way to her bedroom.

Her old room didn't look anything like it had when she was younger. The room now had an en-suite and was painted a completely different color. The windows changed as well, and her window seat where she would do her homework was no longer there.

It didn't matter because the cool late April breeze brought the familiar scent of the ocean air into the room. If she closed her eyes, it was like going back in time. Except she wasn't a naïve teenager in love anymore.

Bethany opened her eyes and grabbed her large suitcase. She struggled to lift it on the bed and practically fell over by the time she got it on top of the mattress. She wasn't going to sleep so she might as well put away her clothes.

An hour later, she shoved her two suitcases into the back of the closet. As she stepped back, she glanced up at the entrance to the attic. The memory of hiding the last thing Aaron gave her up there had her frantically scanning her room for something to climb on. She pulled the armchair over and proceeded to pull herself up until she could manage to push up the square piece of wood.

She wasn't able to reach up into the opening, and she cursed as she hopped down off the chair. She tried to remember how she got up there in the first place. She shoved the chair back and flopped down on the bed. She could ask her nephew to climb up and check to see if the box was still there but that would only provoke a ton of questions she didn't want to answer.

"It probably isn't there anymore anyway," Bethany mumbled to herself as she pushed up to her feet.

If only she'd opened it to see what it was, but Bethany was so angry, she didn't want to see anything from him. It was probably something telling her what a fool she'd been.

Bethany pulled back the curtain and stared out her window. Crunch sat in his car parked in her driveway, and she felt guilty that he had to be outside all night. April wasn't exactly the best time to spend the night in a car. She was about to go down and bring him some coffee, but her sister appeared heading to the car.

It seemed her sister had the same idea, but she also had a plate with what looked like a sandwich. That was Ally, always taking care of everyone but herself. It was how she dealt with grief. Allyson did the same thing when their mother died. She would take care of others to avoid giving into the sadness.

Bethany turned away from the window when there was a light knock on her bedroom door. She moved to the door and opened it. Her father stood on the other side holding a cup in his hand and a smile on his face.

"Warm milk always helped you sleep." He held the cup out to her.

"Thanks, Dad, but I haven't had warm milk since I was eighteen." Bethany stepped back as her father stepped into the room.

"Beth, I needed an excuse to come and see how you were." He placed the cup on her nightstand and turned to face her.

"I'm fine, Dad." Bethany wrapped her arms around his waist and rested her head against his chest. "It was scary to hear someone take another person's life, but I'll be okay."

"I'm not talking about that." He kissed the top of her head. "I'm talking about A.J."

Bethany sighed and tipped her head back to look up at her dad. Her father was over six feet tall and the years of hard work made him strong and lean. He'd gained a few pounds since he'd retired ten years earlier, but he was still the most reliable man she knew.

"Dad, that was a long time ago. He was only here because he's doing his job." His hazel eyes met hers at her statement.

"Beth, since you were able to talk, I've known every time you've lied to me. You never got over that boy even if he did break your heart." Her father narrowed his eyes.

She couldn't deny it to her father because he'd been the one to hold her all night as she cried over being used by Aaron.

"Dad, I'll be fine." She stepped back and picked up the cup he'd placed next to her bed.

"You need to confront him and tell him the real reason you left. Let everyone know what a son of a bitch he was to you, and I don't have anything nice to say about that girl," he grumbled.

"I love you, Dad, but I don't think dragging up old heartbreak is going to make things easier, but there is something you can do for me." She stepped next to her closet door.

"What's that?" He glanced into the closet.

"Can you check and see if there is a box just inside the edge of the attic opening? I put it there before we moved and forgot it when we left. I'd like to see if it's still there." She pointed up to where she'd opened the attic entry.

"I see you tried to reach it, short stuff," her father teased.

"Not my fault I didn't inherit your giant gene." She poked him in the side.

Her father reached up and felt around the attic opening. She was prepared to be disappointed until he pulled down a square box about the size of a book. The purpled paper had faded over the years, and something chewed on the corners but seeing it made her heartache.

"What is this?" He held it out to her.

"Something I should have returned a long time ago." She took it and went to the bathroom to wipe off the years of dust and insulation. "Dad, can you make sure that the attic is closed up? I don't want whatever chewed on the corners to come visit."

"Already done. I'm heading to bed, but if you need to talk, you know I'm here." He kissed the top of her head and left her room.

Bethany placed the tattered gift on the nightstand next to her bed. Her dad was right. She needed to let Aaron know why she left and that she'd never opened his little gift. Sure, she was curious over what was inside, but she couldn't open that wound.

After she prepared for bed, she lay on her side and stared at the box. The paper had been so pretty back then, but she couldn't look at it, which was why she tossed it into the attic. Tomorrow, she would give Aaron back the unopened box and let him know she hadn't fallen for his trick back then.

"You and Raquel will never hurt me again." Bethany sighed and turned onto her other side. "I'm no longer Butterball Bethany."

Chapter 8

Aaron sat in the booth at *Jack's Place* sipping coffee and staring out at the fishing boats unloading their catch. He smiled at the memory of watching his grandfather on the docks when they would go visit him and Nanny Betty.

How could so many great memories be clouded by so many painful ones?

"Are ya tryin' ta scare away all da customers?" Nanny Betty appeared as if out of thin air and eased into the booth across from him.

"I'm too cute to scare away anyone." Aaron grinned at Nanny Betty.

"Doncha try and charm me, lad." Nanny Betty pointed her tiny finger at him as the waitress placed a cup in front of her.

"That's right, A.J. Only I can charm your grandmother now." Aaron chuckled when his grandmother's companion Tom Roberts slid in next to Nanny Betty.

"Oh, stop it." Nanny Betty playfully tapped Tom's hand, but Aaron didn't miss the blush in her cheeks.

"When are you gonna put a ring on that?" Aaron winked at Tom.

"Now doncha go changin' da subject because Tom's here," Nanny Betty warned.

"What subject is that, Nan?" Aaron rested his elbows on the table and wrapped his hands around the coffee cup.

"How ya feel about young Bethany being back in town." Nanny Betty took a small sip of her tea.

"Doesn't affect me in the least except now she's a witness to a murder," Aaron lied.

"I swear if ya lie to me once more I'm going to clout ya." Nanny Betty glared at him with what his father and uncle called the *devil's glare*.

"Nan, Bethany and I were over a long time ago." Aaron couldn't meet her eyes.

"Over or not, ya always pined fer her." Nanny Betty wasn't wrong, but he wasn't in the mood to discuss it.

Before he could respond, he glanced through the window and cursed under his breath. Bethany was walking down Harbour Street toward the beach. He scanned up and down the street, looking for Crash or Crunch, but he didn't see either of them.

"What the fu… hell?" He corrected his near curse because Nanny Betty probably would have slapped him.

"What's wrong?" Tom followed Aaron's line of vision.

"Keith's security is about to get fired." Aaron jumped to his feet and tossed a five-dollar bill on the table.

Aaron stepped out of the diner and jogged to the end of the parking lot. Bethany walked down the beach and Aaron didn't even have to ask where she was going because he knew. It was their place. The place they first kissed, the place where he told her he loved her, and the place he still went when he needed time to clear his head.

"A.J., she's a sneaky little thing." Crash ran to catch up with Aaron.

"How the hell did she get down this far without you seeing her?" Aaron kept heading toward where she'd now disappeared behind the jut of land that separated the main beach from the private cove.

"Her sister brought me a plate of food and distracted me," Crash said sheepishly. "I never let people distract me. What the fuck is wrong with me?"

"Taken in by a pretty face, maybe?" Aaron chuckled. "I got this; you can go back to the house."

Crash nodded and jogged back up the road toward Bethany's house. He couldn't blame Crash for being distracted by Allyson. She was a beautiful woman, but in Aaron's opinion, nobody compared to Bethany.

Aaron checked the waves as they crashed on the shore. The tide was rolling in, and if Bethany didn't get back on the main beach, she was going to have to walk through the cold ocean to get back. He was almost at the jut of land when he saw her running around, but she didn't time the wave correctly, and it caught her around the legs, soaking her from the thigh down.

"Holy shit, that's cold." She squealed and ran out of the water.

She slipped as she made it around the rock and caught herself before she fell onto the rocky beach. As she looked down at her wet jeans and soaked feet, it was hard not to laugh at her.

"Forget how to time the waves?" Aaron knew he startled her when she spun around.

She lost her balance falling on her ass just as another wave rolled in and splashed over her. Bethany tried to jump to her feet and gasped as the cold water rolled in. The rocks were slippery, and she couldn't get to her feet before another wave hit her again.

"Need a hand?" Aaron stepped up to her and his lips quirked as he held out his hand.

"I need a dryer and a hot cup of tea," Bethany grumbled but took his hand, and he helped her to her feet.

Aaron pulled off his jacket and wrapped it around her shoulders. It was as if they stepped back in time except, the last time he did it, she wasn't soaking wet.

"Well, that didn't go well." Bethany groaned.

"Maybe you shouldn't be sneaking off without your security." Aaron raised an eyebrow and bit his tongue to keep from laughing as she rolled her eyes.

"I wanted to take a walk." Bethany stomped ahead of him.

"See where that got you." Aaron snickered.

"I forgot how the tides work. So, sue me," Bethany shouted over her shoulder.

"Let me drive you back to your house before you catch a cold." Aaron jogged to catch up with her.

"I'm like five minutes from my house. I can walk." Bethany walked a little faster as he caught up to her.

"Okay, then I'll make sure you get home." Aaron shook his head.

"I got here myself. I can get home the same way," Bethany grumbled.

"Sorry, you're supposed to be under security detail, and since you slipped out of their sight, I'm it until you get back home." Aaron followed behind her and cursed himself as his eyes fell to her round ass.

The wet jeans clung to it, and his dick instantly hardened. He wasn't going to take a chance and look at what was under his jacket because he was sure that her wet shirt clung to her full breasts.

"Fuck," Aaron mumbled through clenched teeth.

Bethany didn't say another word as they made their way to her house. She stomped up the front steps and practically threw his jacket at him as she walked through her front door. Crash sat on the front step, staring at Aaron in confusion.

"She didn't time the waves, and that's the result," Aaron explained.

"That water got to be fucking freezing. Why didn't you drive her back?" Crash stood up.

"Because that woman is way more stubborn than I ever remember." Aaron shook his head. "Listen, John has Melinda Fox coming to the station tomorrow. We need Bethany to come and give a description of the guy so Melinda can do a composite sketch."

"What time?" Crash pulled out his phone.

"I'll text you or Crunch. I don't know what time she'd be in town. She's coming from Gander." Aaron turned and made his way back to the diner where he'd left his car.

Melinda Fox was a sketch artist they used all the time. She was a police officer as well, but a fantastic artist and her drawings were always near perfect.

Aaron was about to leave when he heard his name shouted from the diner. He waved at Jess and joined her at the entrance of *Jack's Place*. It was almost lunchtime, and he'd wasted the morning drinking coffee at the diner so what was another hour.

"Hey, you coming to get lunch too?" Jess asked.

"Sure, I could eat." Aaron followed his cousin inside the now crowded restaurant.

Luckily, two of his brothers were eating at the booth where his family usually congregated. Ian and John were deep in conversation as Aaron and Jess joined them.

"Do you ever work?" Jess nudged Ian.

"Yes, and I'm also allowed to have lunch. Imagine that." Ian tugged her ponytail.

"I don't know, cuz; you seem to be getting a little thick around the waist. Maybe you should cut back on the burgers." Jess poked Ian in the side.

Aaron watched Ian narrow his eyes and slap his hand against his hard stomach. Ian was a doctor, but he was also a bit of a gym rat. Ian worked out every day, and besides Keith, Ian was the only one of the brothers to make it to a black belt in Karate. He and Jess trained together in Kurt's dojo and taught a lot of the kids in the town since Kurt had cut back on teaching.

"I only have one thing that's thick." Ian wiggled his eyebrows.

"Oh God. Gross." Jess gagged.

"Melinda should be in town tomorrow," John said as he finished the last of his sandwich.

"I told Crash I'd get him to bring Bethany to the station when Melinda gets here." Aaron waved to the waitress that had taken over since Nick's fiancée had gone back to her regular job as an interior designer.

The pretty woman was no more than twenty but was friendly and good at her job. Aaron waved to her, so he and Jess could place their order.

"I heard Bethany gave Crash the slip." John chuckled.

"Yeah and nearly drowned because of it," Aaron grumbled.

The curious stares from his brothers and cousin had him rolling his eyes as he explained what happened after the waitress took their order.

"Crash must be pissed she tricked him." Jess snorted.

"I think he was more embarrassed." Aaron stood up to allow John out of the booth.

"I'm sure it won't happen again," John said as he and Ian headed away from the table.

"How are you doing?" Jess said when his brothers were out of earshot.

"Why is everyone asking me that? I'm fine." Aaron rolled his eyes.

"Come on, A.J., I saw your reaction when you saw her, and I remember how hurt you were when she left without explanation." Jess reminded him.

"She explained plenty. She wanted to move with her dad and sister. End of story." Aaron smiled at the waitress as she placed his hot turkey sandwich with fries and gravy in front of him.

"I don't believe that, and neither do you. There was more to that than just her family leaving. I think it had something to do with Raquel *fuck anything with a dick* Evans." Jess whispered the name she and Kristy had dubbed Raquel during school.

"It's ancient history… are you fucking kidding me," Aaron snapped as he glanced up to see Bethany walking into the diner, alone, again.

"Twice in one day. Ohhhhh… I'm going to give Crash such shit over this." Jess waved to Bethany and Aaron wanted to kick her.

"Before you get bent out of shape, he's outside talking to John." Bethany glanced around without looking at him.

"Are you here for lunch?" Jess asked.

"Yeah, but it looks full." Bethany sighed.

"Sit with us." Jess moved in and glared when Aaron tapped her with his toe.

"That's okay. I can't stay." Bethany's gazed flicked to him then back to Jess.

"That sounds familiar," Aaron said it a little louder than he intended.

"Don't be silly, sit down." Jess pulled Bethany down next to her.

Aaron suddenly became very interested in his plate of food but barely tasted it as he shoveled it into his mouth. He needed to finish and get as far away from her as possible.

Jesus.

Why was he so shaken when he was near her? He had a thousand questions he wanted to ask her, but the minute Aaron was close to her, all he could think about was how much he ached to crush his lips against her or scream at her for leaving.

The only thing worse was the voice he heard heading toward him. He glanced up and wished the floor would open up and swallow him whole.

Chapter 9

"A.J., I've been looking all over the place for you, baby." Bethany turned to see a woman stagger toward them on four-inch heels and clearly inebriated with another overly made-up woman behind her.

"You've got to be fucking kidding me," Aaron growled.

The girl slid into the seat next to Aaron and tried to kiss him. He pushed her back, but the girl was relentless and reached under the table to grab him between the legs.

"Fuck, Jocelyn. Stop this shit. Kylie, why didn't you bring her home?" Aaron managed to grab the woman's hands and push her out of the seat.

"She doesn't listen to me." Kylie shrugged her shoulders as she stared at Bethany.

"I'm horny, baby. So horny for you," Jocelyn slurred.

"Jesus Christ, you do realize you are in the middle of a public place." Aaron grabbed the woman's arm and led her through the door.

"If he hadn't dumped her, maybe she wouldn't be drinking so much," Kylie retorted as she followed Aaron and Jocelyn.

"Wow, that was…" Jess pressed her lips together and then burst out laughing. "Hilarious."

"Jess, you're terrible." Bethany tried to hold in the laughter, but seeing Jess holding her stomach was just too much.

Bethany sat in the seat that Aaron had just vacated. Aaron hadn't moved on from the easy tramps since high school. She didn't know that when she started dating him. At least not until it was too late, and she'd fallen head over heels.

"What are you two laughing at?" Bethany looked up to see Sandy holding a little boy's hand.

"A.J.… Bimbo… Oh. My. God." Jess gasped for air and Bethany covered her mouth to hold in the laughter.

"Okay, so you're useless. Do you know what she's so hysterical over?" The woman's dark-brown eyes kept flicking back and forth between Bethany and Jess.

"She's laughing because A.J.'s girlfriend practically put her hands down his pants here in the seat and proceeded to tell him how… umm… stimulated she was." Bethany tried to keep the conversation child appropriate.

"Alex, why don't you go ask Aunt Alice if you can have a cookie." Sandy crouched down to the little boy who didn't hesitate to run off to the kitchen.

"A.J. has a girlfriend?" Sandy sat next to a laughing Jess and shoved her with her hand. "Pull it together, woman."

"It… was …Jocelyn." Jess said in between trying to control her laughter.

"Fuck, he needs to get some cream to get rid of that hemorrhoid." Sandy rolled her eyes.

"She reminds me of Raquel. Guess that's his type." Bethany forced a chuckle because it killed her to think about them together.

"Who's Raquel?" The confusion on Sandy's face mirrored Jess's expression.

"Do you mean Raquel Evans?" Jess's laughter stopped.

"Yeah." Bethany glanced back and forth between the two women.

"Who's Raquel Evans?" Sandy slapped her hands on the table.

"We went to high school with her. She was in the same class as Kristy. She was the bitch, bully, and slut of the school." Jess stared at Bethany as she spoke.

"A.J. dated her?" Sandy stared at Jess.

"I doubt it. A.J. despised her in school." Jess tilted her head and met Bethany's eyes. "Why would you think he was with Raquel?"

Bethany glanced back and forth between Jess and Sandy. She was confused by the conversation. It wasn't possible that his family didn't know he'd been with Raquel in high school, or had he?

"He was seeing her before I left to go away." Bethany sat back in the seat and watched the shocked reaction on Jess's face.

"Who told you that?" Bethany practically jumped a foot in the air at the sound of Aaron's voice.

"Ahh…" Bethany pressed her body closer to the wall as he placed his fists on the table and leaned over it.

"Who?" Aaron's voice was more of a growl.

"It was common knowledge." It was all she could think to say.

"Not that common because I never knew about it," Jess interjected.

"Who told you I was dating Raquel in high school, Bethany?" Aaron's blue eyes narrowed as he locked his gaze with hers.

"I overheard it in the girl's room." She didn't know why she was so nervous to tell him because she wasn't the one that fucked the biggest whore in the school.

"Who?" Aaron said through clenched teeth.

"Why does it matter?" Sandy asked.

"Because if it's who I think, then I know why Bethany left town all those years ago." Aaron stood up and crossed his arms over his chest.

"Is there something I don't know?" Sandy asked Jess. "I don't like being the only one not to know something. Especially if it's something I can tease A.J. about." Sandy looked like a kid at Christmas.

"Bethany left without telling him why and A.J. was heartbroken for months. She never even said goodbye to any of her friends. Just up and left." Bethany turned when she heard the female voice.

Kristy.

"Hi, Kristy." Bethany gave her a small smile.

"Who said I was dating Raquel, Bethany?" Aaron didn't even seem to notice Kristy next to him.

"I heard Raquel and her shadows talking about it the day after our prom." Bethany folded her arms over her chest. "She said the only reason you were with me was to win a bet you made with Cory and Joey."

"That was a lie." Aaron seemed frighteningly calm.

"I heard you, Aaron," Bethany admitted.

"I think maybe you two need to talk alone." Jess tried to push Sandy out of the seat.

"Not a chance, I want to hear this." Sandy rested her elbows on the table and tucked her fists under her chin.

"There's no way you heard me say I was dating Raquel." Bethany was uncomfortable with the way Aaron glared at her.

"No, but I was in the hallway when you collected the money from the bet. Two hundred from Cory and two hundred from Joey, if I remember correctly," Bethany said smugly.

Aaron didn't say a word as he pulled out his phone and tapped the screen. He put the phone to his ear, but his eyes didn't leave hers.

"Cory, get over to *Jack's Place*. I need you to clarify something for me. I'll explain when you get here," Aaron snapped into the phone and ended the call.

Aaron shoved the phone back into his pocket and sat down next to her on the seat. The booth suddenly seemed very crowded.

"So…. would you like a tea or coffee?" Jess waved to the waitress behind the counter.

Before Bethany could answer, she looked up to see Cory next to the table. He'd certainly grown up, but with the way he was glaring at Aaron, he didn't seem to be pleased about being dragged away from whatever he was doing.

"It's a good thing I was on my way in here to grab a coffee or I would have told you to fuck off. Could you be a little more vague next time?" Cory stood with his hands on his slim hips.

"Ask him, Bethany." Aaron didn't look at Cory or her, but it was comical the way Cory's eyes snapped to where she sat.

"Bethany Donnelly?" Cory glanced at Aaron and then back to her.

"Hi, Cory." Bethany smiled at him.

"Well, get the fuck out here and give an old friend a hug." Cory motioned for her to get out of the booth.

"She can do that when you answer her question," Aaron practically growled.

"What question?" Cory appeared confused by Aaron's nasty attitude.

"What you, A.J., and Joey made a bet about in high school." Sandy filled in the blanks.

"We made a lot of bets in high school." Cory laughed.

"The big bet that I won at the end of grade twelve." Aaron turned to Bethany and her breath caught in her throat.

"Didn't you rub that in enough that summer?" Cory groaned.

"I'm not rubbing it in. I want you to tell Bethany what the bet was." His eyes bored into hers.

"Yes, Bethany, he had the highest average out of three of us. Son of a bitch beat me by three fucking marks." Cory grabbed a chair behind him and straddled it.

"Was there a bet about me getting into someone's pants?" Aaron raised an eyebrow.

"Not that I know of and you know how close A.J., Joey and I were." Cory stared at her for a moment. "Does someone want to tell me what this is all about?"

"Bethany left town thirteen years ago because she overheard Raquel say we had a bet to see if I could get into Bethany's pants." Aaron turned in the seat and looked at Cory. "Oh, and apparently I was fucking Raquel."

"Seriously? That's why you left?" Cory's mouth dropped open.

"Yeah." Aaron stood up and started toward the door.

"Aaron," Bethany managed to say as she stood up.

He stopped and turned around. The shattered look on his face was worse than the one he had the night she ended things.

"I owe you an apology." Bethany took a step toward him only to have him hold up his hand to stop her.

"No, you don't. You believed what you heard. How could I be mad about that?" Aaron spun around and shoved the door open.

"Bethany, you should have talked to him before you ran away." Jess stepped in front of her. "It took him a long time to get over you."

"What the hell are you talking about? He never got over her." Kristy snapped.

Bethany didn't know what to say. She'd spent thirteen years believing Aaron used her to win a bet. The shock of the truth overwhelmed her, and she felt sick. She'd let Raquel's lies destroy the life she could have had with Aaron.

She managed to get outside and brace herself against the side of the pub. Bethany covered her face with her hands and sobbed. She honestly didn't know why she was crying.

"How could I be so stupid?" She rested her head back on the wall.

Was it stupidity or the low self-esteem of a slightly overweight teenage girl? It was hard to remember why she didn't just confront Aaron back then. Give him a piece of her mind when she overheard Raquel. She wouldn't hesitate to do it now, but it was the thought of everyone laughing and making fun of her that kept her from doing that. She was Butterball Bethany, after all.

How was it after thirteen years she still felt like that girl sometimes? Bethany wasn't her anymore. She was a confident, strong woman and not that she was arrogant, but she saw how some men looked at her. She wasn't drop-dead gorgeous like some woman, but she was attractive, and she was thinner than high school, but she still had curves.

"Are you okay?" Sandy's voice said next to her.

"I'm fine." Bethany forced a smile.

"I know as well as any woman that when we say, *fine*, it means we are not fine. Come back to the diner." Sandy touched Bethany's arm, and Bethany glanced over her shoulder to see Crash disappear around the front of the building.

"I don't think that's a good idea and I've got to get back home." Bethany wiped her knuckles under her eyes to wipe away the tears.

"Do you know it took a long time for Ian and me to get together finally?" Sandy smiled.

"Umm… well, no." Bethany didn't know where this was going.

"I see a lot of me in you. Let me guess; you were bullied in school by this Raquel person, which I'd like to meet face to face, by the way." Sandy narrowed her eyes.

"I wasn't the only one she harassed." Bethany smiled.

"I'm sure you weren't, but it made you feel like you were never good enough for anyone. For A.J., right?" Sandy raised an eyebrow.

"Yes." Bethany sighed.

"That bitch probably takes pride in the fact that she split you guys up even if she didn't end up with A.J. in the end, which she didn't. *Ever*." Sandy emphasized the last word.

Bethany didn't know what to say, but part of her was elated that Raquel never got her claws into Aaron. She nodded to show Sandy that she was listening even though she hadn't spoken.

"The point is, don't let her keep you both from seeing if any of the old feelings are there. I think they are. From the way A.J. acted, he's pissed not because he doesn't care but because he's hurt you would think so badly of him." Sandy smiled. "Plus, Kristy, Cory, and Jess told me that they don't think he ever got over you. I guess it's why he's never had a steady girlfriend."

"Never?" Bethany couldn't believe Aaron would be pining over her for that long.

"Never. I'm not going to lie and tell you he's been celibate, because he hasn't." Sandy held out her hand.

"What?" Bethany asked confused.

"Give me your phone." Sandy wiggled her fingers.

"Why?" Bethany pulled out her phone and held it out to the woman.

"Because I'm going to put my phone number as well as A.J.'s in your phone. You can use them or not." Sandy tapped the numbers into her phone. "I've also sent myself a text, so I've got your number. Not that I couldn't get it if you didn't give it to me."

Sandy grinned at her as she gave Bethany back her phone. Bethany couldn't help but smile at the pretty woman. She liked Sandy and knew somehow; she would be a good friend.

"I've got to get back and grab Alex before I go get my girls at school." Sandy smiled. "Don't hesitate to call even if it's just to say hi."

"Sandy?" Bethany smiled.

"Yeah?"

"Thanks, and I usually go by Beth now, but I'm starting to think Bethany is making a comeback." Bethany waved as Sandy walked away.

Bethany may be making a comeback, but it would be a new Bethany. One that wasn't easily intimidated by cruel bitches that wanted to hurt people because their own lives were so pathetic. She also needed to let her father know the truth. It was also time to open the box and see what Aaron had left her all those years ago.

Chapter 10

Aaron couldn't believe he'd spent the last thirteen years wondering what he did to make Bethany dump him when he hadn't done a God damn thing. She left because she believed something she'd overheard in the bathroom from the fucking bitch that tortured her.

"She fucking left because she thought I was a cheating piece of shit that was using her to win a bet." Even when he said it out loud, it was hard to believe.

"What did you do with the money you won?" Aaron jumped when he heard Cory's voice behind him.

Aaron had thought he was down far enough on the beach that nobody would see him sitting on the rocks. He couldn't hide in his spot because the tide hadn't rolled out.

"I'm not in the mood, Cory," Aaron growled.

"I'm not fucking around. You won four hundred dollars back then plus the two hundred you had held aside, and I'm curious what

you did with it because I don't remember you buying anything."
Cory plopped down next to him.

"It doesn't matter." Aaron rested his arms on his bent knees.

"Let me see if I can guess." Cory lay back on his elbows and
stretched out his legs.

"Isn't there a case you could be working on instead of
bugging me?" Aaron sighed.

"I'm an investigator. I live to figure out mysteries," Cory
teased.

"Well, go figure out how we can find who killed Randy
Knight." Aaron glanced back at his friend.

"I can help with that, but this is more interesting now." Cory
hummed to himself, and Aaron wanted to punch his friend.

"Oh, for fuck sake," Aaron grumbled.

"I think you used the money to buy Bethany something."
Cory sat up and folded his hands on top of his legs. "Flowers? No.
Candy? Nope, you would have eaten them yourself. Jewelry?"

Aaron stiffened, but he didn't respond and hoped Cory didn't
see the tension in his body.

"That's it. You bought her jewelry." Cory pushed Aaron's
shoulder. "Fuck, you bought her an engagement ring, didn't you?"

"Fly to fuck." Aaron jumped to his feet and stomped up the
beach toward his truck.

"And I bet you still have the ring." Cory ran to catch up with him.

"That's where you would lose." Aaron stopped and turned toward Cory. "I gave her a fucking ring with a note. I left the box on her step and do you know what she did?" Aaron raised his voice.

"Gave it back to you?" Cory shrugged.

"No, she didn't even have the decency to give it back. Instead, she left without a thought of what I'd written on that note. She took the word of a bitch she overheard in the bathroom over the proposal I wrote because she told me once that she thought handwritten letters were romantic."

Cory stared at him for a moment before he smiled. Aaron shoved him and continued toward where he'd parked the truck Wade loaned him.

"A.J., wait," Cory shouted.

"Fuck off, or I'm going to take my aggression out on your face." Aaron didn't even slow down.

"Maybe she didn't get it." Cory's words brought him to a stop.

"I put it on her step." Aaron stopped next to the truck.

"Did anyone see you put it there?" Cory raised an eyebrow.

"I don't know," Aaron snapped.

"Raquel was obsessed with you back then, and she lived next door to Bethany. She might have stolen the box after you left and before Bethany could see it." Cory raised an eyebrow.

It was possible. Back then, Raquel was almost as bad as Jocelyn. Everywhere he went, she'd show up. She'd even took some of the courses he did in university because she said she was interested in the law.

"Look, I know it's been, what? Twelve years?" Cory held up his hands.

"Thirteen," Aaron corrected him.

"Thirteen? Shit, we're getting old." Cory sighed.

"Speak for yourself." Aaron finally smiled.

"You're older than me, asshat." Cory shoved Aaron's shoulder.

"By two months." Aaron shoved him back.

"Anyway. I know you were head over heels for her back then. I also know how much you hurt when she left, and I'm not blind. You still love her." Cory poked his finger against Aaron's chest.

"I don't know." Aaron shook his head.

"Bullshit. You might be sticking your dick into every willing woman you can find, but none of it means anything to you because there is only one woman you want. I mean truly want because you never got over her and you love her more than you will ever admit to me. At least admit it to yourself." Cory squeezed Aaron's shoulder and then turned to walk away.

Aaron watched his friend and knew everything he'd said was right. He never got over Bethany. As much as he tried to forget her, there was nobody that could take her place in his heart.

"I always knew dat lad was smart. He's right." Aaron turned, startled by the voice.

"Nan, you're sneaking up on conversations now?" Aaron chuckled as he bent to kiss her cheek.

"Only when I tink it's someting I want ta hear." She took his hand and squeezed it.

"What's so interesting about my love life?" Aaron laughed.

"Ya call wat yer doin a love life?" Nanny Betty rolled her eyes as she tugged him toward the bench at the edge of the beach.

"I think I've got a pretty good love life," Aaron lied.

"A.J. ya might be able to lie ta yerself, but ya can't lie ta me. Ya might have a sex life, but dere's no love in dat." Nanny Betty shook her head and slapped her hand against the bench seat as she sat down.

Aaron knew better than to ignore her subtle order. His grandmother was barely five feet tall and probably no more than a hundred pounds, but her personality was bigger than the town of

Hopedale. She'd been living with his parents since his grandfather died and much to his father's dismay, hadn't slowed down even at nearly eighty years old.

"Ya know I don't like to stick my nose in where it don't belong." Nanny Betty smiled.

"Uh huh." Aaron laughed.

"I know why ya run around wit all da less den lady like gals." Nanny Betty gave him that stern glare she gave them when they were in trouble.

"I see."

"Yer afraid ta open yer heart again." Nanny Betty tapped her hand against his thigh.

"Nan, that's not it," Aaron lied.

"Doncha lie to me. I saw ya after she left. I knew wat ya were feelin'. Remember, yer grandfather wasn't my first love." Nanny Betty sat back on the bench and sighed.

"Tom was," Aaron remembered the story of how Tom had been sent to live with a family when his parents and siblings died in a house fire.

Tom was the only one that survived because he was with Nanny Betty that night. Since he was under the age of eighteen, he was sent to live with a family in another town. When he managed to return, Nanny Betty was seeing Jack O'Connor, Aaron's grandfather. Tom left and never saw her again until after his grandfather died.

"Yes, and I don't regret marrying my Jack because he was a good man. I did love him, but a piece a' my heart always belonged ta Tom and God love yer grandfather, he understood dat. It's why he wanted yer father ta have Tom's name as a middle name. He used ta say he was tankful for Tom leavin' because if he didn't, he wouldn't have been able ta marry me." Nanny Betty smiled at the memory.

"He was never jealous?" Aaron didn't know if he'd feel okay with his wife still having feelings for another man.

"A' course he was, but he never let it eat him up. I loved Jack, too. We were happy, and I wouldn't change a day a' my life wit him." Nanny Betty smiled.

"I'm kinda glad you married Grandda too." Aaron wrapped his arm around her shoulder.

"Don't let a lie dat ya didn't know was told keep ya from bein' happy. Don't let anudder day go by witout takin' a chance on love again." Nanny Betty kissed his cheek and stood up. "Ya know Cora was at da diner and saw Bethany."

Here it comes. Cora the Cupid strikes again. His aunt was supposed to have some special gift that she knew when people were meant to be together. As far as he knew, she'd never been wrong.

"Yeah, and what does Cupid think?" Aaron walked with his grandmother toward his parents' house.

112

"Dat ya need ta get yer head outta yer ass and go tell dat girl yer not wastin' no more time." Nanny Betty gave him a shove back toward the truck.

"Nan." Aaron slapped his hand against his chest at the word *ass* coming from his grandmother.

"I'm sure ya heard me say worse. Now go find dat lass." Nanny Betty turned and scurried back toward the house, leaving Aaron on the side of the road staring after her.

"You're right, Nan. As always," Aaron whispered to himself as he ran back to his car.

Aaron should put all his time and energy into finding out who the fuck killed Knight, but not until he knew if she'd gotten his gift, he wouldn't be able to concentrate on anything.

"Bethany first, and then track down the killer." Aaron pressed his foot on the gas pedal and zoomed toward Bethany's house.

Chapter 11

Bethany opened the door to her house and hurried into the living room. There wasn't anyone there, but she could hear voices in the kitchen and called out to them as she plopped down on the couch.

"What's wrong?" Allyson said when she walked into the room.

Bethany chuckled because she'd been crying, her eyes probably looked like a raccoon.

"I got a huge dose of the truth." Bethany laughed.

"Are you nuts? Why would you be laughing at that?" Bethany looked behind her sister and saw a man walking out of the kitchen.

"Elijah," She squealed. "What are you doing here?" She practically jumped into his arms.

"I had some time off and wanted to visit my favorite cousins." Elijah chuckled. "Thanks for letting me know you were back in Newfoundland, squirt."

Elijah was her Uncle Oliver's son, and they were always close even after she moved away. He spent a lot of time in Ontario with his job. He was former military and worked with veterans, helping them get the help they needed after they retired.

"So, you want to explain this dose of the truth?" Allyson waved her hand around.

Bethany pulled Elijah and Allyson toward the couch and sat down. She knew both her sister and cousin would be pissed she hadn't told them the whole story of why she suddenly wanted to leave Newfoundland in the first place but to tell them everything, she needed to start there.

"This should be interesting." Elijah wrapped his arm around her shoulders as she started from the beginning.

Bethany blew out a huge breath after she told them what had happened earlier that day. Allyson stared at her for what seemed like hours but when she finally spoke, her sister was pissed.

"That bitch is the reason you ran away with a broken heart, which by the way, I'm not happy you didn't tell me. She's also the reason A.J. evidently got his torn out as well," Allyson growled.

"I can't blame it all on her. I mean, I should've at least confronted Aaron." Bethany let her head drop against Elijah's shoulder.

"True, but I remember what you were like back then. Shy and would do anything to avoid being the center of attention." Elijah kissed the top of her head.

Before Bethany could respond, the doorbell rang. Of course, Cameron bolted down over the stairs and ran to the door, shouting that it was for him. A few seconds, later he entered the living room with Aaron following.

"Hey, the cops are here, put the drugs away." Cameron snickered as he held up his hands.

"Cameron, that's not funny." Allyson pointed her finger at her son.

"It was a joke, Mom. Relax." Cameron rolled his eyes and sauntered back to his room.

"Aaron, what are you doing here?" Bethany lifted her head off Elijah's shoulder.

His eyes darted back and forth between her and her cousin. His body was tense, and his hands fisted at his sides, but he didn't move any closer.

"I wanted to talk to you." Aaron shoved his hands into his pockets as if he wanted to hide his tension.

"We'll let you talk." Allyson nodded at Elijah, and they both stood.

"Don't hold anything back." Elijah bent and kissed her cheek. "Tell him the truth."

Elijah stood up and followed her sister into the kitchen, but the low growl from Aaron drew her attention back to him. He stood and stared at the empty doorway for several seconds before turning toward her.

"Did you want to sit?" Bethany asked nervously all of a sudden.

"I need you to answer a question." Aaron didn't move from where he stood.

"Sure." Bethany shifted uncomfortably on the couch.

"How long have you been seeing that guy?" Aaron motioned with his head toward the kitchen.

"Elijah?" Bethany raised an eyebrow.

"If that's his name, yes." His voice was hard.

"I've seen him my whole life. He's my cousin." Bethany wasn't letting misunderstandings get in the way anymore.

His broad shoulders dropped a little, showing his relief at hearing Elijah wasn't her boyfriend. He moved slowly toward the couch and eased down on the other end.

"Why didn't you ask me if what she said was true?" Aaron didn't look at her as he sat with his hands hanging between his legs and his eyes downcast to the floor.

"I was going to ask you. That's when I heard you, Joey, and Cory talk about the bet. Obviously, it wasn't what I thought, but I was so hurt, I couldn't face you." Bethany clenched her hands together on her lap.

"The night you ended things, I dropped off a gift for you. Did you get it?" Aaron finally turned, and his eyes met hers.

"Yeah," Bethany whispered.

"And that didn't prove to you how much I loved you?" Aaron turned to face her and rested his knee on the couch.

"I never opened it," Bethany admitted.

"You just tossed it without even opening it?" Aaron sighed.

Bethany didn't say a word as she stood and made her way to her room. She snatched the box from her nightstand and headed back to the living room. When she returned to where she'd left Aaron, he was next to the door with his hand on the doorknob.

"Aaron." The sight of him about to leave caused her voice to crack.

He turned around and glanced at what she held in her hands. His eyes widened with surprise at the sight of what she held in her hands.

"You kept it?" He slowly ambled toward her.

"I never opened it. I was afraid. I tossed it up in the attic, and when we left, I forgot to take it. Stupid, huh?" Bethany held it out to him.

"It's not stupid, but I need you to open it." He pushed it back toward her.

"I don't want to." Bethany swallowed hard.

"Open it," he said again.

Bethany gazed into his eyes. She could never say no to Aaron back then, and that hadn't changed. His dimpled smile gave her the courage to do what she couldn't do thirteen years ago.

Bethany motioned with a nod of her head to him as they made their way back into the living room. When she sat on the couch, he sat next to her. His thigh touched hers, and with trembling hands, Bethany pulled on the frayed ribbon. The box smelled musty, and even though she'd wiped it off, it still felt gritty from being in the attic so long.

As the ribbon dropped to the floor, she placed her hand on the cover of the box. Before she lifted the lid, she blew out a huge breath. Aaron covered her hand with his, and the warmth radiated up her arm through her body.

"I swear if a spider jumps out at me I'm going to hit you over the head with this." Bethany turned her head and narrowed her eyes.

119

"If there's a bug in that box, it would be long dead after thirteen years." Aaron chuckled.

Bethany shook her head and slowly lifted the cover. She pulled aside the yellowed tissue paper and saw a purple envelope with her name scrawled across the front of it. She grinned at the handwriting. Bethany always needled him about his sloppy penmanship looking like chicken scratches.

"I think that says Bethany," she teased.

"Don't start on my writing. I'll have you know I've improved." Aaron rested his elbows on his knees and clasped his hands together.

Bethany lifted the envelope and opened it with trembling hands. So many emotions hit her at the same time as she pulled out the folded paper inside and slowly opened it up. It was a hand-written letter.

Baby,

You told me a handwritten letter was romantic. So here I go. Please excuse my chicken scratches. The day I saw you in the corridor of the school was the best day of my life. It was like something hit me in the chest. I guess it was Cupid's arrow. Funny how that's what they call Aunt Cora.

With every passing day, I fall more and more in love with you, and I hope you know that. There is nothing I wouldn't do for you. Nowhere I wouldn't go to be with you. I'm so happy you decided to stay in Newfoundland and go to university.

Now, we can spend the rest of our lives together in the town we both love. I probably should have talked to your father before doing this, but he's on the mainland, and I don't know how to get in touch with him. Besides I'd be afraid, he'd say no.

So here it goes and if you want me to talk to your father before you answer then I will, but I'm going to ask anyway.

Bethany, I love you with every beat of my heart and nothing on this earth will make me happier than if you say yes. Baby, lift your head and look down at me.

Aaron.

"What is this, Aaron?" She held up the letter and didn't even care that her hand was shaking.

"Look inside, Bethany." Aaron nodded toward the box on her lap.

She lowered her eyes to see a small black velvet box and stared at it as if it was going to bite her. It couldn't be what she thought it was. There was no way.

"I didn't plan on putting it all in a box. The night of the bonfire, I was going to give you the letter, and while you were reading it, I was going to go down on my knee and ask you to marry me." Aaron's voice cracked.

"What? No?" Bethany shook her head as her eyes blurred with tears.

"Yes, the money I won from that bet, I used to buy that engagement ring. Nobody knew I was doing it. Nobody. I wanted you to be surprised," Aaron continued.

"Well, it worked. I'm surprised." Bethany touched the box and then pulled back her hand.

"Open it," Aaron urged.

"I can't." Bethany's voice cracked as a tear ran down her cheek.

"Please." Aaron picked up the box and placed it in her palm as he took the letter and put it on the coffee table.

"Aaron, this isn't mine. Not anymore." Bethany couldn't stop the tears.

"That ring was bought for one person. You. My Bethany. Whether we're together or not. That ring will always be yours." Aaron tucked a piece of her hair behind her ear and ran his thumb across the apple of her cheek.

A couple of deep breaths, Bethany slowly opened the box. Inside was a round diamond set on top of a gold band. Blue and green tiny stones surrounded the diamond. It was beautiful and so much more than she would have ever expected.

"Aaron, it's stunning," Bethany whispered.

"It doesn't compare to you then and now... it looks like a piece of junk." Aaron smiled.

"I'm so sorry." Bethany turned to face him. "I should've had more faith in you. In us."

"Yes, you should've, but I remember how Raquel used to torture you. Especially when it came to me. I never thought you'd ever doubt how much I loved you." Aaron took the ring box and placed it on the table in front of them.

He grasped her hands in his and slowly raised his head until their eyes met. Bethany's heart pounded the same way it did back then whenever Aaron touched her or looked at her the way he was.

"I never lied to you, and I'm not going to start now. I tried to forget you. I'm ashamed to say I used other women to kill the pain. A lot of women, but I'm not telling you this to hurt you. I'm telling you because you need to know you're going to hear stories about me. Sandy calls me a manwhore." Aaron's cheeks flushed.

"I like her." Bethany smiled and then laughed at the shocked expression on his face.

"She's perfect for Ian, but she tends to say things without thinking." Aaron cupped her cheek.

"I don't care what people say about you." Bethany sighed when his thumb grazed her lower lip.

"Really?" Aaron raised an eyebrow.

"Okay, okay. I won't anymore." Bethany smiled.

"Good, but the truth is the last woman I spent any time with was the woman you saw today. I've been months trying to make her understand I wasn't looking for a relationship, but she has a drinking problem, and I'm pretty sure she's doing drugs as well." Aaron shook his head.

"Then why did you go out with her?" Bethany found it hard to believe he'd be with someone like her.

"The truth?" Aaron raised an eyebrow.

"Yes."

"She was … eager." She didn't miss the cringe in his tone.

"I see." Bethany tried to look away from him.

"This is also the truth; nobody ever made me feel like you did. My heart always belonged to you, and there was never any room for anyone else." Aaron held her face in his hands.

"Aaron, I've changed." She closed her eyes.

"So have I." Aaron pressed his forehead to hers.

"I've noticed." Bethany opened her eyes.

"I don't want to…" Aaron's statement was cut off by a loud popping sound outside the house and then the large picture window in the living room shattered.

Before she knew what happened, Bethany was on the floor with Aaron heavy on top of her. After a couple of more pops and the sound of glass breaking around her, she heard the squeal of tires and then Allyson shouting from the kitchen.

"Are you okay?" Aaron lifted off her and scanned her for injuries.

"I'm fine, but I need to check on Allyson, Elijah, and Cameron." She tried to jump to her feet, but Aaron held her down to the floor as he crouched and slowly made his way toward the window.

"Stay down until I check outside." Aaron pulled back the curtain while she watched and prayed there wasn't anyone still outside.

"Beth, are you okay?" Allyson shouted from the kitchen.

"Yes, are you?" Bethany shouted back.

"We're fine." She breathed a sigh of relief when she heard Elijah's voice as well.

"Did someone just shoot at our house?" She almost laughed when she saw her nephew on the floor in the hallway slithering toward her.

"Yes." Bethany motioned for him to come to her and he quickly crawled next to her.

"Fuck," Aaron growled under his breath and then turned. "Sorry, Cameron."

"My friends say worse than that." Cameron rolled his eyes.

"I want you two into the kitchen. I have to check to see if Crash is okay and call John." Aaron held out his hand.

Bethany was afraid to stand in case the gunshots started again. Then she scanned the living room. She'd cut herself to pieces with the glass shards covering the floor.

"Cameron, I need you to stand up but keep your head down while you go to the kitchen." Aaron pulled Bethany to her feet, and she grabbed her nephew's hand.

"Careful of the glass, Cam." Bethany noticed he was in his bare feet, but before he could say a word, Aaron picked him up and set him down away from the shards of glass.

"Stay in there." Aaron met her gaze as he stepped into the hallway and pulled his gun from its holster.

As soon as Cameron saw his mother, he ran toward her. Elijah knelt next to Allyson, his face was red with rage, and her sister looked numb as she clung to her son.

"What the hell was all that about?" Elijah snapped.

"I don't know, but Aaron is gone to check on Crash and call his brother." Bethany sat next to her sister, and they wrapped their arms around each other.

"Why is he calling his brother?" Elijah asked.

"Probably because he's also a police officer and Aaron's boss." Bethany rolled her eyes.

Aaron stomped into the kitchen, and his eyes went straight to her. Bethany saw his face relax and held his hand out to help both her and Allyson to their feet.

"Is Crash okay?" Allyson asked.

Aaron nodded.

"Why would someone shoot at my house?" Allyson pulled her son tighter into her arms.

"And they say Ontario is dangerous." Elijah leaned against the counter and crossed his arms over his chest.

"I'm not sure what this is but this may have something to do with Randy's murder." Aaron stepped toward her, but in a split-second, Elijah had him pinned against the fridge.

"Are you fucking serious? I thought that idiot out there was supposed to protect my cousin. What the fuck was he doing outside?" Elijah shouted.

"Elijah, let him go," Bethany shouted as she tried to pull her cousin away from Aaron.

"You need to listen to your cousin." Aaron's tone was calm, but it sent a shiver down her spine.

Crash stepped into the kitchen. His handsome face tensed when he noticed Elijah holding Aaron against the wall. Bethany shivered at the way he tensed.

"You might want to think before you do something like that." Crash's voice was calm.

"I don't care if he's a cop. What the fuck were you doing out there? Someone could have been killed." Elijah gave Aaron one last shove as he released Aaron and glared at Crash.

"I was returning fire and trying to see the bastards who were shooting at us. By the way, do you guys have some gauze?" Crash turned to Allyson.

"Oh my God, you were shot," Bethany and Allyson said together.

"It's just a graze. I'm fine. I just need to clean it up." Crash pulled his sleeve up.

"You do know Ally's a doctor, right?" Elijah raised an eyebrow.

"Yeah, but I can…" Crash stammered.

Allyson cut him off when she grabbed his arm and dragged him to the laundry room with Cameron following behind them.

"Do I sense a little spark there?" Elijah smirked.

"Maybe." Bethany glanced at Aaron.

"Are you both okay?" Aaron reached for Bethany's hand and squeezed it.

"I'm fine, thanks to you." Bethany stepped toward him and without hesitation wrapped her arms around his neck.

He tensed for a second but then he had her wrapped in his arms so tightly she could barely breathe, but she didn't care in the least. Aaron had her in his arms, and she melted against him.

An hour later, her house filled with police. Most of them being Aaron's family. They kept Bethany and her family in the kitchen while they did whatever police did after a shooting. She didn't want to know, but staying in her house probably wasn't going to be an option.

The only thing that sent her into a spin was her father coming into the house like a raging bull. It took several minutes for Elijah to calm him down and explain what happened. He didn't react to what she'd learned about Aaron and how he hadn't betrayed her. Her father only nodded and pulled both his daughters and grandson into a group hug.

"Bethany, it's nice to see you again. Wish it was under better circumstances." James entered the kitchen.

"Are all your brothers police officers?" Allyson whispered to Aaron.

"Not all. Just John, Nick, A.J. and I. Jess is as well." James smiled.

"How many brothers do you have?" Elijah chuckled.

"There are seven of us." John entered behind James.

"Good to see you, Bethany, Allyson, Mr. Donnelly." John nodded toward each person as he acknowledged them.

Bethany practically flopped down on the chair as the surge of adrenalin from the shooting started to fade. She was suddenly completely exhausted.

"Most of the damage to your house is in the living room. Aaron has Keith on the way to board up that window until we can get it fixed. The forensics guys are finished up there and have everything they need." John held out the small black box. "A.J. said this is yours."

"Yes. Thanks." Bethany wondered where her letter was, but before she could ask, Aaron entered the kitchen holding it in his hand.

"I'd like all of you to stay somewhere else tonight." John glanced back at Aaron.

"We can go to a hotel," Elijah responded.

"Ummm ... I don't think that's going to be happening." James chuckled and stepped to the side.

"Yer not stayin' at any hotel." Bethany smiled at Aaron's grandmother.

The woman didn't look like she'd aged in thirteen years and from what Bethany could see, she still ruled everyone.

"Nan, how did you know they needed a place to stay?" John kissed his grandmother's cheek.

Before she could answer, Kurt and Alice walked in behind her. She knew Kurt was a police officer when she left Hopedale, which was probably why he would show up to a crime scene, but she couldn't figure out why Alice and Nanny Betty would be there.

"I finally figured out why I hate the Bluetooth option in my truck. I was bringing mom and Alice home from the grocery store when Keith called me. Damn demanding women." Kurt looked completely annoyed.

Bethany smiled as Aaron and his brothers snickered at their uncle. She'd always felt a little intimidated by Kurt when she was younger, and he'd seemed to get more intimidating as he'd gotten older, but the sight of Nanny Betty slapping the arm of the over six-foot man was amusing.

"Jus because yer da Chief a' police don't mean ya can talk like dat." Nanny Betty narrowed her eyes and glared at Kurt.

"Sorry, mudder." Kurt sighed and rolled his eyes as his mother turned back to Bethany.

"Stop rollin' yer eyes," she snapped as she headed toward Bethany and her sister.

"It's good to see you again, Mrs. O'Connor." Allyson smiled as she kissed the older woman on the cheek.

"Have ya been away so long dat ya forgot not to call me Mrs. O'Connor? She was me mudder-in-law, and she was a witch. Ya call me Nan jus like ya did before." Nanny Betty turned and glanced at Bethany.

"Hi, Nan." Bethany smiled nervously.

"Well, it's about time ya came back ta put dat boy back on da right path." Nanny Betty pulled Bethany into her arms and hugged her tightly.

"Nan, those two still have a lot to work out, but I'm sure now that all the misunderstandings are out of the way, they'll figure things out." Allyson glanced at Aaron.

"I'm sure dat won't take too long. Now, get yer tings, and we'll take ya outta here until da place is safe." Nanny Betty turned to Cameron.

"Danny and Mason are all excited about ya comin' to stay wit dem." Nanny Betty linked her hand into Cameron's arm, and they walked out of the kitchen.

James had two older boys a little younger than Cameron, but they'd hit it off when Allyson, her father, and the boy were at the family supper.

"Awesome," Cameron said excitedly.

"Why do I get the feeling we'll be telling them to put the games away and go to sleep all night?" James shook his head.

"Because we probably will be." Allyson smiled.

"I'm going to take you and Cameron to my house," James told Allyson.

"Your dad and Elijah will stay with Mom and Dad," John continued.

"What about Beth?" Allyson glanced at her.

"She'll be going to the safe house at The Compound," James explained.

"Is that necessary?" Bethany sighed.

"I'm afraid so." John nodded.

"Crash and I will take you there when you get your things." Aaron stepped back into the kitchen.

This was real. Bethany had a second chance to start over with Aaron, and now someone was trying to kill her. Was this some sign telling her that she and Aaron weren't meant to be? She glanced up and met his blue eyes. No. She was meant to be with Aaron. She knew that thirteen years ago, even if she did doubt it for a while, but gazing at the man walking toward her, she knew they were meant to be together. Now she just had to stay alive.

Chapter 12

Aaron felt shaken to his core. If he hadn't gone to her house when he did, Bethany could be dead. He stared at the couch where he and Bethany sat earlier.

Several holes were scattered across the back of the couch, making his stomach lurch at the thought of how things could have turned out. Ian always got severely stomach sick whenever he was stressed. A lot of times to the point where he'd throw up. At that moment, Aaron could relate.

"A.J.?" Lewis called from behind Aaron.

"Are you ready to go?" Aaron glanced down to where a small suitcase stood next to the man's feet.

"Yes, but I owe you an apology." Lewis dropped his head for a moment and then lifted his eyes to meet Aaron.

"It's not necessary, Mr. Donnelly. I understand why you would be angry with me. If I were a father, I wouldn't have been as calm." Aaron gave him a friendly smile.

"When your little girl comes to you sobbing so much she can barely speak, it tears your heart out. Honestly, I was ready to kick your ass that night, but she begged me to leave you alone. I couldn't deny her that." The memories of what Bethany had gone through that night were painful for her father.

"I wish you would have. At least then it wouldn't have taken thirteen years to clear up the misunderstanding." Aaron shook his head.

"I'm delighted that family doesn't live next door anymore." Lewis chuckled.

"It's probably safer that way." Aaron laughed.

"Do you know how long we'll have to stay out of here?" Lewis glanced around the house.

"A few days at least, but I think it would be safer if Bethany stayed at the safe house until we catch this guy." Aaron held his hand out to Lewis.

"Keep her safe, or I will kick your ass." Lewis pulled Aaron into a hug and slapped him on the back.

"I'll protect her with my life." Aaron shook Lewis hand as he released the hug.

"I'm ready." Bethany walked down the stairs dragging a large suitcase with her.

Aaron grabbed it and grunted at the weight when she released it. She must have packed everything she owned in the damn thing. He grinned when she shrugged her shoulders.

"Is there a body in here?" Aaron teased.

"I honestly don't know what's in there. I just grabbed as much as I could and shoved in there. I don't know how long it will be before I get back here." Bethany went directly to her father and tucked herself under his arm.

"Bethany, you're not going to be kept from your family. It's not a prison you're going to." Aaron dragged the suitcase to the door as Crash opened the door.

Aaron laughed as Crash picked up the suitcase and muttered something about why women's shit was so much heavier than it looked. Bethany giggled as Crash struggled to put the case in the back of the SUV.

"Elijah's waiting outside for you, Mr. Donnelly," James announced as he entered the house. "Allyson and Cameron are settled at the house, and I'll make sure the house is locked up tight when all of you leave."

"Thanks, James." Bethany smiled as she walked toward the door.

James and Aaron both stepped in front of her, stopping her exit. She stared at them in confusion, and all Aaron could do was smile. Bethany was still completely unaware of the danger.

"We need to make sure it's clear before you leave, Bethany." Aaron pulled her out of the doorway.

"Oh, I forgot I'm a dangerous witness." Bethany sighed and leaned against the wall.

"You're not dangerous, but you are a witness that could be in danger." She might be dangerous to his heart though.

Twenty minutes later, Crash pulled up in front of the secure house on Keith's compound. Aaron drove with him while Crunch drove behind them in Aaron's car. The whole drive Bethany clung to Aaron's hand as if he would disappear.

"That isn't what I expected." Bethany smiled when he helped her out of the SUV.

"What were you expecting?" Keith walked up behind them.

"I don't know. On television, this type of place is usually old cabins or rundown houses." Bethany slowly turned around as she took in the small house.

"It's nothing fancy, but it's comfortable." Keith wrapped his arm around Bethany's shoulder and squeezed. "You'll be safe here."

"Let's get you inside." Aaron took her hand and led her up the two steps leading to the white front door.

"It's cute," Bethany whispered.

"Yeah." Aaron chuckled as he pushed open the door and they walked through.

The front door led into a small foyer probably only big enough for two people to stand comfortably. As they stepped further into the house, they walked into a large open area with a kitchen on the left and the living area was on the right.

Straight ahead was the hallway leading to the bedrooms. Aaron had been in the house several times and knew it well. He tugged Bethany toward the back and showed her where she'd be sleeping.

There were four small bedrooms, two on each side. Aaron pushed open the door closest to the kitchen and motioned for Bethany to walk in ahead of him.

"This is where you'll be sleeping." Aaron stared at her as she looked around the small room.

"It's cozy." She smiled.

"Yeah, that door is a bathroom." Aaron pointed to a door in the far corner. "That door there leads into the other bedroom." He pointed to the door closest to where they entered the room.

"That's convenient, I guess." She sat on the foot of the bed and wrapped her arms around herself.

"It's just in case one of the security has to move you fast." Aaron crouched in front of her.

"So, someone could still …" Her voice trailed off.

"Bethany, Keith's property is like Fort Knox. He built it before he finished the gates around the property." Aaron rubbed his hand up and down her arms.

"I'm scared." She closed her eyes.

"You've got every right to feel that way, but I want you to know one thing." Aaron waited for her to open her eyes before he spoke again. "Now that I have you back, I'll move heaven and earth to make sure that bastard doesn't get near you."

"You could have gotten shot today." Bethany choked as she cupped his face in her hands.

"I didn't." Aaron knelt on the floor and wrapped his arms around her waist. "I guess I'm pretty presumptuous when I say I've got you back, but I do want you back."

He stared into her green eyes that looked even more beautiful than he remembered. She slowly leaned toward him, and he held his breath as he let her take the first step to them again.

Her lips lightly brushed against his as her eyes stayed locked with his. She pulled back a little, and her eyes traveled across his face, down to his mouth and back to his eyes. She pulled his face to her and pressed her soft, warm lips against his.

With a sigh, Aaron molded his lips to her and slid his hands up to cradle her head in his hands. His tongue glided across her lips, and he moaned when she opened to his invasion. She wasn't tentative like the first time they kissed. No. Bethany swirled her tongue around his, and when she sucked it further into his mouth, Aaron's cock hardened instantly.

He groaned when her hands threaded into his hair, and she fisted it as she tilted her head. It gave him better access to her mouth, and he took full advantage of it.

The small part of his brain that hadn't disappeared screamed at him to slow down. Aaron cursed it but pulled away from her, leaving both of them gasping for air.

"As much as I want this, and fuck, do I want this. I think we should probably slow this down. We just found each other again, and I have to meet John at the station. I would rather poke hot sticks in my eyes than leave you right now, but it's important." Aaron pressed his forehead against hers.

"I understand." She sighed. "Will you be coming…"

She stopped as if she was afraid of his answer. He sat back on his heels and cupped her face in his hands.

"I'll be back tonight. I promise." Aaron gazed into her eyes. "Just so you know, you're stuck with me."

"I guess if I'm stuck with you, I'll have to deal with it," she teased, and he narrowed his eyes as he pressed his lips hard against hers.

"And by the way, I won't be waiting eight months to have you under me again," Aaron growled as he gave her one more searing kiss before he forced himself to move away from her.

"Good to know." She braced her hands behind her and leaned back. "Eight months is a long time at our age."

"Damn right." Aaron winked as he pulled open the door. "I'll be back as soon as I can."

He blew her a kiss as he made his way out of the house. Even with the danger surrounding them, he couldn't wipe the smile off his face if he tried.

"Well, Aunt Cora, I guess you were right after all." Aaron chuckled as he jumped into his car and headed to meet John.

Chapter 13

Aaron left a couple of hours earlier, and Bethany was bored of flicking through the channels on television. Crash wasn't exactly a huge conversationalist and tended to be more interested in reading than talking.

She'd explored the small house and checked out the fridge, surprised to see it stocked with food. Bethany made herself a sandwich and offered one to Crash who happily accepted.

"Have you worked for Keith long?" Bethany sat across the table from the large man.

"About ten years. Rusty hired me when I got out of the army." Crash took a bite of his sandwich.

"Rusty?" Bethany held her sandwich in front of her mouth.

"It's Keith's nickname." Crash laughed.

"I guess I don't need to ask where he got the nickname." She snickered as she thought about Keith's red hair.

"No, but nobody else but us can use it," Crash warned.

"You were in the military?" Bethany wasn't surprised because he carried himself the same way Elijah and her late brother-in-law did.

"Yes, I did two tours overseas and retired after the second. I'd had enough." A sad expression clouded his eyes but disappeared so quickly that Bethany was starting to think she'd imagined it.

"Elijah is retired as well and works with veterans. Allyson's husband was killed overseas a few months back." Bethany glanced down at her half-eaten sandwich.

"I didn't know." Crash's body tensed.

"It was the main reason she wanted to move home again. It was hard to stay there after Trent died." Bethany met his eyes.

"Sorry, I need to do a check around the house. I'll be back in a few." Crash shoved his empty plate in the dishwasher and quickly left the house.

He reacted very strangely but she assumed since he'd probably seen some pretty awful things during his tours, he didn't want to think about anyone not making it back. Elijah never talked about his time overseas, and when anyone mentioned it, he would change the subject.

Bethany's phone buzzed, and she pulled it out of her back pocket. A message on the screen confused her at first, but then she burst out laughing.

We're coming, and we're bringing booze. We want information. Got it?

The message was from Sandy, and she assumed she was bringing her sisters-in-law. Bethany wasn't sure about the alcohol because it didn't seem like a good idea considering how the last couple of days had gone. Then again maybe she needed a good stiff drink.

A few minutes later, she heard several footfalls on the front steps. It didn't frighten her since she heard Sandy shout through the door.

"Open up. We got you surrounded." Sandy shouted through the door as Bethany pulled it open.

Crash stood at the bottom of the steps, shaking his head as several women filed by her and headed into the house. Total shock hit her when she saw one of the women.

"Marina?" Bethany gasped.

"I know. I was shocked when James introduced his wife." Allyson laughed.

"How do you know Marina?" Sandy asked while she placed several glasses across the counter.

"My boss and Bethany's boss are brothers." Marina hugged Bethany.

"Seriously?" A beautiful woman placed two platters on the counter.

"Yeah, and Marina once kidnapped me and dragged me to this bar where we barely got out alive." Bethany laughed.

"It was a dangerous abduction, but we had fun." Marina winked.

"Okay, we need to do introductions because I know she doesn't know everyone." Kristy wrapped her arm around Bethany and whispered. "I'm so happy you're back."

"Me too." Bethany hugged her old friend.

"Okay, you know Sandy and Emily. You remember Isabelle and Pam?" Kristy pointed to her sister and cousin.

"I remember them." Bethany hugged both women.

"So, this is Billie; she's married to Mike. That's Stephanie; she's married to John." Kristy pointed to the dark-haired woman and a pretty blonde.

"Steph's my sister, too." Marina pulled the plastic off the platter Billie had placed on the counter.

"You both married brothers. Wait, wasn't James engaged to Sarah Mason?" Bethany remembered how excited Aaron had been about being in a wedding party.

The smile dropped from all the women's faces, and she felt terrible for bringing it up. Bethany met Sarah when she first dated

Aaron and liked the perky woman. James and Sarah were so much in love that it seemed strange they weren't still together.

"Sarah passed away from breast cancer ten years ago. She and James got married and had a baby, but she got sick shortly after Mason was born and passed away," Marina explained.

"You met James when you came home?" Bethany sat next to Marina at the table.

"Before I left. Steph and John were dating when I came back." Marina smiled, but Bethany had a feeling there was more to the whole story.

"I'm Lora. I'm engaged to Nick. They tend to forget me since I'm just new to the group." The woman sat by Kristy nudged Aaron's cousin.

"How could I forget the woman that I escaped a crazy man's house with?" Kristy snickered.

"Huh?" Bethany glanced back and forth between the two women.

"Oh, honey have we got stories to tell you." Sandy placed a shot glass in front of every one of the women. "But first, welcome to the group."

Bethany clutched her stomach two hours later as it was hurting from laughing. It was the first time she'd laughed so hard in a long time. She met her sister's smiling face and realized she hadn't seen her sister smile so much since her husband died. It was good to see.

"You know this is the first time we've all been together, and all of us can drink." Isabelle pointed her finger at all the glasses each woman held.

"True," Marina agreed.

"Well, it's the first time one of us hasn't been pregnant in a long time." Kristy snickered.

"I can't believe you and Aaron were almost engaged." Marina eased next to her on the couch.

"Neither can I. What was he like back then? Was he a huge flirt back then too? When we ask the guys about it, we get this dangerous silence. Like they're afraid to say anything." Billie leaned her elbows on her knees and rested her chin on her fists.

"No. Aaron was sweet and funny. Every time he came to pick me up he'd have some sort of flower. I don't know where he used to get them, but he always had one." Bethany smiled.

"That's so sweet," Stephanie cooed.

"Yeah, she used to press every flower he brought," Allyson teased.

"I wonder where he got them," Emily said as she poured another glass of wine.

"I'd steal them from the flowers Mom used to put around the house every day." Bethany turned at the sound of his voice, and her heart flip-flopped in her chest.

"I'm telling Aunt Kathleen," Jess joked.

"Why are there a bunch of half-drunk women in the safe house?" Bethany looked behind Aaron at a large bald man.

"Like you're disappointed. You reap the benefits of this half-drunk woman." Kristy wiggled her eyebrows.

"Kitten, you don't need to be drunk for me to reap the benefits." The man grinned at Kristy.

"That's Kristy's husband. Dean Nash but everyone calls him Bull," Marina whispered. "He and Keith are business partners as well."

"He's huge." He was at least a couple of inches taller than Aaron.

"You have no idea." Kristy wiggled her eyebrows.

"Yeah, Bull, it's time to take her home," Aaron groaned.

"Didn't we tell you? We're all staying tonight." Sandy looked completely serious.

"Yeah, it's a big slumber party," Emily agreed.

Aaron opened the front door and motioned to someone outside. Crunch walked in with another man that Marina said was another of the security that worked for Keith and Bull. She called him Trunk.

"Take all these drunks home." Aaron swirled his finger around the room.

"You're such a party pooper, whoreboy." Sandy tossed a pillow at Aaron.

"Goodnight, ladies." Aaron stepped back and bowed as each of the women hugged Bethany and followed Crunch and Trunk through the door.

"Kitten, I think we need to go too." Bull grasped Kristy's hand and pulled her to her feet.

"Fine," Kristy grumbled.

Kristy walked next to Bethany and pulled her in for a tight hug. Kristy had been her best friend back then, and Bethany had missed her almost as much as Aaron. Not keeping in touch with her friend was one of her biggest regrets.

"I'm so happy you're back," Kristy whispered into her ear. "Please, do whatever the guys tell you. They'll keep you safe."

"I'm glad to be back too, and I'll do whatever they say." Bethany smiled as Kristy pulled back from the hug.

"A.J., don't fuck this up." Kristy kissed Aaron's cheek as she linked into her husband's arm and walked through the door.

Aaron closed the door and fell against it as he blew out a huge breath. Bethany giggled at his expression. It was as if he had just cleared a minefield and was relieved to have gotten out alive.

"I didn't know they were coming over." Aaron shook his head.

"It's okay. I was so glad to see Marina and meet the rest of her sisters-in-law." Bethany moved around the open space, picking up glasses and bringing them to the kitchen.

"You know Marina?" Aaron tidied up the living room.

"We met when she lived in Ontario. Her boss and my boss are brothers," Bethany explained as she closed the dishwasher.

When she turned, he was directly behind her. Startled, she stepped back but smiled when he placed his hands on her hips and tugged her closer.

"How did your meeting go?" She pressed her hands against his hard chest, and her body buzzed at the heat of him against her.

"We have to bring you to the station in the morning so that you can describe the suspect. Melinda will be there around noon." Aaron's hands slipped around her waist and linked at the middle of her back.

"Okay." Bethany leaned closer and inhaled, filling her senses with his scent.

"Did you just sniff me?" Aaron chuckled.

"I love the smell of your cologne," she admitted.

"I guess I'll be picking up a bucket of that if it keeps you this close to me." Aaron grinned and leaned down, brushing his nose against her cheek.

"Aaron," Bethany whispered as his lips grazed her cheek and moved slowly down to the corner of her lips.

"Bethany," he breathed as she turned her head enough so that she could press her lips against his.

Again, the kiss was slow and tender but made Bethany tingle with anticipation and need. Aaron's hand pressed against her back, pulling her flush against his hard body and flicking her libido switch into overdrive as he slid his tongue into her mouth.

Her arms slipped around his neck and tilted her head to give him better access to her mouth. He tasted of coffee and the mixture of the wine that she'd been drinking and would never strike her as an aphrodisiac, but it was driving her crazy.

"Jesus, Bethany." Aaron gasped as he pulled his lips from hers.

She could feel his excitement against her belly and knew he was as affected by this as she was. With her inhibitions lowered because of the wine, she was sure she'd pounce on him if he didn't pull away. She knew it wasn't only the wine; it was Aaron. The only man to own her heart.

"You're driving me crazy, baby." Aaron cupped her. "And as much as I want you, I don't want to rush this. I want you to fall in love with me now. Not the memory of who I used to be."

"I guess I need you to do the same because, Aaron, I'm not the same timid girl I used to be. I won't let anyone walk all over me." She gazed into his eyes.

"Makes me want to find Raquel and her shadows and let you loose on them." Aaron chuckled.

"Do you know where they live?" She grinned.

"I don't, and I really couldn't care less where they are." Aaron pressed his lips against her forehead, and she slid her arms around his waist.

"I guess I should get some sleep." Bethany sighed as she pulled back. "Unless you have something you want to do to keep me awake longer." She grinned, and he shook his head.

"You have changed, and you're going to be trouble, aren't you?" Aaron tapped her nose with his finger.

"A good kind." Bethany smiled.

Aaron turned and pulled her into his side as he walked her to her bedroom. She didn't want him to leave her all night, but he was right. They needed to get to know each other again. The attraction was still there, but she wasn't the same person. Maybe taking their time would be a good idea.

"I'll be in the adjoining room. Goodnight, Bethany." Aaron gave her a tender kiss and then continued down the hallway to the other room.

Yeah, she'd get to know him again and hopefully build a relationship that she'd dreamed about all those years ago. That was if she didn't get caught in the crosshairs of a cold-blooded killer.

Chapter 14

Aaron sipped the hot coffee and prayed that it would be strong enough to give him the boost of energy he needed after a restless night. He'd tried every sleeping position known to man, but nothing helped him fall asleep.

The fact that he had a raging hard-on that refused to go down every time his mind went to Bethany didn't help in the least. He'd peeked in on her several times during the night and was glad to see that she was getting some rest.

The problem was she'd kicked off the blankets, and he got a clear view of the lace panties that covered her firm round ass. He'd groaned and closed the door. It was at that moment he decided to do something about the wood straining against his boxers.

It didn't help him sleep, and at five in the morning, he'd given up on getting any more sleep and took a shower to wake himself up. Now he stood tired and slightly cranky, waiting for Bethany to get out of bed.

"Crunch is here, and I'm heading home to get some shut eye." Crash entered the safe house.

"I hope you have better luck than I did last night," Aaron grumbled.

"Little lady kept you up all night?" Crash joked.

"Not the way you're thinking." Aaron narrowed his eyes.

"Are you kidding me? I walked in last night when you two were going at it in the kitchen. You guys didn't even notice." Crash laughed.

"We kissed, asshole." Aaron tossed a napkin at him.

"The kiss I saw either leads to a hot night of sex or a painful night of blue balls." Crash chuckled as he made his way to leave.

"Thanks, Crash. I hope your day of sleep was a good as mine was last night," Aaron shouted.

"Bastard," Crash shouted back.

"I'm really not a morning person." He heard her sleepy voice coming from the entrance to the kitchen.

"You're certainly beautiful in the morning." Aaron winked.

Bethany rolled her eyes as she gently pushed him away from the coffee pot. He laughed as she leaned against the counter and sipped the coffee as if it contained the best tasting liquid in the world.

"Why are you up at seven in the morning?" Bethany yawned as she plopped down on the stool next to the island.

"I was actually up at five." Aaron almost choked on his coffee when her eyes widened, and she shuddered.

"People actually get out of bed that early?" Bethany sipped from her cup again.

"Yes, they do. During the police academy, I had to be up at five every morning for physical training." Aaron rested his arms on the counter.

"That's why I wouldn't have made a good cop." She snorted.

"I wonder how all the girls are doing this morning." Bethany grinned.

"Probably hung over. I don't think any of them will be much good at their jobs today." Aaron laughed.

They talked about his family and her life in Ontario. He was surprised to know that Elijah was former military. She told him that he traveled back and forth between Newfoundland and Ontario working with some other military guys.

By the time they were ready to head to the station, they'd practically caught up on thirteen years in a few hours. Aaron could never remember talking to a woman as much as he did with her. Even when they were teenagers, they would spend hours talking. It seemed that was the one thing that didn't change between them.

"Whatever happened to Joey Mayo?" Bethany asked as Crunch drove them to the station.

"Joey's a dentist," Aaron explained when Crunch turned into the parking lot.

"Is he married?" It was apparent she wanted to distract herself from the thought of remembering what she heard and seen.

Aaron knew from experience sometimes describing a suspect made people uneasy. Especially if they felt traumatized over the memory.

"Not yet, it's only been legal for him to marry for a couple of years. They only allowed gay marriage a few years ago," Aaron explained.

"Joey's gay?" Bethany's eyes were as big as saucers.

"Yeah, he came out in university. He and his partner have been together since then. Braden is a little flamboyant, but he's a great guy." Aaron didn't feel any different about Joey or Braden than he did any of his other friends.

Joey helped out at Holy Cross with the after-school programs and sports. Since Joey was one of the best basketball players in high school, Father Wallace asked him to help coach the teams if he had the time.

"I'd love to see him again and meet this Braden guy," Bethany said as they walked in through the entrance of the building.

"Maybe when this is all over we can get together with them." Aaron clasped her hand in his.

He was surprised at how much her hand shook. As much as she acted brave, she was scared. Aaron couldn't blame her. It terrified Aaron as well. He'd lost her for thirteen years and wasn't about to let anyone take her away from him again.

John sat with Melinda in one of the conference rooms. The tall, athletic woman stood when Aaron entered with Bethany next to him. Melinda had short blonde hair with pink streaks in the front when her hair fell to the side.

Aaron often flirted with her in the past, but they'd never dated. Suddenly, he felt utterly nervous about being around the cute cop. The last thing he needed was Bethany to think he couldn't talk to a woman without flirting.

"Hey, A.J." Melinda held out her hand to Aaron.

"Hi, Melinda." Aaron shook her hand and then pulled it back quickly.

"Nice to see you again." Melinda's lips quirked as she glanced between Bethany and Aaron.

"This is Bethany Donnelly. My girlfriend." Aaron lay his hand on the small of Bethany's back.

"Girlfriend?" Melinda's eyes glanced back and forth between Aaron and John. "You're pulling my leg."

"No." Aaron was a little ticked off at the fact that Melinda seemed so shocked over him having a girlfriend.

"Wow, well you must be an extraordinary lady to get this one to commit to a relationship." Melinda sat across from Bethany and snickered.

"Could we get on with this?" Aaron grumbled.

"Don't be such a grump." Melinda rolled her eyes. "Okay, Bethany, the first thing I want you to do is to try and remember as much detail about this guy as possible. We'll start with the shape of his face, the color of his hair, eyes, and so on. I'll show you what I have once we get that and then we'll fill in the little details."

"Okay." Bethany glanced up at Aaron and then back to Melinda.

"You two can go grab a cup of coffee while we work." Melinda waved her hand toward the door.

"I'm staying." Aaron leaned against the wall.

"No, you're not." John opened the door and gave him a look that said not to argue.

"What is it about the married people in this family and that devil's glare? Does Nan give you a lesson after you get married or something?" Aaron said when he stepped outside the conference room.

"Yes." John chuckled.

"Why can't I stay in there with her?" Aaron cringed when he realized how he sounded.

"Our little brother has finally grown up, but you do sound like a spoiled brat right now." John wrapped his arm around Aaron and guided him away from the room. "Let me buy you a coffee, and I'll tell you about the birds and the bees of relationships."

"Fuck off." Aaron pushed John to the side, but both of them laughed.

"We'll keep her safe, bro." John clamped his hand on Aaron's shoulder.

Aaron heard that statement so often over the last ten years that it became like a motto for the O'Connor family. With the danger that plagued all his siblings' relationships, it was surprising they came out of it as happy as they were.

It gave him the hope that he and Bethany would be able to do the same. The first thing they had to do was find the guy who killed Randy Knight. Somehow the man knew that Bethany had seen him and found out where she lived.

"Is there any word on the bullets they found at Bethany's house?" Aaron asked John as they sat in the lunchroom.

"Looks like two guns. Both forty-five caliber." John placed the report in front of him.

"Well, that's something, at least." Aaron glanced through the forensics report.

"We think we know how this guy found out where she lived." John pushed several photos toward Aaron.

"What is this?" Aaron shuffled through the photos taken by the forensics team.

"They're pictures from over a dozen bugs planted at that office. Two were in the office where the shooting happened. Four in Knight's office. One in the bathroom and several more around the reception area," John explained.

"They would have heard us say she saw the shooter and that she was going back to Hopedale. It wouldn't take much for him to figure out what she looked like." Aaron tossed the pictures on the table. "Fuck."

"Yeah, and we've got Sandy and Smash working to see if they can trace the server that they connect to but according to Sandy, that may take some time. She went on about some techie stuff that made me feel like a complete moron. I just nodded and told her to let me know if she finds anything." John smirked.

"When Sandy and Smash start talking computer stuff I feel like Charlie Brown listening to that teacher. Blah Blah Blah." Aaron laughed when John nodded.

"I also have her looking into Knight and Craig Molloy as well. Marina said there's no way he would be involved in something shady, but I figure we better check him out anyway." John stood up as his phone buzzed.

"Melinda?" Aaron shot to his feet.

"Yeah, she said they're done." John made his way out of the office and Aaron close behind.

When they got to the conference room, they could hear laughter from inside. John pushed open the door, and the laughter stopped. Aaron didn't like the guilty look in their eyes.

"What do you have?" John asked as he walked behind Melinda.

"She's incredible." Melinda beamed.

"You don't have to tell me that." Aaron met Bethany's gaze.

"Seriously, she's so descriptive. It made it so easy to draw this loser." Melinda turned the sketch so Aaron could see it.

"Melinda's pretty amazing too. That looks exactly like the guy that shot Randy." Bethany pointed at the drawing.

"Great, we'll get this out and see if anyone recognizes the guy." John took the drawing. "Thanks, Melinda. We owe you one."

"You can pay me back by getting me transferred out here," Melinda shouted as John left the office.

"I'm working on it, Mel," John called back.

Melinda packed her things as she chatted with Bethany. Aaron sat between them and listened to the conversation but didn't pay attention to what they were saying. He was too entranced with

Bethany's mouth, and all he could think about was how soft her lips were when they kissed.

"A.J., snap out of it." Melinda shoved him, startling him out of his haze.

"What?" he grumbled.

"Wow, you got it bad, but I have to say, this one at least has a brain, and I like her. Don't fuck it up." She tapped the back of his head and winked at Bethany.

"I need to make sure John doesn't get you transferred here," Aaron teased.

"He loves me and so do you." Melinda stuck out her tongue as she hefted her bag on her shoulder.

"It was nice meeting you." Bethany stood up and hugged Melinda.

"You too. I hope they catch this guy and soon. Then we can take a trip to George Street." She grinned as she eyed Aaron.

"Not a fan of George Street but we could go to Jack's Place." Bethany laughed.

"Considering all the hot men I've seen around here lately, you got a deal." Melinda made her way to the door. "Don't lose this one, A.J."

Then she was gone from the doorway. Aaron stood up and wrapped his arms around Bethany from behind. She leaned back against him and sighed.

"I'm never losing you again," Aaron whispered into her ear.

"Good. You'd score some major points if you took me to get some food." She tipped her head back and looked over her shoulder at him.

"*Jack's Place* it is." Aaron spun her around and pressed a kiss to her lips.

"Isabelle said she owns the restaurant on the corner of Beach Street," Bethany said as they walked out of the station.

"We can go there if you want." Aaron didn't mind going to *A Taste of Hopedale* because Isabelle's food was great as well.

"I don't think I'm dressed for that place." Bethany waved down at her jeans and t-shirt.

"Do you think Isabelle cares about that?" He snorted.

"No, but I'd rather wait until we can go just the two of us without the Secret Service behind me." Bethany motioned to Crunch leaning against the SUV.

"It's a date. When we catch this guy, I'll take you on the most romantic date you've ever seen." Aaron winked and kissed her cheek.

Aaron wrapped his arm around her shoulder and pulled her into his side. He glanced at Crunch and the hair on the back of Aaron's neck prickled. A dark, older model Ford drove slowly down the street next to the parking lot.

Aaron instinctively shoved Bethany behind him and made sure she was out of the direct vision of the car. Crunch opened the back door of the SUV, ready for Bethany to get inside.

"Bethany, as soon as we get next to the vehicle, get in and stay down until we say it's safe." Aaron kept his focus on the car as they hurried across the parking lot.

"Okay," Bethany whimpered behind him.

Bethany practically leaped into the back of the SUV and Aaron slammed the door. Aaron made his way around to jump into the front as Crunch hopped in the driver's seat.

They sat in the truck and watched the car turn into the parking lot behind *Snippy Gals*, the beauty salon on Harbour Street. Emily and Sandy's sister owned the only salon in Hopedale, and though Emily was in her last few months of maternity leave, she still spent at least a couple of days a week dropping into the place.

Aaron hovered his hand over his weapon and waited to see what the people in the vehicle had in mind. Crunch turned his dash cam toward the car, and they waited.

"Can I get up?" Bethany whispered from the back.

"Not yet, baby," Aaron answered.

The back door slowly opened, and two women stepped out. They said something to the driver and chatted as they made their way inside the salon.

"You can get up, Bethany." Aaron blew out a breath.

"Do you want to tell me why I was laying down in the back?" Bethany leaned on the seats and stared at Aaron.

"Not sure. Crunch seemed nervous about that car." Aaron nodded toward the van that was now pulling back out of the parking lot.

"Crash said the shooters were driving a black Ford Tempo with tinted windows. He said it was an older model probably late nineteen nineties. Hence the suspicion." Crunch started the SUV and pulled out onto the road.

"Well, that was fun, but can we go to *Jack's Place*? I'm still starving." Bethany sat back and pulled her seatbelt over her shoulder.

"Hey, I'll take any excuse to get a plate of fish and chips at *Jack's Place*." Crunch grinned.

Aaron reached back over the seat and snagged Bethany's hand. He gave it a little squeeze, and she blew him a kiss. Yep, Aaron was a goner.

Chapter 15

Bethany moaned at the taste of the fresh, deep-fried codfish. She'd had fish in Ontario but there was nothing like deep-fried codfish, and Alice O'Connor knew how to cook it.

"A.J., if I were you I'd start to feel a little jealous over the way she's moaning over that food," Crunch teased.

"Trust me; I'm not jealous. She'll moan a lot louder for me," Aaron growled, and she slapped his arm.

"Aaron," she gasped.

"Why do you call him Aaron? Everyone else calls him A.J., except his mother when he's in shit." Crunch laughed.

"It's the way he introduced himself to me. It seems weird to call him A.J., at least to me." She glanced up at Aaron and had to keep herself from sighing at his smile.

After they'd finished eating and Alice practically ordered her to try a piece of her blueberry pie, Bethany felt as if she was going to bust. She sat back and listened to Crunch and Aaron chat about the renovations Crunch was doing to the house he'd bought in Hopedale.

"I'm not in a big hurry to renovate the other bedrooms. It's just me, and I don't see any prospects in the future." Crunch chuckled, but there was something in his grey eyes that said he certainly wanted someone in his life.

Bethany didn't say anything but watched him as he kept glancing toward a young waitress serving the tables behind them. She might be mistaken, but there was a hint of interest there, at least on Crunch's part.

"Is that okay, Bethany?" Aaron and Crunch were both looking at her.

"I'm sorry. I zoned out there for a minute. What did you ask me?" Bethany smiled sheepishly.

"I can see that." Aaron nudged her with his shoulder.

"I have a lot on my mind." She nudged him back.

"I know, but I need to go by Holy Cross School to drop off some papers to Father Wallace. I've been helping him with the one-hundredth anniversary. I thought you might want to go and see the old school." Aaron smiled.

"I'd love to, but is it safe for me to go there? I don't even know when I can go back to work. Oh, wow, I should call Craig and see if there's anything I can do. Is he a suspect? I know it wasn't him. He would never…." Bethany stopped when Aaron put his hand over her mouth, halting her rambling questions.

"Can you imagine her and Stephanie in a room together when they are both excited?" Crunch laughed.

"Sorry, I just had all that go through my head at once." Bethany felt the heat of a blush warm her cheeks.

"I see that hasn't changed." Aaron kissed her cheek. "And to answer your questions, you can go back to work, but for now it will have to be from the safe house. He is on the list, but I'm pretty sure he's not involved. It will be safe to go visit the school because Crunch is coming with us." Aaron grinned as if he was pretty proud of himself.

"I think he answered every question." Crunch stood up, and again his eyes glanced at the pretty waitress.

"You should ask her out," Bethany whispered as she walked by Crunch.

It was incredibly funny to see such an alpha male drop his head to hide the blush that turned his cheeks red. Bethany winked as she linked her hand into Aaron's arm and walked toward the exit.

"I don't think she'd be interested," Crunch whispered back as Aaron paid for the food.

"If you don't ask, you won't know." Bethany poked Crunch's chest. "But don't introduce yourself as Crunch."

It appeared that Hunter 'Crunch' Crawford might be a brave and protective bodyguard, but when it came to women, he was as shy as a teenage boy.

Bethany felt odd walking into her old high school. The building looked and smelled the same. Even though it was the end of the school day, there were still some students roaming the corridors, some of them waving or saying hello to Aaron.

The girls told her the previous night that he volunteered with the after-school programs and from the way the kids acted when they saw him, the students liked him.

They made their way to the office, Aaron frequently stopping to point out something new in the school or chatting briefly with a student. Crunch seemed at ease which made Bethany feel calm.

"Hey, Ivy, is Father Wallace in his office?" Aaron asked the familiar woman behind the desk.

"Hi, A.J." Ivy smiled at Aaron. "He's in there. Go on in."

"Bethany, come on in and see him. He was asking about you not long ago." Aaron motioned for her to follow him.

"I knew that was you." Ivy came around the desk and wrapped Bethany up in a hug.

Bethany felt uncomfortable with the woman hugging her because she didn't recognize her. She glanced at Aaron for some help, but all he did was laugh at her expression.

"Ivy, I don't think she remembers who you are," Aaron informed the excited woman.

"I'm sorry. I've been away for a long time." Bethany felt terrible that she didn't remember the smiling woman.

"Does the name Ivy Ray mean anything to you?" Ivy grinned.

"Oh my God. How could I not recognize you?" Bethany embraced her sister's former classmate. "I thought you moved to England?"

"I did, but my husband and I came back about five years ago." Ivy smiled. "Is Ally back as well?"

"Yes, I should give you her number, and you can give her a call." Bethany stepped back from Ivy.

"That would be great." Ivy handed Bethany a piece of paper to write the number.

"I thought I heard familiar voices out here." A raspy male voice boomed.

Bethany glanced up to see Father Wallace walking out of his office. He had aged but still had the friendly smile that made you feel as if you could tell him anything. He'd been head of the school for as long as she could remember, and she guessed he wasn't retiring any time soon.

"Father Wallace, it's so good to see you." Bethany wrapped her arms around the chunky priest in a tight hug.

"It's good to see you back, Ms. Donnelly." Father Wallace smiled down at her.

"Father, I have the addresses for the list you gave me. Should I leave them with Ivy?" Aaron asked, pointing the papers toward where Ivy had taken her place back at her desk.

"We have some students that are sending out the invitations. They are in the art room preparing them now." Father Wallace motioned for them to follow him.

"See you again, Ivy." Bethany waved as Ivy picked up the ringing phone.

The art room was at the end of the corridor next to the music room. Bethany had spent a lot of time in both places during her year in Holy Cross. She was part of the choir and had her piano lessons there as well.

Inside the art room, a dozen students scurried around a large table in the middle covered with colorful papers and envelopes. Crunch waited at the entrance of the room while Bethany followed Aaron and Father Wallace inside.

"Mr. Watts, we have more addresses for you." A young man looked up from the computer he sat behind and jumped to his feet.

"This is Mr. O'Connor and Ms. Donnelly." Father placed his hand on the teenager's shoulder. "This is our student council president, Quintin Watts."

"I know Mr. O'Connor from basketball." Quintin nodded at Aaron.

"That's right, Quintin is one of the best point guards on the team." Aaron's compliment made the young boy perk up instantly with pride.

"Mr. O'Connor, could I talk to you for a minute?" Quintin asked shyly.

"Sure, what's up?" Aaron showed so much interest in the young man, and that was the Aaron she remembered.

"No offense, but could I talk to you in private?" Quintin blushed as his gaze went from Aaron to Father Wallace and then to Bethany.

"Sure, you want to step outside?" Aaron nodded toward the door of the art room.

Quintin nodded, and Bethany gave him a wink as he followed Aaron outside. She scanned the room, watching the remaining students scurry around as they prepared what looked like hundreds of envelopes.

"All these students are in grade twelve," Father Wallace explained.

"It's great they are willing to help with this." Bethany glanced behind her where Crunch stood near the entrance.

The door opened, and Bethany expected to see Aaron and Quintin returning but instead, the last person she wanted to see walk through the door, tapping frantically into her phone.

Bethany glanced at Crunch, and part of her wanted to tell the bodyguard that the woman that walked through the door needed to be taken down. It was childish and probably wouldn't go over well, but the vision of Raquel Evans tackled by Crunch made her smile.

Although, if Raquel were anything like she was in school, she'd probably enjoy being tackled by a handsome, muscled man. No. Bethany wouldn't do that to Crunch.

"There you are, Father Wallace." Raquel scurried toward where Bethany stood by the priest.

The once teenage boy's dream had aged and not well. Bethany knew Raquel was the same age as she was, and it was a little shocking to see the deep creases in Raquel's once perfect features. She still dressed in clothes that showed her ample breasts and too much makeup.

"Raquel, how can I help you?" Father Wallace gave Bethany a soft smile as he turned to the woman still tapping into her phone.

As Raquel spoke to the priest, Bethany didn't miss the glances she kept throwing her way. The fact that Raquel didn't seem to recognize Bethany was a relief. Not that she could intimidate Bethany anymore.

When Raquel finished her conversation with Father Wallace, she turned. Bethany tried hard not to show any hint of recognition as she nodded to the woman and slowly walked toward Crunch.

"I'm sorry, you look familiar. Do we know each other?" Raquel asked as Bethany stopped next to Crunch.

"I'm not sure," Bethany lied.

"I'm Raquel Evans." She smiled, and Bethany saw a hint of the pretty girl from high school.

"I'm sorry, the name isn't familiar." Bethany didn't want Raquel to think she was memorable enough that Bethany would know her the minute she saw her.

"Beatrice?" Raquel said slowly.

"No, my name isn't Beatrice." Bethany tried not to roll her eyes.

"Goodness, right. It's Bethany, right?" Raquel stood taller and smiled like the bitch she was.

"Yes, but I still can't remember you." Bethany tilted her head and met Raquel's gaze.

"I'm sure A.J. would be surprised to see you here." Raquel tossed her frizzy hair over her shoulder.

"I doubt that." Bethany turned to Crunch who appeared completely confused.

"Who's this handsome guy?" Raquel cooed as she reached over and touched Crunch's arm.

"Hunter Crawford, this is Raquel Evans." Bethany introduced Crunch to her old nemesis.

"My, you're so strong." Raquel ran her long fingernail up Crunch's arm, and he stepped back.

The move seemed to give her the hint that Crunch didn't want her to touch him. Bethany touched his arm, and he smiled down at her. It was a childish move, but she wanted to show Raquel Crunch didn't mind Bethany touching him.

"It's so great to see you again, Bethany." Raquel pulled Bethany into an awkward hug.

"You too." Bethany pulled out of the hug as soon as she could.

"It's been so long. I thought you moved away?" Raquel crossed her arms under her ample breasts, pushing them practically out of her low-cut blouse.

"I did. I just moved back recently." Bethany glanced toward the entrance as Aaron and Quinton walked back into the art room

"Oh A.J., honey, look who's back in town." Raquel reached her hand out to Aaron as if they were a couple.

"I'm aware she's back." Aaron didn't look amused.

"And why didn't you tell me?" Raquel put her hands on her hips and glared at Aaron.

"Probably because I haven't spoken to you in more than ten years." Aaron stepped around Raquel and wrapped his arm around Bethany's waist.

"Ah... Umm… you two are together?" Raquel stammered over her words, and her eyes were as big as saucers.

"Yes, we are." Aaron kissed Bethany's temple.

"I just thought after the way she left…" Raquel fidgeted with the bracelet on her arm.

"Yes, she left because she'd overheard someone saying something that wasn't true and misunderstood a conversation between me, Cory, and Joey, but we worked things out, and we're picking up where we left off." Aaron grinned.

"I see." Raquel's cheeks were flaming red, and Bethany wasn't sure if it was anger or embarrassment.

"Well, we need to go." Bethany nodded to Raquel. "I'd like to say it was nice to see you, Raquel, but we both know that would be a lie."

With that statement, Aaron led Bethany out of the art room and out of the school. Bethany practically held her breath as they hurried outside and toward the SUV. They stepped next to the vehicle and Bethany started laughing.

"I can't believe you said that." Aaron chuckled.

"Me either, but I couldn't help it." Bethany laughed.

"She kind of scares me. She doesn't have a sense of personal space," Crunch grumbled as he opened the doors to the vehicle.

"I think she probably thought you and I were together and it was her way of trying to irritate me." Bethany rolled her eyes.

"I honestly have not seen her in at least ten years. I've been volunteering at that school since then and not once have I seen that woman there. I'm guessing she's trying to take credit for all the planning of the anniversary party." Aaron shook his head.

"Who cares? At least she knows we both know what she did back then, and I don't want to give her another thought." Bethany clicked her seatbelt. "She's already consumed too many of my thoughts over the years. No more."

Aaron reached back from the front seat and grabbed her hand. He squeezed it in support and even though she was probably in the sights of a murderer, she felt like a weight lifted off her shoulders. No more would Raquel Evans keep her from what she wanted.

Chapter 16

It wasn't natural for a man to have a hard-on for an entire week. Aaron was sure that men probably died from the condition, but here he was at his desk trying to concentrate on the information Nick had given him, but all he could think about was the kisses between him and Bethany every night before she'd go to bed.

She was frustrated too and made it known to him the previous night. It wasn't that he didn't want her, because God knew he did. It just terrified him that the last time he'd made love to her, she disappeared, and it was hard to shake that fear.

"I think we should probably set the whole thing on fire and blame it on Nanny Betty." Nick sat in the chair from Aaron's desk.

"What the fuck are you talking about?" Aaron stared at the weird statement from his brother.

"I was just checking to see if you were listening since you haven't heard anything I've said for the last five minutes," Nick smirked.

"Sorry, just something on my mind." Aaron glanced down at the papers in front of him.

"Something or someone?" Nick crossed his ankle over his knee.

"Can I tell you something?" Aaron leaned his elbows on the desk and folded his hands.

"Do you need to ask that question? Of course, you can." Nick leaned back in the chair.

"I'm scared shitless," Aaron admitted.

"Of what?" Nick reached behind him and closed the door to Aaron's office.

"These feelings are coming back so damn fast, and I'm not sure if it's from remembering how I used to feel about her or if I never really stopped feeling this way about her." Aaron flopped back in his chair.

"You can't even say what the 'feelings' are?" Nick chuckled as he used his fingers as air quotes around the word feelings.

"I know what the feelings are, asshole," Aaron grumbled.

"Then say it." Nick raised an eyebrow and smirked.

"Nick," Aaron sighed.

"Until you say it out loud, you're never going to figure this out." Nick pointed his index finger at Aaron.

"Fine, I care about her. A lot. I…I love her. I don't think I ever stopped." Aaron blew out a breath.

"You did a good job of hiding it, but you never stopped loving her. You played with sex and women to forget her, but it didn't work, did it?" Nick was right, but it pissed Aaron off because it wasn't long ago Nick had his share of one-night stands.

"What was your excuse when we would do the double pick-up at the clubs?" Aaron smirked.

"I was just a sex hound." Nick winked.

"Now that you're in a relationship, you aren't anymore?" Aaron laughed.

"No, now I'm worse. I just don't have to leave my house to get some." Nick stood up and grinned.

"Anyway, the slug they pulled out of Randy Knight and the rounds they collected at Bethany's place. Not the same guns." Nick tapped his finger on top of the papers in front of Aaron.

"How many fucking shooters are we looking for?" Aaron scanned the document.

"Well, we know there are three different weapons. Shooters? Who knows." Nick turned to leave the office. "Your first step, tell her how you feel. Maybe you'll find out she feels the same way." Nick gave Aaron a mock salute as he left the room.

He knew Bethany was going through the invoices that Randy Knight had submitted. He'd warned her not to call any of the pharmacies or people. Aaron wanted her to make a list of people from her files. Craig agreed it was the best way to go and gave the police full access to anything they needed.

Aaron didn't know where to go next with the case. The composite of the shooter had gone to all news programs and social media, but all leads they received were dead ends.

Then there was the conversation he'd had with Quintin. He was a great kid, and Aaron knew he was going places. The day at the school he asked Aaron if he could talk privately, Aaron honestly thought it was about girls.

When he asked what to do if he knew of someone selling drugs in and around the school, Aaron asked for the name of the person. Quintin was resistant to giving anyone's name for fear of retribution because he'd said the person selling was working for a dangerous group.

When Aaron tried to push Quintin, he shut down and walked away. By the time they'd gotten back into the art room, Aaron had eyed Bethany dealing with the last person she'd probably wanted to see. She'd handled it well, but it took everything he had not to tell Raquel precisely what he thought of her.

"Hey, they just pulled a body out of St. John's Harbor, and I was told to take you to the scene." James stuck his head in through the doorway.

"Male or female?" Aaron snatched his jacket from the back of his chair and followed James out to the parking lot.

"Male," James replied as they both hopped into the cruiser.

"Age estimate." Aaron didn't know why they'd call him for this particular body.

"Rick said late teens or early twenties," James replied

"I don't understand why we are going to this scene. Shouldn't this be St. John's jurisdiction?" It wasn't that they didn't join with the city in cases, but they never called unless they were sure it involved the instances from the Hopedale division.

"They found your card in the guy's wallet." James glanced at Aaron.

Aaron tried to remember the number of cards he'd handed out over the last couple of weeks. With all the cases he'd worked on, he probably handed out a hundred or more.

James was quiet as they made their way down the highway toward St. John's. Aaron's thoughts raced as he tried to think about who it could be that they'd pulled out of the water.

The docks on the harbor front practically glowed from the lights of police cruisers. Spectators crowded behind the police tape, curiosity getting the better of them. It sickened Aaron to see how people flocked to see someone else's misfortune.

James cursed several times as he tried to maneuver his way through the crowds of people blocking the entrance to the apron of the dock. It took several minutes to finally pull up to the several rookie police holding the spectators back.

"What the fuck is wrong with people?" James grumbled as Aaron followed him to where Rick stood next to a blue tarp on the ground.

"How the hell did you get here before the medical examiner?" Rick was frustrated.

"It took us almost ten minutes to get through the people, and we had lights flashing." Aaron stepped toward the tarp and grabbed the corner.

He lifted it off the body, and his stomach turned. Aaron knew the deceased, and it made him sick to see the kid laying on the damp concrete a bluish color to his skin.

"I know this kid." Aaron dropped the tarp.

"Who is he?" Rick asked.

"His name is Levi Watts. His younger brother is on the basketball team I coach. I haven't seen Levi since he graduated two years ago." Aaron shook his head as he stared at the covered body.

"How did he get your card?" James asked.

"I think Quintin may have given it to him." Aaron started to put the pieces of the puzzle together.

Quintin had asked about someone selling drugs. He didn't want to tell Aaron because it was his brother. This situation would kill Quintin. Aaron knew how much he looked up to his older brother.

"Quintin?" Rick asked.

"Quintin is one of the kids I coach at Holy Cross. Hell, I coached Levi, too." Aaron plowed his hand through his hair.

"I want to go tell the family." Aaron glanced at James.

"You'll have to check that with Rick." James nodded toward where Rick had turned his attention to the coroner who had finally arrived.

Aaron waited impatiently while he scanned the crowd of onlookers for anyone that could be of interest. From the quick glance he'd gotten of Levi's body, he had a wound on his chest that looked like a knife had pierced his shirt.

"See anything?" Rick walked up behind Aaron.

"Nope, just a lot of nosey people." Aaron turned to Rick.

"James said you know the family and want to go inform them of the death." Rick shoved his notebook into his pocket.

"I would. I only know Quinton and Levi. I've never met the parents, but Quintin's a good kid." Aaron pinched his nose with his fingers.

"I'll come with you. Just give me a second." Rick jogged toward another officer questioning a couple of men that looked like fishermen.

"I'll let Bethany know you're probably going to be late getting off today." James joined Aaron at the edge of the chaos of people.

"Thanks, I'll get Rick to drive me back to Hopedale." Aaron nodded when Rick motioned for him to follow.

Aaron called Father Wallace to get the address for Quintin's family. He made sure to tell the priest that he should probably head to the house as well.

Quintin lived in another of the small communities outside St. John's. It was one of several towns where the students attended Holy Cross School. It wasn't much different from Hopedale, and he knew it wouldn't be long before everyone knew about the death.

Petty Harbor was smaller than the town where Aaron grew up, but he knew the area since many of his friends during his school days were from the city. Rick drove up a long unpaved road and then turned onto a short driveway.

The house was dilapidated, but the yard was well maintained. A couple of bikes were on the ground or leaned against the cracked railing of the front deck. Rick and Aaron made their way up the steps and knocked lightly on the door.

Rick turned to glance around the property while Aaron listened for someone inside. He was about to knock again when the front door opened and a pretty dark-haired girl answered the door.

"Hi," She said glancing between Aaron and Rick.

"Hi, is your mom or dad at home?" Rick asked.

The girl stared at him for a minute and then glanced back inside the house. She looked to be about twelve years old, and Aaron remembered Quintin talking about a younger sister.

"Mia, who's at the door?" Aaron heard Quintin's voice shouting from the back of the house.

"They're looking for our mom or dad," the girl shouted back.

A few seconds later, Quintin appeared next to his sister. He looked scared at first, but when he saw Aaron, he smiled. Aaron hated to tell him the news and wipe that bright smile off the kid's face.

"Mr. O'Connor, what are you doing here?" Quintin asked.

"Quintin, is your mom or dad home?" Aaron gave him a friendly smile.

"Umm… my dad… well…" Quintin stammered.

"Our dad took off with some whore a few years ago," Mia blurted out as if it was nothing odd.

"Mia," Quintin groaned.

"Well, that's what happened." Mia rolled her eyes and left Quintin to deal with Aaron.

"I'm sorry. She's kinda rude sometimes." Quintin nervously shoved his hands into his front pockets. "My mom died a few years ago, and my older sister takes care of us. She works, but she should be home any minute."

"Can you call her?" Rick asked.

"Umm, our phone doesn't work." Quintin's cheeks turned red.

"Do you have a number we can call her?" Aaron didn't want to embarrass the kid any longer.

It was obvious they didn't have a lot, and from what Aaron could see, their father had left, the mother was dead, and their sister worked to support them. He knew the kids were well cared for because they were clean and well fed.

A car pulled into the driveway before Quintin could respond to the question. Aaron stepped back to let Quintin meet the vehicle that pulled in. A woman got out of the car, a hat pulled down over her head, and Quintin helped her lift several grocery bags out of the trunk.

Aaron shook his head as the woman got closer to make sure his eyes weren't playing tricks on him. The woman was wide-eyed as she walked toward him with recognition in her expression.

"Denise?" Aaron stared at one of Raquel Evans shadows from high school.

"A.J. O'Connor." She stopped at the top of the stairs and glanced between him and Rick.

"You're Quintin's sister?" Aaron must have had a comical expression on his face because Denise laughed.

"What? You didn't think I would end up like this?" She smiled, but Aaron could see the sadness in her voice. "It's probably karma for the things I did when I was younger."

"Rick, this is Denise Rowan." Aaron introduced Rick.

"Take that into the kitchen." Denise gave the bags she was carrying to Mia who'd appeared in the doorway.

"Denise, we need to talk to you." Aaron glanced at Mia as she disappeared back into the house.

"What's wrong? Is Quintin in trouble? He's a good boy, and I knew you were his coach. I would have loved to get to his games, but I work two jobs since Waylon ran off." Denise seemed genuinely concerned that her brother was in trouble.

"No, Quintin is not in any trouble, Denise, but I'm afraid we have bad news." Aaron motioned to the dirty wicker chair on the steps.

"What is it? Oh my God, my grandparents? Are they okay?" She eased into the chair and pulled the hat off her head.

"It's not your grandparents. Denise, it's Levi." Aaron swallowed as he crouched in front of her. "His body was pulled from St. John's Harbor."

"His… body." Denise stared at Aaron as if he was speaking a different language.

"Yes," Aaron confirmed.

"He's only nineteen. He was getting ready to go to college. Oh my God." Denise covered her mouth with one hand and held the other to her chest.

"We do need someone to identify him, but I'm pretty sure it's him. I coached him as well," Aaron said as Rick held his phone out to Aaron.

Aaron looked at the screen. It didn't seem like a photo he should show the family of the kid, but it was the only one they had. The picture showed Levi's face only after he came out of the water.

"I have a photo of him. Would you be able to look at it?" Aaron asked.

"I'll do it." Quintin stepped through the door.

"Quintin, it's fine." Denise held out a shaky hand and took a huge breath before she looked at the screen. "It's him."

She shoved the phone back at Aaron. Tears were streaming down her cheeks, but she wasn't making a sound. Quintin stood stock still. His face had no expression, and it worried Aaron.

"Do you have any idea why he was in St. John's?" Aaron asked.

"His friends are from town," Quintin said with a hint of anger.

"Do you know their names?" Rick asked.

"No, I just know they are a bunch of jerks and Levi changed when he started hanging with them." Quintin placed his hand on Denise's shoulder.

"Levi has been different lately, but I never thought he'd kill himself." Denise shook her head.

Aaron glanced up at Rick and then back to the stricken woman. She clung to Quintin's hand like she was afraid he'd vanish, and Aaron never thought he'd see the day that his heart would go out to Denise Rowan.

"He didn't kill himself. It's not confirmed, but he had a couple of wounds that were not self-inflicted," Rick told her.

"Are you saying he was mur...murdered?" Denise stood up and wrapped her arms around Quintin.

"It looks that way. We'll know more after the autopsy." Rick's voice was soft and compassionate.

"I need to call my grandparents and Levi's dad." Denise turned to go into the house. "I should probably go there and tell them."

"Why don't we go inside and give yourself a few minutes to get your head around this?" Aaron allowed Quintin to guide his sister into the house.

Aaron and Rick followed them into the small kitchen. Considering how the house looked outside, it looked clean and well cared for inside.

"Would you like a cup of coffee?" Denise asked as she aimlessly moved around the kitchen.

"No thank you." Rick glanced at Aaron.

"Denise, is there someone you can call to come here?" Aaron had noticed Mia enter the kitchen.

Quintin entered behind her; it was apparent he'd told his little sister the bad news. She had tears streaming down her cheeks as she ran into Denise's arms. It seemed to help Denise focus, and she stood with her arms wrapped around the young girl.

"Just my grandparents and Levi's father." Denise met Aaron's gaze. "My mom remarried after dad died, she had Levi, Quintin, and Mia from that marriage. Waylon left six years ago, and I moved back in with mom to help with the kids. Mom passed away three years later, and I've been taking care of them because my grandparents are not well and weren't in a situation to care for them."

"That's a lot to deal with." Aaron felt terrible for the woman.

"Now I have to bury my brother." Denise sank onto the kitchen chair, leaving her sister and brother holding each other.

"Denise, can I get you anything?" Aaron crouched in front of her.

"Do you believe in karma?" She lifted her face from her hands and met his eyes.

"A little, I guess." Aaron didn't know where she was going with this.

"It's ironic that you would be the one to come and tell me about this." She sat back in the chair. "Quintin, can you take Mia upstairs and give me a few minutes?"

Quintin and Mia left the kitchen and Aaron could hear the young girl sobbing as she walked upstairs. Rick stood against the wall with his hands in his jacket pocket. Rick Avery didn't seem to be comfortable with where the conversation was going.

"Why is it ironic?" Aaron asked.

"Considering I helped Raquel Evans terrorize your old girlfriend. I wanted to be cool back then, but once Raquel got what she wanted out of people she tossed them aside. My family wasn't well off, and I did things to make money so that I could keep up with Raquel." She dropped her head. "I just didn't brag about it."

"That was a long time ago, Denise." Aaron clenched his jaw.

"Levi was hanging with a group that reminded me of Raquel and how she treated people. The only thing was, I think they were into things that were dangerous." She stood up and opened a cupboard over the fridge, pulled out a large bag and placed it on the table.

"What's this?" Aaron asked.

"Levi gave me this last week." Denise opened the bag and pushed it toward Aaron.

He opened the bag and looked inside at bundles of cash. Aaron didn't want to touch it too much, but he motioned for Rick to take a look. It didn't look great that Levi gave his sister a lot of money and then ended up dead.

"He wouldn't tell me where he got the cash, but he said to use it to pay off some bills and put the rest away." Denise plopped down in the chair again. "I was afraid to use it."

"Do you think Quintin knows what Levi was doing?" Aaron asked.

"Quintin is a good kid. He would never be involved…" Denise dropped her face into her hands. "What do I know? I thought I'd raised Levi to be a good kid. I've screwed them up so much."

"Denise, don't blame yourself for this, and you're right, Quintin is a good kid. I ask because last week he asked me about what to do if someone was in trouble." Aaron touched her shoulder. "Would you mind if I talk to him?"

Denise lifted her head, and her eyes went to the bag on the table. For a few minutes, she stared at it and then she shook her head.

Aaron motioned to Rick to stay with Denise while he went to find Quintin and his younger sister. Before Aaron got to the top of the steps, Quinton stepped out of a bedroom that had the name Mia on the door.

"How is she?" Aaron asked as he got to the top of the steps.

"She's calmed down a bit." Quintin stared out the window at the end of the hall.

"Want to take a walk with me?" Aaron motioned downstairs.

Quintin didn't speak, but he walked ahead of Aaron and straight through the front door. Aaron followed but gave Rick a shout to know they would be back.

Quintin scuffed across the street from his house. Aaron followed and stopped when Quintin stood at the edge of the road, staring out at the harbor.

"I knew he was in trouble," Quintin whispered.

"He told you?" Aaron shifted so he could see the kid's face.

"He didn't have to. I could tell by the way he acted. He'd come home, and it was as if he was afraid of something. I asked him what was wrong, but all he said was make sure I took care of Mia and Denise. He said what he was doing was important to people." Quintin glanced at Aaron with tears in his eyes.

"Do you know where he got the money he gave Denise?" Aaron hated to push, but something told him there was a connection to Randy Knight's murder.

"No, but with the idiots he was hanging with, I'd say it was from drugs or something. Mr. O'Connor, my sister busts her ass for us and works two jobs to support us. I don't think Levi was doing it for fun. I think he was doing it to help Denise, but he got in too deep." A tear slipped out of Quintin's eye and he wiped it away angrily.

"Do you know the names of any of the people he associated with?" Aaron asked.

"He just called them stupid nicknames." Quintin took a huge breath and shrugged.

"That's okay. Tell me the nicknames." Aaron pulled out his notebook.

"Okay. Well, there's Buzzer, Grease, Doom, and the worst of them is a guy they called Slash." Quintin rolled his eyes. "They think they are badasses because they have lame nicknames."

"You don't know any of their real names?" Aaron hoped but from the look on Quintin's face that he didn't.

"No, but the guy Slash, he's like your age and has a huge scar on his forehead." Quintin ran his finger across his forehead and Aaron's blood ran cold.

"I'm going to show you a sketch, and you tell me if it looks familiar." Aaron pulled out his phone and brought up the picture of the composite of the guy that killed Randy.

Quintin looked at it for a few seconds and then handed the phone back to Aaron.

"Looks like Slash," Quintin told him.

"Okay, I'm going to go talk to your sister. I think it would be better if all of you stayed somewhere else tonight. Maybe with your grandparents." Aaron wrapped his arm around Quintin's shoulders and led him back to the house.

Levi was probably dead because of the money, and if Slash thought for a minute the money was in the house, it would be trouble. There wasn't any doubt in Aaron's mind that Quintin, Mia, and Denise were in danger, but at least now he had a name for the guy he was after.

Chapter 17

Bethany stared at the piles of invoices on the table. Her eyes started to burn with irritation. It always happened when she spent a lot of time reading the small print. She pulled her glasses out of her purse and put them on.

Bethany didn't wear them very often, and she could probably get away with not wearing them at all since her laser eye surgery. It didn't correct her vision to perfect, but when she strained her eyes, the glasses helped ease it.

She picked up another invoice and took note of the order, how much, and which pharmacy. Bethany noticed the name of who placed the order was not on all the invoices. The company required the contact name on every invoice, but Randy left that line blank on most of the orders.

Bethany had a pile that had all the required information and seemed like they were legitimate invoices. There was another pile that was suspicious, and the last collection from the pharmacy that

Craig already called and confirmed they hadn't placed any of the orders.

"That's the girl I remember." Bethany glanced up at the sound of Aaron's voice.

"Did you forget me since you left this morning?" She laughed.

"Not a chance, but when we met, you were wearing those cute glasses that matched the color of your eyes." Aaron stalked toward her.

"I hate glasses, and I only wear them when my eyes are tired." Bethany turned in her chair as he crouched in front of her.

"You're beautiful." Aaron cupped her cheek.

"Maybe you need glasses. I've been hunched over these invoices since you left, my hair is in a messy pile on top of my head, and dressed in an old t-shirt and yoga pants. Beautiful is not a word I would use right now." Bethany's breath caught with his intense gaze.

"You could be covered with tar and feathers, and you'd still be the most beautiful woman in the world to me." Aaron leaned forward and pressed his lips to hers.

"You look tired." Bethany ran her fingers through his hair as he pulled his lips from hers.

"It's been a long, shitty day." Aaron pulled a chair next to her and sat down.

"I'm sorry you had a bad day." Bethany touched his cheek.

"Remember Denise Rowan?" Aaron linked his fingers with hers.

"Yes, I remember Raquel's shadows very well." Bethany nodded.

"Trust me, she's not like that girl from high school anymore. She's raising her three younger siblings on her own. She's working two jobs to do that." Aaron leaned back in the chair.

"Wow, that's a lot of responsibility." Bethany managed to show a little empathy.

"Remember Quintin at the high school?" Aaron was playing with the birthstone ring on her finger.

"Yeah."

"He's her brother. Her mom remarried but the hard part was today we pulled the older brother of the three siblings out of St. John's Harbor. Not only that, I found out Levi was running around with the guy that killed Randy." Aaron tipped his head back and blew out a breath.

"Do you know how to find him?" Bethany hoped so because she wanted to get back to a normal life.

"We have a name but finding him could be an issue." Aaron pulled her from her chair and onto his lap.

"Why?" She absently played with the hair at the nape of his neck.

"Quintin only knew the guy's nickname, and we don't have anyone on file with the alias Slash. Sandy is looking into it too. Hopefully, she'll find something." Aaron tucked his face into her neck and his warm breath feathered across her skin, causing goosebumps to rise on her body.

"Are you hungry?" Bethany whispered.

"Starving." Aaron lifted his head and cupped the back of her head.

Bethany felt the evidence of his erection against her hip and when she met his eyes, the arousal in them was screaming at her. They'd been holding off on intimacy. Well, Aaron kept stopping things before they got too far but the look in his eyes at that moment told her he wasn't going to hold back anymore.

"Where's Crash?" Bethany sighed as he brushed his lips against her jaw.

"He's outside at his post." Aaron nipped her lower lip and then ran his tongue across to ease the sting.

"Aaron, if we start this, are you going to pull away again?" Bethany pulled back and stared into his eyes.

"I've been pulling away because I didn't want you to think that's all I wanted with you. It's been killing me not to make love to you." Aaron traced her lips with his finger. "I need you, Bethany. I want you more than I need to breathe. I've been drifting through the last thirteen years, and it wasn't until I saw you again that I realized that."

"Aaron, how could my feelings for you still be so strong after all this time?" Bethany pressed her forehead against his. "I need you too."

Bethany squeaked when he shot to his feet with her hoisted into his arms. He didn't bother to turn off anything as he carried her to the bedroom. Bethany reached and turned the knob to open the door, and Aaron kicked it shut once they were inside.

"Bethany, I love you. I never stopped." Aaron held her head between his hands, and his words sounded strangled as if he was overwhelmed with emotion.

"My heart always belonged to you. Even when I thought you didn't want it." Bethany pressed her hands against his chest and slowly slid them up and around his shoulders.

"My heart stopped when you left, and it didn't start beating again until you came back." Aaron lowered his head and covered her mouth with his.

The kiss was soft but desperate. Aaron's tongue demanding entrance and Bethany opened to accept it. They'd kissed over the last few days, but something about this one was different. It was more of a promise of forever.

"Bethany." Aaron pulled back long enough to strip his t-shirt over his head and toss it aside.

His arms wrapped around her and pulled her tight against his hard body as he moved her backward until the back of her legs touched the bed. Aaron eased her back until she was lying under him and his lips feathering across her jaw and down the side of her neck.

She tilted her head to give him better access and gasped as his hand slide under the hem of her shirt. His hands were hot against her skin, and her body tingled from head to toe as he nipped the side of her neck.

"Aaron," Bethany moaned as she raised her hips to press against him.

"Fuck, your skin is like silk." Aaron pulled his head back as he raised the shirt up and over her stomach.

He straddled her legs, and his hands caressed the skin across her abdomen. It was as if he was mesmerized by what he was doing, but all it was doing was driving her to the brink of insanity.

"Aaron, I have a lot more skin on my body." She smirked when he raised his eyes to meet hers.

"Baby, I never thought I'd get the chance to touch you again so forgive me if I want to take my time and relish every minute." He slipped his hands up her sides, and his fingers grazed the sides of her breasts.

Bethany took the opportunity to take in the man currently worshiping her. His body was chiseled and tan with well-defined pectoral muscles covered in a dusting of hair a little lighter than the hair on his head. He had a tattoo of a lion head on his right shoulder that covered it completely and on the right side of his chest was a bible quote.

Her eyes traveled down to his prominent abdomen muscles that flexed as his hands caressed her. Her eyes followed the trail of light hair that disappeared into his jeans and her gaze dropped to the bulge in the front of his jeans. It looked painful, and all she wanted to do was free it from its confines.

Bethany reached for the button of his jeans and popped it open. Aaron growled as her fingers slid across the top of the waistband and grazed the head of his cock.

"I want to see all of you." Bethany slowly lowered the zipper of his jeans.

"You will, but I want to get rid of all these clothes you're wearing." Aaron slid the shirt over her head and tossed it aside.

Bethany smiled at the way his eyes widened when his gaze moved to her bra. He released the hook in front with one quick flick, and it popped open, exposing her breasts to his view.

"You're so fucking beautiful," Aaron growled and gently cupped her breasts in his hands.

Bethany arched toward his touch and squirmed under him as the ache in her core begged for attention. She needed him to touch her there.

"The way your skin flushes from being turned on is so damn sexy." Aaron gently pinched her nipples and twisted them gently between his fingers as he lowered his mouth toward her chest.

"Ahh… Aaron… yes." Bethany moaned as he pulled the tight peak of her nipple into his mouth and sucked.

He moved back and forth between both for several minutes, sucking a little harder with each exchange. Bethany's hips were thrusting up as he sucked her tight nipples into his hot mouth. She could practically feel it through her body right to her clit.

"I need you to touch me, Aaron," Bethany begged.

"I am touching you." He sat up and grinned mischievously.

"I don't remember you being so evil." She reached for the waistband of his jeans, making sure she circled the head of his protruding cock with her finger.

"I'm just enjoying your body." Aaron groaned.

"You could be enjoying my mouth if you'd get rid of those jeans," Bethany smirked and giggled when his eyes rolled into his head as her finger found the sensitive spot under the head of his dick.

"Fuck, you win." Aaron pulled her hand away and jumped off the bed.

She watched while he stripped away his jeans, boxers, and socks in less than ten seconds. When Bethany tried to slide her panties and yoga pants off, Aaron pulled her hands away and took over stripping her naked.

Aaron put his hands on her inner thighs and pushed them apart as he knelt between them. He slid his hand up to the apex of her legs, and his fingers grazed the edge of her pussy as he lowered his head down.

Bethany watched him until his tongue slid between her folds and her head dropped back in pleasure. His tongue slowly glided up and down between her wetness as one hand pressed against her stomach. The fingers of his other hand found the swollen clit, and he gently pinched it between his fingers as he drove his tongue inside her.

"Oh…oh… God." Bethany lifted her ass off the bed and thrust against Aaron's mouth.

"You taste like heaven," Aaron whispered against her pussy, and his hot breath made her shiver.

He drove his tongue inside her again and again as he applied pressure to her throbbing clit. She was so close, and she couldn't stop herself from pinching her nipples as he pleasured her.

"That's it, baby. Pinch those beauties," Aaron urged her.

"I'm so close," Bethany moaned.

"Come for me, Bethany," he whispered.

Aaron shoved two fingers inside her and sucked her clit between his lips, flicking his tongue against it. His fingers thrust in and out. Within seconds, her body convulsed as an intense orgasm slammed through her body.

Aaron continued to suck her clit, as his fingers thrust in and out of her. She grabbed his head and pulled him away because she thought she might pass out from the pleasure. Before he moved Aaron gave her sensitive clit another quick flick that made her shudder one last time.

"Are you trying to kill me?" She panted as she tried to catch her breath.

"You just taste so damn good." Aaron pulled his fingers out and sucked them into his mouth. "So, fucking good."

Aaron was on his knees, and her eyes dropped to his hard dick standing straight out. The moisture at the tip dripped onto her stomach, and she ran her finger through it. She brought it to her lips and met his eyes as she licked it from her finger.

"Fuck," Aaron growled.

"Not yet. I want more than that little taste." Bethany sat up and wrapped her hand around his thick shaft.

"Baby, as much as I would love to have your mouth around my dick, I don't know if I will last two seconds if you wrap your lips around me." Aaron gasped when she cupped his balls in her other hand.

"Three hundred and sixty-nine divided by fifty-three." Bethany glanced up and grinned.

"You remember that?" He chuckled.

"Yes, I remember you used to have to do long division to be seen in public after we made out." Bethany ran her hand down the length of him.

"Fuck, I don't even know if that will work tonight." The statement came out strangled as she stroked him slowly.

Bethany leaned forward. With him kneeling between her legs his cock was at the right level. She kept her eyes locked with his and slowly licked her tongue around the swollen head. Aaron's body was practically vibrating as she continued her slow tease.

"As much as I would love you to continue doing what you are, I need to be inside you." Aaron jerked once more as she gave him one last lick.

"Sorry, you just taste so good." Bethany got up on her knees and pressed her body against his.

"Anytime you want to do that, just ask." Aaron cupped her ass and pulled her against him.

"Make love to me, Aaron." She gasped as he slid his finger between the cheeks of her ass and rubbed his thick cock against her clit.

Aaron eased her back on the bed. She didn't know where it came from, but he had a condom between his fingers. He tore the top off with his teeth and rolled it onto his erection.

Bethany let her legs fall to the sides as he positioned himself at her entrance. He stopped, and his eyes met hers as he hovered over her. The last time they made love he'd been slow and careful with her. They were both virgins, and he didn't want to hurt her. There was something in his eyes. Fear? Doubt? She couldn't read it.

"I've never been with anyone who makes me feel the way you do. I've only ever loved you, and there was never any space for anyone else." Aaron pressed slowly inside her. "I'm never letting you go again."

With his last statement, he pushed entirely inside her and covered her mouth with his. His hips were pressed hard against hers as he devoured her mouth. Then he started to thrust, his hips driving his cock deep inside her.

Bethany could feel the beginning of another orgasm and gasped when Aaron pulled his mouth away from hers. He changed his movement, and it pressed his pelvic bone directly against her clit as he circled his hips.

Bethany grabbed his ass to keep the pressure against her throbbing nub. Aaron leaned down and sucked one nipple then the other. She was so close to a cataclysmic orgasm that she could barely speak.

"Ah... yes." Bethany screamed as Aaron clamped his teeth down on her nipple and slammed into her one last time.

"Fuck, baby." Aaron roared as his body shook above her.

He pulled back twice and slammed back into her, setting off small tingles that traveled through her body. She tried to open her eyes, but her vision was hazy. His cock twitched inside her, and with each movement, Aaron moaned.

For a few minutes, the only sound in the room was their heavy breathing and the rustle of the wind blowing through the trees outside the open window. Bethany ran her hands up and down his back as she placed soft kisses across his damp shoulder.

"I think you killed me." Aaron groaned and tucked his face into her neck.

"I don't think dead people talk." Bethany giggled.

"You sure? It's that, or I'm paralyzed." Aaron lifted his head and grinned down at her.

"Oh, that's too bad. I guess we won't get to do this again." Bethany feigned a sigh.

"Trust me; we'll be doing that again, and again, and again." Aaron placed a kiss on her lips for every time he said *again*.

"You're pretty confident in your stamina, Mr. O'Connor." Bethany lowered her hands and squeezed his tight ass.

"I've got a lot of catching up to do." Aaron gave her a sweet smile as he brushed the hair back from her forehead.

"Hmmm… sounds good to me." Bethany smiled.

"I need to ditch the condom. Don't move." Aaron pulled out of her and made his way to the bathroom.

Bethany grabbed the blanket and pulled it over her naked body. She hadn't felt so content in a long time. It was kind of funny she was in a safe house so that a murderer couldn't find her and it was the first time she'd been truly happy in a long time.

"That's a beautiful sight." He jumped on the bed next to her, laying on his side.

"Yes, you are." Bethany let her eyes travel down his naked form.

"Are you okay?" Aaron took her hand and laced his fingers with hers.

"I'm incredibly happy." She turned onto her side and smiled at him.

"Bethany, I know you're aware of my reputation since you left but I promise you I'm clean and I've never been with anyone without a condom." Aaron blurted it out so fast that it was hard for her not to laugh.

"Aaron, I'm no angel either, but I'm clean too, and I've never had sex without a condom. Plus, I'm on the pill." Bethany narrowed her eyes. "So can that be the last conversation of any previous partners."

"Definitely." Aaron turned on his back and pulled her into his side.

She laid her head on his chest and closed her eyes as she listened to the rhythm of his heartbeat. He was moving his hand up and down her back, and every few minutes he'd kiss the top of her head. It was sweet, but it was like he was afraid she'd vanish.

"I'm not going anywhere." Bethany tipped her head back and looked at him.

"I know." Aaron ran his finger along her jaw.

"Then why are you holding me like I'm going to run away?" Bethany grinned.

"Maybe I should've been holding you like that thirteen years ago, and we wouldn't have wasted all that time." Aaron turned on his side, facing her and he pulled the blanket over him.

"Aaron, I should've had faith in you, in us. I had such low self-esteem back then and even knowing Raquel and her shadows were doing it to get to me didn't matter. I needed to believe in myself more, and that's why it was a good thing I left. I can be the partner you deserve." Bethany snuggled into his chest and his arms wrapped around her.

"That's the thing. I never thought I deserved you and still don't, but I'll be damned if I let that keep us apart. I'm going to be the man you need. I'll keep you safe and I damn well sure won't let anyone ever come between us again." Aaron pressed his lips to her forehead.

His kiss moved down between her eyes to the tip of her nose and then to her lips. His lips moved against hers, tender and loving. He pulled her tight against him as his tongue slipped inside her mouth and she met it eagerly. Aaron was the man she'd never been able to forget. The man who owned her mind, body, and soul.

Chapter 18

Aaron stood in the kitchen a towel wrapped around his waist as he prepared coffee and breakfast. He probably looked like a complete idiot grinning like he was but he couldn't help it. It had been a long time since he'd woken up with a woman and not felt like a piece of shit because he wanted to get as far away from her as possible.

Guilt did dig at him a little for his happy mood. What Quintin and his family were going through, it was hard not to feel some sadness for being so lucky. His life was at a standstill though until he was sure that Bethany was safe.

"Jesus, man, put some clothes on." Aaron spun around at the sound of the male voice and barely caught the towel as it slipped off his hips.

"What the fuck are you doing here at this hour?" Aaron adjusted the towel and glared at Hulk.

Bruce 'Hulk' Steel was another of the men who worked for NSS. He'd almost lost his life the previous year when he came face to face with a stalker hell-bent on getting his hands on Lora, Nick's fiancée.

"Crunch had something he needed to do." Hulk plopped down in the armchair.

"I didn't know you were back to work." Aaron should have felt weird standing in the kitchen wrapped in a towel with Hulk in the kitchen, but the guy was like another brother.

"I'm not. That bastard brother of yours won't let me back fully until the end of May because that's when the doctor okayed it. I can bench press three hundred pounds and run fifteen kilometers, but I can't go back to work." Aaron chuckled at Hulk's sarcasm.

"They're just making sure everything is completely healed," Aaron replied.

"Whatever, so is this another of the O'Connor brother love stories where the woman is in danger, and you fall in love?" Hulk pointed to the side of his neck.

"What?" Aaron crouched to look at his reflection in the toaster.

"Well, you got laid, or you got in a fight with a vampire." Hulk chuckled.

"Ummm… hi." Aaron turned to Bethany peeking out from the hallway.

"Now I see why this guy is grinning from ear to ear and whistling like a lunatic." Hulk smiled.

"Bethany, this is Hulk." Aaron motioned for her to come into the room.

"I have two questions." Bethany glanced between Aaron and Hulk.

"Shoot." Hulk leaned back in the chair and crossed his arms over his chest.

"Where's Crash and what's your real name?" She grinned.

Aaron couldn't help but smile because the old Bethany probably would have turned and bolted back to the bedroom instead of facing the large man in the chair.

"Crash had something he needed to do, and my real name is Bruce Steel." Hulk smiled. "Now can you tell the stud there to put on some clothes? You may like to look at that, but it does nothing for me."

Aaron flipped off Hulk as he made his way back to the bedroom to get dressed. Bethany was comfortable chatting with Hulk when he returned.

"Keith tells me you're looking for the bastard that killed that kid," Hulk growled.

"Yeah, we figured out he's the same guy that killed Bethany's co-worker." Aaron slid the picture over to Hulk.

"Looks like an asshole." Hulk picked up the picture and studied it.

"The only thing we know is he goes by the name Slash." Aaron glanced at Bethany.

She was staring into her mug and was suddenly quiet. Her smile had faded, and her shoulders were tense. Aaron wrapped his arm around her and pulled her into him.

"He won't get close to you." Aaron kissed her temple.

"I feel so awful for Quintin. He seems like a sweet kid, and I know Denise wasn't my favorite person in the world, but she must be so upset over losing her brother." Bethany lifted her tear-filled eyes and glanced between Aaron and Hulk.

"She's with her grandparents now, and Quintin and Mia are with them." Aaron wiped a tear from her cheek.

"Are they in danger?" Hulk asked.

"We aren't taking a chance. Blake Harris is undertaking their security." Aaron informed Hulk.

"Why didn't you recommend NSS?" Hulk raised an eyebrow.

"There's no way they could afford it, and I didn't want to embarrass her any more than she was. They live in a pretty dilapidated house, and she works two jobs to get by." Aaron rested his arms on the counter.

"You think Raquel would be there to help her friend or Celine." Bethany shook her head.

"I got the impression they aren't friends anymore." Aaron covered her hand with his.

"What time are you off today?" Hulk asked.

"I should be back around five." Aaron glanced at his watch.

"Damn." Hulk sighed.

"Why?" Hulk's reaction was odd.

"I usually meet a friend in town on Mondays, Wednesdays, and Fridays at three." Hulk sat back casually on the stool.

"Got a woman in St. John's, do ya?" Aaron teased.

"Fuck off; I said a friend." Hulk gave him the middle finger.

"Now is that any way to act around a lady." Sandy sauntered into the house.

"You know for a safe house people walk in here a lot." Bethany laughed.

"You don't need to worry. The only people getting on this property are people that work here or family." Sandy gave her a side hug. "Although, they should probably start to keep some family members out of here."

Sandy poked Aaron in the ribs, and he rolled his eyes. Out of all his sisters-in-law, Sandy was the one that gave him the hardest time. It wasn't that he minded her digs because he knew she did care about him.

"I kind of like having that family member here." Bethany winked.

"Oooo… tell me all the dirty details." Sandy leaned across the counter with a massive grin on her face.

"I think I need to have a chat with Ian. You seem to be lacking in the dirty department since you're so interested in everyone else," Aaron teased.

"Oh honey, trust me I'm not lacking, and neither is Ian. As a matter of fact, last night…" Sandy's story stopped as Aaron covered her mouth with his hand.

"No. Bad Sandy." Aaron pulled his hand away when she licked his palm and pointed his finger in her face.

"They're so easy." Sandy winked at Bethany.

"I do have a question. Why are you here at this hour in the morning?" Aaron shrugged on his jacket.

"James said Bethany has a ton of invoices with names of pharmacies as well as some names. I thought it might be a good idea to run them through my databases and see if I can find any links to this Slash guy or Randy Knight. Ian is off today, so he's on kid duty." Sandy dropped the bag from her shoulder on the counter and pulled out a laptop.

"Sounds like a good idea. I'm going to check on Denise and her siblings. Maybe they've thought of something." Aaron clasped Bethany's hand and tugged her toward the front door.

Leaving Bethany was hard after the previous night. All he wanted to do was take her in his arms and hide in the bedroom. They'd made love several times during the night and as creepy as it sounded, he'd stayed awake for a while watching her sleep. He was afraid if he closed his eyes she'd disappear.

"Tell Denise I'm sorry for her loss." Bethany wrapped her arms around his neck.

"I will. Are you okay with these two?" Aaron nodded toward where Sandy and Hulk were chatting

"Yes, I'm fine. I like Sandy. She's a blast." Bethany ran her fingernails through his hair, and he shivered.

"You're trying to drive me out of my mind, aren't you?" Aaron growled into the side of her neck.

"Maybe or maybe I just want you to hurry back." Bethany winked.

"If I didn't have to go to work, I'd have you on the bed naked and be taking my time exploring every damn inch." Aaron cupped the back of her head and stopped her response as he devoured her mouth.

He pulled away gasping for air and grinned at the dazed look in her eyes. His cock was painfully hard, and he stepped back to adjust himself.

"Need help with that?" She wiggled her eyebrows.

"You're truly an evil woman." Aaron shook his head as he pulled open the front door.

"Be safe today." She clung to his hand.

"Always, and Bethany?" Aaron tugged her closer.

"Yeah?" She sighed.

"I love you," he whispered as he stared into her green eyes.

"I love you too," she whispered as she gave him a quick kiss on the lips.

Aaron sat in his car for a few minutes, staring at the closed door. He didn't want to leave, but he had to get rid of the threat against Bethany. Not that anyone had made a direct threat, but bullets shot at her family wasn't exactly subtle.

He stopped at the station and checked for any new information on his investigation. Several messages were waiting for him but not from anyone he would call back. Since he'd blocked all Jocelyn's calls, she'd started harassing the reception of the police department.

"She's a little insistent that she speak to you immediately," the reception officer said, a little annoyed.

"I'm sorry, Natalie. She doesn't seem to understand that things between her and me ended." Aaron slapped the bundle of messages against his hand.

"Maybe you need the direct approach. Something that would slap her right in the face. How about a two-by-four?" Natalie smirked.

"I don't even know if that would work with this one but remind me not to piss you off, and I'm gonna warn any of your future boyfriends." Aaron chuckled.

"I tell them that up front," Natalie shouted to him as he walked away.

Natalie French grew up in Hopedale. She was a few years younger than Aaron, but both their families were friends. She'd always been spunky, and that didn't change when she completed her academy training.

She'd been excited when she was assigned to the Hopedale division of the Newfoundland Police Department the previous year. She was a rookie but had graduated at the top of her class, but as a rookie, she had to take her shift behind the reception desk. Aaron just felt shitty that she had to deal with Jocelyn for the first hour of her shift.

He didn't know what to do about Jocelyn, but he wasn't worried about her. Aaron had too much to deal with, including finding a killer.

"A.J., I hate to tell you this, but there's a woman out front looking for you." Natalie stuck her head into his office.

"Fuck," Aaron growled through clenched teeth.

"I told her you were in a meeting. I know, not good for a police officer to lie, but she looks like a complete skank." Natalie said, using the derogatory term meaning the woman looked like a slut.

"I don't want to deal with her right now." Aaron stood up and plowed his fingers through his hair.

"She doesn't seem like she's going away," Natalie smirked as she disappeared from his doorway.

Aaron pulled all the patience he could muster and made his way to the front of the station. He stepped through the security door and out into the lobby. He didn't recognize her from behind, but at that point, he was just relieved it wasn't Jocelyn.

"Excuse me, I'm Sergeant Aaron O'Connor." He walked up behind the lady.

She turned around, and he wanted to spin back and run. It was the last person on the face of the earth he expected or wanted to see again.

"How is it you O'Connor men still look as hot as you did in high school?" She smiled and ran a finger down the center of Aaron's chest.

"Raquel, what a surprise to see you in Hopedale," Aaron said with a less than welcoming tone.

"A good surprise, I hope." She winked.

"Let's just say a surprise and leave it at that." Aaron didn't smile.

"Oh, come on A.J. Don't tell me you're still pissed at me?" Raquel stuck out her lower lip in a fake pout.

"Did you drop by to rehash old times? I'm swamped, and I don't have time for it." Aaron crossed his arms over his chest.

"Wow, talk about cold shoulder." Raquel rolled her eyes.

"What did you expect? A parade?" Aaron snapped.

She stared at him for a moment, but Aaron didn't flinch. Raquel tried to fuck up his life and she was the reason Bethany left Newfoundland. Then there was the night he tried to forget. The night Raquel showed up at his house with her father and blamed Aaron for something that was impossible.

April, thirteen years ago…

Aaron was on his way home from walking Bethany to her house. He had a skip in his step since he'd finally told her that he loved her and asked her to the prom.

He'd just passed his Uncle Kurt's house when he heard someone shout his name. He turned around and saw his brothers Mike and Nick run toward him.

"We've been all over Hopedale looking for you." Mike puffed when they caught up with him.

"I was with Bethany." Aaron grinned.

"You got to get your ass home. Now." Nick looked pissed.

"I'm going there now." Aaron turned to continue on his way.

"Raquel's at the house with her dad." Mike stopped Aaron when he grabbed his arm.

"What's she doing there?" Aaron furrowed his brow.

"A.J., she says she's pregnant." Mike's blue eyes, so much like his own, narrowed.

"Good for her, but she was bound to get caught with all the guys she fucks around with." Aaron didn't understand what this had to do with him.

"She says the baby is yours," Nick blurted out.

"What? Not a chance in hell." Aaron's eyes widened so much that it hurt.

"When did you sleep with her?" Nick growled.

"I never slept with her. Are you fucking nuts?" Aaron snapped.

"You do know he means sex and not actual sleep?" Mike asked.

"I'm not an idiot." Aaron turned and stomped toward his house.

He wasn't getting blamed for something he didn't do. Mainly because he was still a virgin and there was no way he would betray Bethany to sleep with anyone. Especially Raquel Fucking Evans.

Aaron walked into the house with Mike and Nick close behind. His mother sat on the edge of one of the kitchen chairs looking like she was about to throw up, but it was his father's clenched jaw that had Aaron ready to turn and run.

Aaron glanced up to the top of the stairs leading to the bedrooms. Keith and Ian sat on the top step with James and John behind them. He rolled his eyes at them because it seemed even though the four oldest brothers moved out, they seemed to want to be there for Aaron's drama.

"Michael, Nicholas, upstairs. John, James, Ian and Keith you can join the other two in their room until we get this resolved." Sean O'Connor raised his voice to that tone they dreaded as kids.

The fact that Mike and Nick turned and practically shot up the stairs and the other brothers almost tripped over each other to do what they were told gave Aaron the impression his parents believed what Raquel said. He had to fix that and fast.

"Aaron Jacob, you come in here and sit," his mother quipped with a tone he'd never heard before.

"Kathleen, let me handle this." His father spoke with a calm rumble that scared the shit out of Aaron.

"I'm sorry, A.J." Raquel gave him a look that he'd seen on her a thousand times because she thought it was seductive and sweet.

"Raquel, quiet," her father snapped.

Aaron knew Alan Evans from school. He drove one of the buses and was the mechanic that looked after all the school buses. He wasn't a big man, but he wore a long beard that looked like it hadn't been cut or brushed in years. He was always friendly, but at the moment he looked ready to kill.

"A.J., Raquel just told us something we never expected to hear." His father sat across the table from Aaron.

"I didn't want to say anything." Raquel dropped her head when her father glared at her.

"Mike and Nick told me." Aaron glared at her.

"What do you have to say for yourself?" His father folded his hands on the table in front of him, but his knuckles were white.

"If she's pregnant, it's not mine. It's impossible." Aaron looked right into his father's eyes.

"You little liar," Alan growled.

"Dad, please." Raquel sighed and rolled her eyes.

"A.J., you need to be honest with us." His mother rested her hand on his arm. "We'll deal with things, but you need to tell the truth."

"Mom, I can tell you one hundred percent there is no way I'm the father of her baby. I've never had sex with her." Again, Aaron made sure he looked his mother in the eyes.

"There you have it." His mother stood up and glared at Alan. "A.J. says he isn't the one who got Raquel pregnant."

"And you believe him?" Alan scoffed. "Your sons are like a bunch of oversexed animals."

"That's enough." When his father shot to his feet, Aaron thought he would jump over the table toward Alan.

"Raquel, I don't know why you lied, but you need to tell the truth." Aaron didn't want his father in the middle of a fist fight.

"I... I'm not ..." Raquel started, but Aaron held up his hand.

"The truth or I'll start telling a few truths of my own." Aaron knew a lot about Raquel and how many boys in school could be the father of her baby.

She glared at him for a minute, but Aaron didn't falter. She turned to her father and then back to Aaron.

"Fine, he's not the father, and I'm not even sure if I am pregnant." Raquel sighed.

"Are you fucking serious?" her father shouted.

"Yes." She rolled her eyes as if what she did was nothing more than a joke.

"Get your ass out to the car." Alan pointed toward the front of the house.

"Take a pill, Dad." Raquel groaned as she left the house.

"I'm so sorry." Alan glanced between his parents and then to Aaron. "I hope we can keep this between us. I'll deal with her when I get home."

"I don't know why she would do something like this but Alan, I think you need to sit down and have a long talk with your daughter." His mother wrapped her arm around Aaron.

"I will." Alan turned and left the house.

"Well, that was fun." Aaron tried to joke, but his father turned and glared at him.

"Why would she blame you?" His father still seemed to think Aaron did something wrong.

"I don't know." Aaron shrugged.

"Because she's been trying to bag an O'Connor since grade ten." Mike leaned against the door jamb of the kitchen door.

"Didn't I send you upstairs?" His father didn't turn around to look at Mike.

"Yeah, but that didn't mean we couldn't hear. The air vent is better than an intercom." Mike sauntered into the kitchen and plopped down in a chair. "For the record, I didn't believe her."

"Well, now we can all be satisfied." his father grumbled sarcastically.

"Sean, can't you be happy that it wasn't true?" His mother sat down and sipped her tea.

"I am, but I don't like the fact that my sons have a reputation of being a bunch of oversexed animals. I thought I taught them better than that." His father looked genuinely pained over the insult.

"Dad, none of us are like that." Mike leaned on the table. "I'm sure none of us are virgins anymore, but it's not like we're jumping from one girl to the next."

"Michael." His mother sighed.

"You've always told us to be honest with you guys." Mike smiled.

The fact that he was still a virgin didn't need to be family knowledge, but if Raquel's little trick got out the rumor would be around town within hours. The last thing he wanted people to think was he cheated on the girl he loved. That would kill him.

Present…

"You told your father I knocked you up. That was low, even for you." Aaron turned his head as the memory faded and came back to reality.

"I can't believe you still hold that over my head." Raquel stood staring at him as if he'd just smacked her.

"We were never friends, Raquel," Aaron reminded her.

"Well, that's going to make working together really difficult." She sighed.

"I'm sorry? Work together?" Aaron narrowed his eyes.

"I'm on the committee for the hundredth birthday for Holy Cross." She tipped her head and smiled.

"I didn't see you on the list." Aaron raised an eyebrow.

"I just signed up." Raquel smiled with what she probably thought was seductive.

"I'm sure you have your job to do, and I have mine. I don't think the jobs will require us to work closely together." Aaron couldn't help but sound annoyed.

"I figured you would have grown up a little by now." Raquel rolled her eyes.

"I have because if I hadn't, I wouldn't have stood here this long," Aaron countered.

Raquel pulled out a folder from the large bag she had on her shoulder. She shuffled through the papers and yanked out a couple. As she held the documents out to Aaron, he glanced at her hand.

"It's paper, A.J. Not a barracuda," Raquel grumbled.

"Can't take a chance with some people." Aaron didn't take the papers from her hand.

"Oh, for Christ's sake. It's a list of students that I pulled from the archives," she snapped. "I brought them to Father Wallace, and he told me you were dealing with finding addresses."

Aaron tentatively took the papers from her hands and scanned the names. Most of them were family names he knew from Hopedale.

"You're welcome, by the way." Raquel shoved her bag up on her shoulder and spun on her spike heels. "I hope to God you don't hold on to that anger with everyone, but I guess it would explain your bad attitude."

With those words, she pushed through the door, and he watched her disappear. He had a feeling Raquel only volunteered her time because she'd seen him and Bethany at the school. It didn't matter because she wasn't going to interfere in his life ever again.

Chapter 19

Bethany had spent the entire day with Sandy going through invoices and searching for the names that appeared on some of the invoices.

Nothing out of the ordinary had come up, and she was frustrated. Sandy wasn't giving up though. The woman was clicking on the computer keys like a speed demon. The only other sound was Hulk tapping his finger on the arm of the armchair as he watched a ball game without the sound.

Bethany hadn't heard from Aaron all day, but she figured he was probably busy with his cases. She had seen the report of the body they'd pulled out of the harbor on the news, and her heart went out to the older man who spoke with the reporter. He was Levi's grandfather, and he could barely talk.

"Is everything okay?" Hulk asked as she sat on the couch.

Bethany stared at him with a raised eyebrow and a smirk on her face. Was he serious?

"Well, except for the obvious." He chuckled.

"I'm just starting to feel a little secluded. I'm used to seeing my family every day or at least when we all lived in Ontario, and I figured when I came back we'd spend more time together." Bethany sighed. "I know I shouldn't be whining considering what Denise and her family are going through."

"You've got every right to whine. I don't see why your family can't visit you here. I'm sure they know that." Hulk reached over and patted her knee.

"It's not that I haven't talked to them, but oh, I don't know," Bethany huffed.

"Look, I didn't get to see my brother and sister very often until I got shot last year. Now my sister lives in the apartment over Emily's salon, and my brother just got a position with the Hopedale fire department. I never thought I'd miss being close to them, but with all the time I spent with them after, I realized what I missed. You seem like you're close to your family and it makes sense that you miss them." Hulk smiled.

"You know, that is the most I've heard him say at once since I've known him." Sandy stared at Hulk.

"That's because all conversations with you lead to you being nosey." Hulk narrowed his eyes.

"I'm going to find out who she is, Hulk," Sandy smirked.

"I guess I don't have to worry because there is no she." Hulk sat back in the chair and linked his fingers behind his head.

"So it's a he, then?" Sandy grinned.

"No, it's not a he." Hulk tossed a pillow at her.

"Hulk, I'm going to find out who your little friend in the city is and then I'm going to tell her how you got your nickname." Sandy snickered.

"How did you get it?" Bethany leaned on the arm of the couch.

"That's a story for another time." Hulk focused back on the television and Bethany knew she wasn't getting an answer.

"Me and Emily will tell you later." Sandy winked.

She pulled out her phone and scrolled through social media while she waited for Aaron to return. She wanted so badly to see him and ask him about her family coming to see her. She'd already left to go to the school, so maybe he'd even bring her to see them.

Allyson had called her earlier and said the house was ready for them to go back and according to her, Keith had installed a security system and upgraded all the windows on the bottom floor of the house.

When Bethany had apologized for putting them in a dangerous situation, Allyson had gotten angry and told her it wasn't her fault. Bethany still felt like if she'd told Craig she wouldn't do the investigation on Randy, her family wouldn't be in danger. Then again, she wouldn't be back in Newfoundland and back with Aaron.

"That's a very content sigh." A comforting male voice had Bethany's head snap up at the sound.

"Dad," Bethany ran into his arms and hugged him tightly.

"How are you doing, Beth?" He kissed the top of her head.

"I'm okay. I wish all this was over, but I'm dealing with it." She rested her cheek against his chest.

"That's my strong girl." He gave another squeeze and turned to Hulk.

"Good to see you again, sir." Hulk reached out and shook her father's hand, and Bethany was a little surprised that her father already had met the quiet man.

"You too, young man. Nanny Betty said to tell you there's a container of her fish and brewis in the box for you." He nodded towards the Rubbermaid container next to the door.

Fish and brewis was a traditional Newfoundland dish that consisted of dried salt cod boiled and mixed with hard bread and fatback pork. It didn't sound very tasty, but it was delicious.

"I swear if Tom weren't in the picture, I'd marry that woman." Hulk rubbed his hands together as he picked up the box and carried it to the counter.

"She also sent food for you and A.J." Her father wrapped his arm around her shoulder and led her toward the couch.

"She sends stuff over every second day." Bethany laughed. "I don't know if there is any room in the fridge."

Her father stared at her for a moment and then smiled. Her father looked pretty content himself, and she knew that was because he was back in the town where he grew up.

"What's the smile for?" she asked.

"You're glowing." He cupped her cheek.

"Dad, I'm not wearing any makeup, so it's probably the shine from my slightly oily skin." She rolled her eyes.

"No, I see that sparkle in your eyes that you lost a long time ago." He tapped her nose with his finger.

"The O'Connors must be treating you well because you look happy." She poked his stomach. "And a little pudgy."

"Hey, that's good home-cooking." He winked.

"Are you saying that Allyson and I starved you?" She feigned shock.

"No you didn't, but you can't get the good old Newfoundland cuisine on the mainland." Her father wasn't wrong there.

"Well, fuck a duck," Sandy shouted.

"Sandy?" Bethany stared at the woman who was slapping her hands on top of the counter.

"Sorry, Mr. Donnelly." Sandy smiled sheepishly.

"What did you find?" Hulk stood behind her.

"That kid that drowned. He wasn't working with the dealers. He sent several emails to what looks like the Narcotics unit telling them he had information on a group selling drugs in the center of the city." Sandy pointed to something on the screen.

"Should you be looking at emails for that unit?" Hulk raised an eyebrow.

"I go where the paths lead me, and Levi Watts led me to this. It's Levi's email. Jordan Foster emailed him and told him to get as much information as he could, and he'd make sure he got paid well. That is not the way that works. I'm pretty sure Foster is the head of that unit and should know better." Sandy shook her head.

"Aren't you also a police officer?" Bethany's father asked.

"Umm... yeah, but I always find ways around that." Sandy gave them a huge grin.

"But that kid is only what? Nineteen years old?" Hulk glanced at Bethany. "That's what the news said, right?"

"Yeah, and Aaron said it too." Bethany nodded.

"I'm sure there's a reason this Foster guy didn't tell Levi to back off, but it's not going to go over well that he got killed because of this." Sandy pulled out what looked like a long tube and put several pieces of paper through it.

"Is that a printer?" Hulk stared at the small contraption.

"Yep, courtesy of Newfoundland Security Services." Sandy smiled.

"Does NSS management know they bought it?" Hulk laughed.

"Bull does, Keith? I have no idea." Sandy shrugged.

"What does Keith not know?" the sound of Aaron's voice caused her heart to flutter.

"Sandy is buying expensive computer shit." Hulk poured a cup of coffee.

"I see. Hi, Mr. Donnelly. Glad you got my message about coming to see Bethany." Aaron shook her dad's hand.

"Ally said she and Cameron would be over tomorrow. Cameron has something at school today," her father said.

"You doing okay?" Aaron didn't move toward her, and it was almost as if he was wary of her father being there.

"I'm good, but Sandy found something." Bethany nodded toward where Sandy was printing off several documents.

Bethany watched Aaron's expression go from curiosity to pissed-off in a matter of minutes. The more of the documents he read, the redder his face turned.

"What the fuck is wrong with this department? Letting a kid put himself in the middle of all that shit." Aaron slapped the papers down on the counter and pulled out his phone as he disappeared into the bedroom.

Everyone exchanged worried glances as Bethany followed him. He had the phone to his ear and was practically shouting at someone on the other end.

"I don't give a shit where Foster is. You have him call me right away. This is not proper protocol." Aaron tossed his phone on the bed and pressed his fists into his eyes.

"Aaron?" Bethany whispered.

He dropped his hands and turned his back to her. She placed her hand on his shoulder, and the muscles tightened. She moved around him until she could see his face.

"Are you okay?" She cupped his cheek, and he immediately covered her hand with his.

"Yeah. I'm just furious that some fucking asshat thought it would be a good idea to let a teenager help bring down a drug dealer. I mean, we have fully trained cops that can pass for high school kids. Men and women who are trained to deal with danger." Aaron pulled her into his arms and hugged her. "Why use a kid that doesn't have a clue what he's got involved in?"

"I don't know." She wrapped her arms around his neck, and he buried his face in her neck.

For several minutes, Bethany held him like that until his body started to relax. The reaction was to be expected because he knew Levi and his family personally. She was angry about it herself and would like to know why the young man got tangled up with the situation.

"I'm sorry," Aaron whispered.

"For what?" Bethany pulled back so she could see his face.

"For the outburst." Aaron rested his hands on her hips and kissed her forehead.

"Aaron, you're angry because Levi got put in such a bad situation and it cost him his life." Bethany smiled and held his face between her hands. "It's because you have such a sensitive heart. You always have."

"Your dad must think I'm a hot head." Aaron pulled her against him and hugged her again.

"I doubt that." Bethany squeezed him around the waist.

A few more minutes and Aaron led her out of the bedroom into the kitchen. To her surprise, Allyson was there with Cameron and Ian and Sandy's two daughters, Lily and Evie. They looked worried, and the kids were whispering to each other.

"Hey." Bethany wrapped her sister up in a hug.

"Hi, Beth." Allyson's voice sounded strained.

"A.J., the kids have something they need to tell you." Allyson's eyes glanced between Aaron and Sandy.

"What's going on?" Sandy's ordinarily happy-go-lucky attitude was gone, and her eyes filled with concern.

"I don't know." Cameron looked at Lily.

"We have to tell them." Lily glanced at Evie.

"Cameron, I know we promised her, but…" Evie stopped and looked at her mother.

"Spill it now." Sandy's hands were on her hips.

"The kid that they found in the harbor, we know his sister." Evie didn't look at her mother.

"And?" Aaron stepped forward.

"Mia's in my class," Cameron told him.

"We all sit together at lunch and… well… Mia told us last week that her brother was a spy for the police." Lily tucked her hands into the pocket of her hoodie.

"We didn't believe her, but she wasn't at school today, and she sent me a text." Evie handed her phone to Aaron.

Aaron looked down at the phone and then back up at his niece as he passed the phone to Sandy to read. Aaron motioned for the three pre-teens to sit on the sofa.

"What does it say?" Bethany asked.

"They killed my brother, and now they're going to come after my family because he stole money from them." Sandy read the text aloud.

"I need to call John." Aaron was crouched in front of the couch, whispering to Cameron, Lily, and Evie.

"Uncle John's going to be really mad we didn't tell you before now, isn't he?" Lily glanced at her mother and then back to Aaron.

"I don't know about Uncle John being mad, but I'm pretty upset with you girls right now." Sandy sat between her daughters and pulled them into a hug. "You never keep something like that from your dad or me."

"It was a secret," Evie said in a soft voice.

"Dangerous secrets." Sandy's voice cracked.

"I'm sorry, Mom," Lily said.

"Me too." Cameron dropped his head.

"You guys didn't do anything wrong and the fact that you came to us and told us this shows how mature you are," Aaron told the upset kids.

"Is Mia really in danger?" Evie asked.

"I tell you what, you worry about getting good grades and being kids and let us worry about keeping everyone safe." Sandy kissed both her daughters on their heads and glanced up at Aaron.

"That's right. We got the superheroes, remember?" Aaron winked at Sandy.

"Right." Lily stood up and walked over to Hulk. "We got the best superheroes in the world."

Chapter 20

Aaron sat on the bed with his back braced against the headboard. Bethany was in the bathroom getting ready for bed, and his thoughts were going a mile a minute.

Did Levi think he was a spy for law enforcement or was it just something he told his sister to impress her? He'd read several of the emails that Levi sent and read the ones he got in return.

He knew Jordan Foster and always thought he was a great police officer. It didn't make any sense that he would put a kid in danger. It was possible he didn't believe Levi and was just appeasing the kid.

John took the emails and was going to talk with their Uncle Kurt about the situation. Something was needling in the back of Aaron's brain. From what John had found out so far, there was no formal investigation on Slash by the St. John's division of the Newfoundland Police Department.

Aaron didn't like the fact that Jordan was running an investigation off the books. Not only that he used at least one teenager and that kid was dead. Were there any more out there?

"That's a serious face." Bethany crawled onto the bed and straddled his legs.

"And that's a beautiful face." Aaron ran a finger down Bethany's cheek.

"This is a lot bigger than you expected, isn't it?" Bethany's beautiful eyes stared into his.

"It is, and now I'm worried about my nieces and your nephew." Aaron slid his hand under her tank top and smoothed his hands against the soft skin on her back.

"I'd never be able to do your job." Bethany placed her hands on his shoulders and tried to work the tension out of his muscles.

"That feels fantastic." Aaron closed his eyes and moaned.

"Yeah." He felt her lean forward and place her lips against his chest. "How about that?"

"Uh huh." Aaron's hands slid slowly up and down her back.

Her tongue circled his nipple, and she gently scraped her teeth across the tip. Her hands slowly caressed their way down over his chest as she moved to his other nipple, sucking it hard into her mouth.

"Damn," Aaron groaned.

She kissed her way down over his abdominals and slid her body lower down his legs where he couldn't reach her anymore. Her tongue circled his navel, and she gripped the side of his boxers slowly sliding them off his hips.

Aaron lifted his hips so she could get them down over his ass. He opened his eyes and almost ejaculated at the sight of her hovering over his hard dick. She was touching every inch around his throbbing member, and it was the sexiest fucking thing he'd ever seen.

"Fuck, your mouth so close to my cock is driving me crazy." Aaron lifted his hips, so the tip touched her lower lip.

"Impatient, are you?" Bethany flicked her tongue quickly over the swollen head.

"Damn," Aaron moaned.

She wasn't done with her exquisite torture as she ran her tongue around the head and blew lightly on the tip before doing it a second time. Aaron was squirming under her tease and just wanted to flip her over and drive himself deep inside her.

Before he could finish that thought, Bethany took the head of his dick into her mouth and slid her lips down his thick shaft. Her hands cupped his balls, and he was sure he saw stars.

"Fuck, baby." Aaron roared as she sucked the tip for a moment then slipped her mouth quickly down over him again.

Aaron grabbed the headboard and tried to keep from shooting off when she did it once more. As Bethany wrapped her other hand around the base of his hard-as-steel-cock, she slipped her lips up and down over his shaft making his body quiver.

"Jesus, that feels… Fuck… so damn good." Aaron gasped and opened his eyes to watch.

He couldn't move his eyes from her plump mouth taking his cock almost all the way into her mouth and out again. Her teeth lightly scraping over the top and bottom had his whole body tingling from the top of his head to his toes.

"Bethany, I'm gonna come. If you don't want me doing it… ahhh… down your throat, you need to … fuck…" Aaron didn't finish his sentence as she took his entire dick down her throat and he lost it.

Every muscle in his body tensed and his body convulsed as she kept sucking every drop of his seed down her beautiful throat. Bethany didn't stop, and Aaron grabbed the pillow and bit it, so they didn't hear his cries of pleasure all over Hopedale.

He didn't know when he closed his eyes, but he heard the light pop of her releasing his dick from her mouth. His couldn't speak, and he didn't even know if he was breathing. All he knew was he'd never experienced such an intense orgasm by just a blow job.

When he was finally able to open his eyes and focus, Bethany sat on the bed next to him sporting a seductive smile. He reached for her and pulled her down, so he could kiss her. The taste of his ejaculate on her tongue had him semi-hard.

"Did you enjoy that?" She grinned when she pulled her lips from his.

"I think I'm still enjoying it. My dick keeps twitching and driving aftershocks through my legs." Aaron sighed.

"Good, huh?" Bethany pressed her tongue against his nipple.

"Good would be a severe understatement. I don't think there's a word that could describe what you just did to me." Aaron grinned.

"Are you relaxed now?" Bethany cupped Aaron's cheek.

"Not enough that I don't want to return the favor and then make love to you until we're both too boneless to move." Aaron flipped her over and did exactly that.

Chapter 21

Bethany sat behind Aaron's desk at the station while she listened to Aaron and John make plans to confront Jordan Foster about why he enlisted a kid to do such a dangerous job. Kurt had called the officer and told them they needed him at the Hopedale station to help with a drug case.

"He can't deny what he did with all these emails." Aaron slapped his hand on the pile of emails on his desk.

"No, but you need to let me and Uncle Kurt handle this. I know this is your case, but this could be a case for Internal Affairs," John warned, and he was right.

Bethany knew if the cop was doing something illegal or endangering people, it could be grounds for suspension or even criminal charges.

"I know, but I just can't see him doing this." Aaron shook his head. "He's a good guy, John. You know that as well as I do."

"I know, but these emails say it all." John flopped down in one of the chairs.

"Is it possible someone is using his email?" Bethany felt bored and had seen a crime show where a similar thing happened.

"I doubt it." Aaron picked up one of the emails and scanned through it.

"Why am I here?" Bethany asked because she didn't know why Aaron had dragged her out of bed at the ass crack of dawn.

"She's not a morning person." Aaron chuckled.

"We just want to see if you recognize Jordan from anywhere." John smiled.

"You couldn't send me a picture?" She sat back in the chair and glared at Aaron's grin.

"I promise I'll make it up to you tonight." Aaron winked.

"You damn well better." Bethany tried not to smile, but she couldn't stop herself.

"And another one bites the dust." Crunch, who'd been quietly sitting in the corner, snickered.

"Your day is coming when I get talking to that pretty waitress," Bethany teased.

"Keep her away from Sandy, would ya?" Crunch sighed.

"I don't think that would work. Sandy got all the girls corrupted." John linked his fingers behind his head and laughed.

"She's like the X-rated version of Nan." Bethany snorted at Aaron's description of his sister-in-law.

"But you all love her." Sandy stuck her head into the room.

"Jesus," John groaned.

"Who's the pretty waitress we need to talk to, Bethany?"

Crunch grumbled something about nosey women, and everyone in the room burst out laughing. All except for Crunch of course.

"Why are you here?" John wasn't rude, but from what Bethany knew, Sandy worked mostly from home.

"I was kind of curious about something and did some digging. Jordan Foster's email address didn't have any incoming emails from Levi's email." Sandy had a file folder in her hand.

"He probably deleted them." Aaron shrugged.

"He can't. All emails get saved on the main server. You guys can only delete them from your computers, not the server." Sandy explained as she pulled the system to everyone in the room.

"Our system is the same way." Bethany figured most places did the same thing.

"There's no way he could get into the server?" John asked.

"Nope. I set up that system and Jordan doesn't have the type of skills to get into that system," Sandy replied.

"Something is fishy about this whole damn thing." Aaron shuffled through the emails on his desk.

Several minutes later, Bethany sat with Sandy, Crash, and Aaron behind a one-way mirror listening to John and Kurt talk to Jordan Foster.

"Chief, I have no idea what you're talking about. I don't know Levi Watts. I've heard of this Slash guy, but nobody seems to know his real name or who he works for." Jordan sat straight up in the chair, and from the look on his face, he was entirely in the dark.

"We have dozens of emails going back and forth between you and Levi. How do you explain that?" John placed the papers in front of Jordan.

"I swear, Chief, I've never seen any of these before. I would never put a kid in that kind of situation. I don't even like putting my team in that situation." Jordan was flipping through the pages frantically.

Bethany saw Aaron and Sandy share a confused look and Kurt and John mirrored their confusion. Bethany didn't know Jordan, but something told her he was telling the truth.

"Wait." Jordan flipped back to the top email and slowly went through them again. "This isn't my email address."

"Yes, it is. We checked it." John opened a folder and slid it across the table.

Jordan put down the paper John had and one of the emails he had and slid them back across the table. He tapped on each sheet without saying a word.

"Do you see the difference now?" Jordan asked.

"How the fuck did we miss that?" John growled. "Sandy, come here."

Sandy scrambled to her feet and into the room. She looked back and forth between both sheets John pushed in front of her, and for a few seconds, she didn't seem to see it.

"Well, fuck me." Sandy slapped her hands on the table.

"I didn't do this." Jordan sighed.

"How did I miss that?" Sandy kept staring at the papers.

"It's my email, and I didn't see it at first either." Jordan shook his head.

"What the fuck are they talking about?" Aaron grumbled.

"Someone pretending to be you gave Levi an email address that is almost identical to yours except that one dot at the end of your name. Lured this kid in thinking he was helping catch a drug dealer only to get him killed." Kurt sounded like he was about to explode.

"Someone who knows I'm the head of the Narcotics unit." Jordan's face was red, and Bethany could tell he was angry.

Aaron was pacing in front of her, and she stopped looking in the room and concentrated on Aaron. Like Kurt, Aaron seemed like he could tear someone's head off at the moment.

"Whoever Slash is working for had to be the one to recruit Levi. We need to find out who," Aaron muttered to himself because the big question was, who did slash work for?

The rest of the day passed with Aaron, Jordan, John, James, and Nick crowded around Sandy and her laptop. Nick's fiancée, Lora and John's wife, Stephanie, came to the safe house to keep Bethany company.

"I swear this is like Deja vu." Stephanie smiled as she sipped her tea.

"Why do you say that?" Bethany asked.

"I was hired to be John's physiotherapist. That's how we met, but someone wanted me dead, and this scene happened more than once with all of us." Stephanie glanced at her.

"You were his therapist after his accident, right?" She'd heard the girls talk about it the night they'd come over to get together.

"Yes, it was some dangerous therapy." Stephanie sighed.

"Sounds like it." Bethany nodded.

"At least yours didn't have dangerous delusions." Lora chuckled.

"This is true." Stephanie laughed.

Bethany glanced toward the table as if she sensed his eyes on her. The way he gazed at her made her squirm in the chair. Aaron had a look that said I want to get rid of these people and spend the rest of the night naked.

"Okay, I'm getting hot just watching the way he's looking at you." Stephanie nudged Bethany with her foot.

"I know I need to fan myself," Lora teased.

"I'm sure you guys get those looks frequently." Bethany had no problem returning the teasing.

"Oh honey, those O'Connor men have a way with the eyes." Stephanie wiggled her eyebrows.

Bethany's gaze went back to Aaron who was still looking at her. That was until James hit him in the back of the head and whispered something that had Aaron shoving his older brother and shaking his head.

It was a little after ten at night and Bethany was barely able to keep her eyes open as she, Stephanie, and Lora watched an episode of *Cold Water Cowboys*. It was a show about local Newfoundland fishermen and their struggles on the cold Atlantic Ocean.

"You know I was born in Newfoundland and I have trouble understanding these guys." Lora laughed.

Bethany yawned and tucked her hands under her head as she rested against the arm of the chair. Stephanie had already fallen asleep, and Lora looked like she wouldn't be awake very much longer.

The women were waiting for their husbands. Their kids were with grandparents for the night, and Bethany felt awful that they were spending the childfree night dealing with something she brought into the family.

"Baby, come on, let me get you into bed," Aaron whispered, and Bethany opened her eyes.

"Where did everyone go?" Bethany stretched and glanced around the empty room.

"They went home about ten minutes ago." Aaron chuckled.

"I guess I fell asleep." Bethany stood up.

"Yep, you, Stephanie, and Lora." Aaron pulled her into his arms and gave her a soft kiss on the lips.

"See, that's what happens when you wake me before the sun comes up." Bethany wrapped her arms around his neck and rested her head on his shoulder.

"Baby, the sun was up by the time you got up, but let's go get into bed and get some sleep." Aaron backed up toward the bedroom, tugging her with him.

"Did you figure anything out with the email?" Bethany asked after they were both under the covers.

"Sandy is working on trying to track the email address. She's going to get Smash on it too." Aaron pulled her to his side, and she put her head on his chest.

"Smash?" She yawned.

"He's the other computer analyst that works for Keith. His actual name is Gage Hodder." Aaron's hand gently caressed her back.

"I wonder what your nickname would be if you worked for Keith." Bethany lifted her head and looked into his smiling eyes.

"Stud." Aaron wiggled his eyebrows.

"Nah, how about Songbird?" Bethany grinned.

"Oh, that's so manly." Aaron snickered.

"I haven't heard you sing since I got back." Bethany folded her hands on his chest and rested her chin on them.

When they were teenagers, Aaron would sing to her all the time. One of her favorite songs was a Collin Ray song called *In This Life*. Every time they were alone, he'd pull her close and sing it.

"Do you remember what song you used to sing for me?" Bethany raised an eyebrow.

Without missing a beat, Aaron cleared his throat and started to sing. For some reason him not even thinking about it for a second caused her eyes to blur with tears and a lump to form in her throat. To know that he'd never forgotten made her realize that he hadn't ever forgotten her.

Aaron smiled as he sang and wiped a tear from her cheek that had slipped out. He didn't question why she was crying just pulled her into him and continued to sing their song. She closed her eyes and let the gentle vibration of his voice lull her to sleep.

"I love you," she whispered right before she drifted off into a contented sleep.

Chapter 22

Aaron stood in the back of the church holding Bethany's hand as if she would disappear. He wasn't happy that she'd demanded to go to the funeral service for Levi.

He couldn't sit still as he continually scanned the church for the one man they wanted. They weren't alone. Crunch, Crash, Hulk, and his brothers were all surrounding them. As well as all of his sisters-in-law, Kurt, Alice, Cora, Brian, his parents, and grandmother.

Having all his family at the church when there could be a potential murderer in attendance didn't make the situation any better. He didn't win the discussion of why it wasn't a good idea for all of them to go.

At the end of the pew where he sat with Bethany sat Jordan Foster and scattered through the church were several other officers both from Hopedale and St. John's.

His heart went out to Denise and her siblings as they entered the church. Quintin carried the urn up to the front of the church at the start of the service. The kid's face was emotionless as he slowly made his way up to the altar with his sister and other family members behind him.

"Quintin looks ready to explode," Bethany whispered.

Aaron nodded as he continued to scan the crowd for anyone that looked out of place or suspicious. Sandy and Allyson had allowed Cameron, Lily, and Evie to attend the funeral since they were friends with Mia but they sat close to his family.

Father Wallace started the service, and the only other sounds besides his voice were the sobs and sniffs of people in mourning. Aaron noticed Denise glancing behind her several times and only relaxed when she met his eyes. He nodded and her shoulders relaxed.

She was scared, that was obvious. He wouldn't question her on anything that day, but he had a feeling she had something to tell him. Aaron started to relax as the service progressed and was able to listen to Father Wallace's Homily. He talked about what a great student Levi had been and how he was headed to university to become a teacher.

The click of the church door made Aaron turn toward the entrance. Two men walked into the church dressed as if they were going to a biker bar. They scanned the church and stopped at the urn in the front of the church.

"They look creepy," Bethany whispered.

"They are definitely out of place." Aaron moved Bethany to his other side, further from the men and closer to Hulk.

"They don't look familiar." Jordan leaned over the back of the pew toward Aaron and John.

Aaron glanced toward the family in the front of the church to see Quintin glaring at the newcomers as if they were the devil. Something told Aaron that these were probably two of the men that Levi had been associating with. Aaron tried to get the kid's attention, but Denise had made her brother turn back to the front of the church.

"How about you and I casually walk to those guys and ask them to leave?" Keith leaned forward over the pew.

Aaron nodded and after making sure Bethany was secure with Hulk followed his brother to the church entrance. The man's eyes widened when they saw Keith heading toward them. It wasn't hard to understand why they would be intimidated by his older brother. Keith was a big guy even next to Aaron's six-foot-one inch.

"Gentleman, I'm afraid this service is just for friends and close family of the deceased," Keith spoke in a hushed tone.

"What makes you think we aren't friends or family?" The shorter of the two smirked.

"Because we know the family and friends." Keith's voice stayed monotone, but his stance was filled with intimidation.

"Shows what you know, we were close personal friends of Snitch." The taller guy smirked.

"I don't want to cause a scene at such a somber time, but if you both don't turn around and exit right now, I will physically remove you from this church." Keith dipped his head and glared at the men.

Aaron didn't need to look to know that there were now several other men behind him and Keith. The color draining from the faces of the two young men who looked barely out of high school.

"Good day, gentlemen," Aaron whispered.

The shorter guy glanced once more toward the front of the church before he and his pal exited quietly. Aaron turned back to the front of the church as his brothers, Jordan, Crunch and Crash made their way back to their seats.

Luckily nobody noticed the scene at the back of the church and Aaron made his way back to Bethany's side. He wanted to run after the two men to see who the hell they were and how they knew Levi.

"Rick and Blake are outside waiting for those two," John whispered as if he had read Aaron's thoughts.

Aaron gave his brother a thumbs up as Father Wallace ended the service and the choir start singing the recessional hymn, *Precious Lord, Take My Hand.*

Quintin's grandparents were hosting a reception at their house. Aaron wasn't comfortable with Bethany going to the house, but Crash and Hulk had assured him that the home would be secure. It made him feel slightly better, but he made sure Bethany was close to him.

"My condolences to you and your family, Denise," Bethany said as she gave one of her old bullies a hug.

"Thank you. It doesn't feel real yet." Denise forced a smile.

"It probably won't for a while." Bethany clasped Denise's hand between her own.

"I'm glad to see you and Aaron together. I've realized something in the last few years. Life is short, and you get what you give. My life has been a mess for years, and I blame it on the things I did as a bitch of a teenager. I'm truly sorry for everything I ever said or did to you in high school. I wanted to be cool and being one of Raquel's shadows made me feel that way. At least for a while." Denise had tears in her eyes.

"It's water under the bridge. As you said, life is too short to hold grudges." Bethany's eyes were glistening with unshed tears.

"You're a bigger person than I would be." Denise dropped her head. "It was Raquel's idea to start that rumor in the bathroom the day you broke up with Aaron. We saw you go in and she came up with this plan to break you up."

"That was a long time ago. Let's start over. If you need anything, let me know." Bethany hugged Denise again and motioned for Aaron in the direction of Father Wallace and Quintin.

"Thanks, I may take you up on that." Denise turned and made her way through the numerous people crammed into the house.

"Mr. Watts, you need to leave this to the police. The last thing your sister needs is you getting hurt or worse." Father Wallace's voice carried to Aaron's ears.

"They killed my brother and then have the nerve to show up at the funeral. Those two are the reason Levi is dead." Quintin's voice was a low rumble.

Aaron stepped next to Father Wallace and saw Quintin's eyes. They were cold, and he had vengeance written all over his young face. Aaron didn't like it and knew he had to do something to keep Quintin from being another victim in this whole situation.

"You need to listen to Father Wallace, Quintin. We'll find these guys." Aaron placed his hand on the kid's shoulder.

"They were there. Why didn't you arrest them?" Quintin pulled away from Aaron and shouted.

"They didn't get off the church steps." Aaron kept his voice calm and low. "You need to calm down before you upset your sisters and grandparents, more than they already are. Don't screw up your life over these idiots. Levi wouldn't want that and neither would your mom."

Quintin locked his angry glare with Aaron for a few minutes, but it was as if he realized Aaron was right and he dropped his head. Aaron wrapped his arm around the young man's shoulder and gave him a side hug.

"You're stronger than any of those bastards think and ten times smarter," Aaron whispered.

"The two at the church were Buzzer and Grease," Quintin whispered.

"Thanks. The only thing I need you to do for me is let me know if you see these guys hanging around, call me right away. Don't engage them, don't talk to them. We'll make sure they get what's coming to them." Aaron glanced over Quintin's shoulder to where James tried to get his attention.

"Thank you, Mr. O'Connor." Quintin gave him a half smile before turning to the priest. "I'm sorry for being a jerk, Father."

"You've got every right to be a jerk today, Mr. Watts. Just don't think that this attitude will work at school." The priest winked as he nodded his head at Aaron.

Outside the house, Hulk accompanied Bethany to the SUV and sat with her inside while Aaron spoke with James, Kurt, and Jordan. James had the phone to his ear, and Aaron waited for him to end the call.

"I'm assigning a couple of plain-clothed officers to stay with Levi's family," Kurt told Aaron while they waited.

"Good." Aaron shoved his suit jacket back from his hips as he pushed his hands in his pockets.

"Okay, that was John. He said Rick found out the two guys from the church have outstanding warrants." James shoved his phone into his pockets.

"Quintin told me that their nicknames are Buzzer and Grease." Aaron assumed if Rick found warrants he knew their real names.

"Yeah." James chuckled. "They won't answer Rick unless he calls them by those stupid names."

"Let me guess; they got files as long as my arm." Kurt shook his head.

"What's their real names?" Jordan asked.

"That's the good news. Getting their real names lead us to the other nickname Quintin gave us. Doom aka Jeremy Lambe and Buzzer aka Darryl Lambe are brothers from Placentia. Grease aka Ruben Finn is from St. Mary's. They were all in juvenile detention together," James explained.

"So that's where they met. Any word on who this Slash guy is?" Aaron asked.

"They say they don't know anyone by that name." James rolled his eyes.

"So, until we get something out of these guys we are at a standstill. A.J., take Bethany back to the safe house and if she's okay with you leaving her with Hulk, meet us at the station." Kurt raised an eyebrow as he glanced over his shoulder.

"Uncle Kurt, don't even try to keep me out of this." Aaron glared at his uncle.

"I've learned that even when I try to do that, you boys don't listen. I want to have a pow-wow and see where you are going with the investigation from here." Kurt backed up as his wife headed toward him. "I'll see you in a bit."

Aaron got into the back of the SUV with her. Hulk sat behind the wheel and Crunch in the passenger seat. Several cars pulled out of the parking area across from the row of houses. Hulk waited for his chance to pull out.

As the SUV eased into traffic, something started hitting the side of the vehicle. At first, Aaron thought someone was spinning rocks, and they were hitting them until he heard Hulk shout.

"Son of a bitch. That van is shooting at us." Hulk spun the SUV and pulled off in the opposite direction.

Keith purchased several vehicles for his company. He had bulletproof windows and armor-plated panels installed in the doors. Aaron remembered him complaining it cost him big money, but it was just to ensure the safety of his clients. Aaron was never so thankful as he pushed Bethany to the floor and covered her while Hulk weaved and sped away from the van.

"I'm really tired of bullets directed at me," Bethany complained from under him.

"You and me both, sweetheart," Hulk shouted.

"Turn down this road, Hulk," Crunch yelled.

"Are they following us?" Aaron called out to the two men.

"I don't see them behind us, but I'm getting us right to The Compound," Hulk shouted, and Aaron felt the vehicle accelerate.

"Stay down until we tell you it's safe." Aaron felt Crunch's hand tap him on the shoulder.

Aaron could feel rage bubbling up inside him as he tried to keep himself and Bethany from being tossed around by the speeding vehicle. When he got the bastard who shot at Bethany, someone better be there to stop Aaron from killing the fucker.

Chapter 23

Bethany's heart was still racing by the time they pulled into the safety of Keith's property. Crunch gave them the okay to sit up in the seats about ten minutes before they got to Hopedale, but she wasn't scared. Okay, well maybe a little but mostly she was pissed.

Not only did the assholes shoot at her, Aaron, Hulk, and Crunch, but there were still several vehicles on the street and people walking to the cars that had been at the reception. She waited with her hands folded in her lap while Aaron checked to see if anyone had been hurt or worse.

"Did anyone get a plate or a look at the shooter?" Aaron asked Jordan, who'd stayed at the scene.

Bethany glanced to the front at Hulk and Crunch. They were quiet as they pulled in front of the safe house and she wondered what they were thinking.

"Well, at least nobody was hurt. Make sure you send John and me all the reports on the evidence you find. When I get inside the house, I'll call someone to come to check the SUV to dig out the slugs." Aaron ended the call and glanced at Bethany as Hulk turned off the vehicle.

"You want us to do a sweep before we bring her inside?" Hulk's voice sounded strained.

"It's probably not necessary because nobody is getting by the security on this property, but I'm not taking chances. So yeah." Aaron reached over and covered her hands with his.

"Someone could have been killed." Bethany lifted her head and met his gaze.

"True but nobody was." Aaron put his finger under her chin. "Are you okay?"

"Okay? I'm fucking furious." Bethany fisted her hands under Aaron's hand. "All this is because Randy decided it was a good idea to sell drugs to a fucking drug dealer and then figured he could run the whole situation, but what did that get him? A bullet in his chest. Now, these dickwads are shooting real bullets at me. Real fucking bullets, Aaron. So, no I'm not okay. Right now, I'd like five minutes alone with these assholes and a baseball bat in my hand."

Bethany took in a deep breath and blew it out slowly to try to calm her anger. Yeah, she did feel the fear, but her rage was overriding that fear. She was about to tell Aaron that very thing when she heard Crunch and Hulk laugh and Aaron snicker.

"I think I just fell in love with you." Crunch winked.

"Back off, ass," Aaron growled.

"Come on, that was awesome. Reminds me of Emily and Sandy." Hulk laughed.

"I'm ready to beat someone to death with a bat and you three are making jokes. Seriously?" Bethany opened the door to the SUV and got out.

"We aren't joking, baby." Aaron caught up to her as she was about to enter the house. "That was the best damn thing I've ever heard."

"Aaron, you're not making any sense." Bethany sighed.

"What he means is, a lot of people would fall apart in your situation. The fact that you're ready to rip someone's head off means you're strong enough to handle this." Bethany glanced over Aaron's shoulder at Hulk.

"Fine, now what?" Bethany relaxed a little and allowed Aaron to lead her into the house.

"I'm going to the station to see what information they got out of the two, what was it you called them? Oh, yeah, dickwads," Aaron chuckled. "I honestly don't think I'd ever heard you curse."

"I curse plenty. When I'm mad." Bethany tried to keep herself from smiling.

"I'll have to remember that," Aaron whispered in her ear, and she couldn't keep from laughing.

"I need a hot bath and a stiff drink." Bethany rested her forehead on his shoulder.

"There's wine in the fridge, and I think I hear that bathtub calling out to you." Aaron kissed the side of her head. "I'll be back before you know it."

"Okay, but be careful. We may be safe in here, but those guys could be waiting for you to leave." Bethany pulled back and cupped his face in her hands. "I can't have anything happen to you."

"I'll be careful. I love you, Bethany. So damn much." His blue eyes glistened as he stared deep into hers.

"I love you too, Aaron." Bethany leaned forward and pressed her lips hard against his.

"Go get that glass of wine and bath." Aaron gave Bethany another quick kiss and stepped back.

He blew her a kiss as he winked and left the house. Bethany turned around to head to the kitchen. She smiled when Crunch met her with a glass of wine and pointed her toward her room.

"You want to take the bottle with you." Crunch smirked.

"I don't think that would be a good plan. I might just put the bottle on my head and guzzle it down." Bethany smiled and headed toward her bedroom after she thanked both Hulk and Crunch for what they did for her earlier.

The hot water surrounded her body as she eased into the tub. It was the first time she'd been alone in a room for more than two minutes since Randy's murder. It wasn't that she didn't like the guys or appreciate what they were doing for her, but she missed being able to take a walk to clear her head.

She closed her eyes and let her body relax. It was hard to do with her mind going a mile a minute, but there was nothing she could do about that. Bethany couldn't keep her brain from replaying the last few weeks in her head.

Her eyes popped open when she remembered something she hadn't told police or Aaron. She'd completely forgotten.

Bethany sat up in the tub and scrambled out. She had to call Aaron and tell him what she remembered.

Chapter 24

"You have all three of them here?" Aaron saw Rick leading a young man into one of the interrogation rooms.

"Yep, and they aren't going anywhere but jail. All three have outstanding warrants." John handed Aaron the files he'd carried out of the office.

"So, what's the plan?" Aaron looked through each file, scanning through the previous charges and convictions of all three men.

"Keep them here until we get info. They haven't asked for a lawyer yet, so I guess they're stupid or don't think we have anything." John nodded to Rick as he came out of the interrogation room.

"We'll leave them in the rooms for a while and then start with the youngest, Darryl. He's edgy and scared." Rick pointed to the room behind them where the shorter of the two from the church paced the room nervously.

"He'll probably flip before the other two." John nodded.

Aaron didn't care which one they got to flip; they just needed the name of the guy who shot Randy and was trying to get to Bethany. The fact that the fucker came way too close twice only made him more desperate to get something on the asshole.

"I'm a little worried about Quintin and his family. Have you talked to Jordan?" Aaron hadn't been able to get hold of the narcotics officer since he'd talked to him a little while earlier.

"I haven't heard a word, but maybe you and Cory should drop by their house and see if everything is okay." John motioned for Cory as he sauntered down the hallway.

Aaron wanted to be there while the three men were questioned but he also wanted to make sure that Quintin, Denise, Mia, and their grandparents were safe. The family had such a stressful day and then the shooting. They had to be traumatized by the whole thing.

Aaron and Cory pulled into the parking area across from Denise's grandparents. After a quick scan of the area, they made their way to the house. An unmarked police car parked at the side of the house and an officer inside.

Denise opened the door and invited them inside. The house was quiet with only Denise and Mia in the kitchen. The grandparents had gone to lay down for a nap before supper.

"They're exhausted." Denise sighed as she placed a cup of coffee in front of Cory and Aaron.

"Nana has a bad heart, and it's been a long day for her." Mia didn't look up at them as she stared down into her cup of hot chocolate.

"You all must be tired. Is Quintin resting too?" Aaron asked, noticing he hadn't seen the kid since he'd arrived.

"He went upstairs a while ago. Said he needed to be alone for a while." Denise turned and stared out the window.

"I'll run up and get him." Mia stood up and left the kitchen.

"She's so quiet. Normally she's got a smart mouth and sarcastic attitude, but she's like a different kid." Denise sighed. "She thought Levi was some sort of spy. It was the only thing she's never tattled about her brother."

"She's young, and it's hard enough for adults to understand this kind of thing. It's got to be impossible to understand for a twelve-year-old." Cory glanced at Aaron.

"I was eighteen when my grandfather died, and it was still hard for me to get my head around." Aaron glanced behind at the sound of footsteps pounded down the stairs.

"Denise, Quintin is gone. He left this note." Mia had tears streaming down her cheeks. "He's going to get himself killed too."

Aaron took the note while Denise pulled Mia into her embrace and tried to calm the hysterical girl. Cory looked over Aaron's shoulder at the note. As he read it, Aaron's heart dropped. What the hell was the kid doing?

Denise,

I'm going to get these animals that killed Levi. I know it's hard to do but don't worry about me. I've got Pappy's rifle. Don't call the police. I love you and Mia. I'm doing this for you.

Love Quintin.

Aaron made sure Denise was okay before he hurried to the side of the house where the officer sat. How the fuck could he let Quintin sneak off? He didn't know the young cop, but he certainly wanted to punch him at that moment.

"How the fuck did you let him get past you?" Cory was already tearing the guy a new asshole.

"He didn't come out this way. I would've seen him," the young officer replied.

"Aaron, he must have climbed out on the roof," Denise called out and pointed to the open window above the awning. "All of us used to sneak out that way one time or another. There'd be no way for the officer to see him."

"Damn it." Aaron plowed his hands through his hair.

"Do you have any idea where he'd be going to find these guys?" Cory asked.

"None, I just asked Mia the same thing." Denise had her arms wrapped around herself.

"We'll find him, Denise. Go inside and if you hear from him call me right away," Aaron shouted as he and Cory ran to his vehicle.

Aaron sped out of the parking area and headed toward the area where they found Levi's body. It was probably a waste of time, but at the moment he didn't know where to start. The kid didn't have a cell phone, so he couldn't even track Quintin's phone.

When they pulled up to the harbor apron, there weren't many people walking around. Aaron hoped to see Quintin, but something told Aaron he wasn't going to have any luck.

"I just called John." Cory stood next to Aaron and scanned the harbor front.

"I don't have a fucking clue where to start looking for the kid." Aaron tossed his hands in the air.

"The only one of the guys we don't have in custody is that Slash guy." Cory turned to look up the west end of the road.

"Yeah, and from what I can figure out, he's the worst." Aaron sighed.

He was getting back into his car when his cell phone vibrated in his pocket. He pulled it out hoping it was Denise telling him Quintin was back home. He glanced at the phone and saw Bethany's number.

"Hi, baby," Aaron answered.

"Aaron, I remembered something. There was a woman. She was there. She didn't call the guy Slash. She called him Melvin." Bethany rambled.

"Bethany, what are you talking about?" Aaron was completely confused as he put her on speaker so Cory could hear as well.

"The day Randy was killed. I completely forgot until I was in the bath. I was relaxing and closed my eyes, and I started to go through that day. I remembered the woman. I didn't see her because I hid in the bathroom, but I heard her. She called the guy who shot Randy by his first name. His name is Melvin." Cory shook his head and smiled as Bethany frantically told her news.

"That's great, baby. I'll see if the name helps but right now we're trying to find Quintin," Aaron explained as he headed out into traffic.

"What happened to Quintin?" Her gasp caused him to cringe at her panicked question.

"I'll explain when I get home. I've got to get a BOLO put out on him." Aaron turned and headed on the highway toward Hopedale.

"Okay, be careful. I love you." Bethany ended the call before he had a chance to answer her.

He needed to find Quintin before he got himself killed. Then Aaron was thinking about kicking the kid's ass for running off like some vigilante and worrying everyone. Especially Quintin's family. They'd already been through enough.

Chapter 25

Bethany was worried sick about Quintin. He'd been gone
more than twenty-four hours, and nobody had seen or heard from
him. She knew Aaron was ready to explode by the way he snapped
at everyone. It was hard not to say something about his behavior, but
he was concerned about the kid.

She sat focused on the television with several of Aaron's
family, her family, and most of the men who worked for Keith. The
news anchor was reporting on the missing young man and the
connection with the arrests of the three men.

"Quintin Watts was last seen yesterday a little after three. He
left his home through an upstairs window. If anyone has seen him,
please contact the Newfoundland Police Department…" Bethany
stopped listening when she saw Aaron heading outside alone.

She slipped out of the living room where everyone sat around
the television and stepped outside. Aaron had his back braced

against the house with his hands clasped and resting on top of his head. Bethany's heart broke at the stressed expression on his face.

"You need a hug?" Bethany stepped in front of him.

"I can always use a hug from you." Aaron dropped his hand and wrapped his arms tightly around her as he tucked his face in the nape of her neck.

"You'll find him, Aaron," Bethany whispered into his ear as she wrapped her arms around his neck.

"I'm just praying he's not involved in any of this." That was when she realized most of Aaron's concern was that Quintin was involved in the situation.

"I don't believe that, and I don't think you do either." Bethany pressed her lips against the side of his head, and he hugged her tighter.

"He runs off; half-cocked with a fucking rifle. If he kills anyone, no matter if it's in self-defense or not, he'll never come back from that, Bethany." Aaron lifted his head, and she could see the tears in his eyes. "I care about all the kids I coach at that school. I want to see them all succeed, and it kills me this kid was dealt a tough hand. His mom died, his dad took off, and his brother murdered. Sure, Denise is doing her best, but that's a lot for a kid to take. He and Mia have had a tough time."

"Maybe he'll come to his senses and come back home before he does something foolish." Bethany cupped his face between her hands.

"Hey, A.J." Jordan appeared in the doorway of the safe house.

"What's up?" Bethany stepped back, but Aaron kept his arm around her.

"My cousin Larry is a pharmacist at one of the pharmacies on the list John just showed me. He's given me some great leads in the past on some of the people he suspected of selling narcotics. I tried calling him, but he hasn't gotten back to me yet. You want to ride along with me and drop by his house to see if he knows any of these guys?" Jordan stepped outside and closed the door.

"Are you talking about Larry Foster?" Bethany remembered Craig had told her he was one of the pharmacists that he'd spoken with and had confirmed that he didn't place any orders with Randy.

"Yeah, do you know him?" Jordan asked.

Bethany explained she only knew the name but how he'd been one of the pharmacists that Craig spoke to before Bethany returned to Newfoundland. The drug store he owned was also one of the ones that had the most invoices written out. Bethany figured Randy probably thought Craig wouldn't question a regular customer.

"I'll come with you, and maybe we should have John come along as well." Aaron motioned for Bethany to go into the house ahead of him.

"Good idea." Jordan followed them inside.

Bethany hoped this would get settled soon. The only person that they had to arrest was Slash, and she'd be free to take a walk on the beach or even a stroll down Harbour Street. What Bethany looked forward to the most was starting a life with Aaron. The one she should have had thirteen years ago.

"Are ya doin okay, ducky?" Nanny Betty handed a cup to Bethany.

"I'm doing okay. I feel a little guilty about your family having to be involved in all this." Bethany stared down into the cup of tea.

"Ya got nothin' ta feel guilty about. We're here cause we care fer ya and A.J. loves ya. Me grandson has always loved ya and even though ya both were apart for a while, doesn't change da fact dat family helps family." Nanny Betty pushed a plate with a huge date square on it.

"I don't want anyone to get hurt, and it seems like this whole thing is bringing more people into it every day. I'm so worried about that boy, and I only met him once." Bethany sighed.

"Bethany, it's because you've got a huge heart, just like my son." She raised her head at the sound of Kathleen O'Connor's voice.

"Thank you, Mrs. O'Connor." Bethany smiled.

"You call me Kathleen or Mom. All my daughters-in-law call me Mom." Kathleen sat next to her and gave her a side hug.

"That's right. The only woman that has a better mother-in-law than we do is, Mom O'Connor." Billie sat next to Nanny Betty.

"I'm so glad you came home." Jess grinned as she leaned on the back of Kathleen's chair.

"Me too. As soon as this dumbass gets caught, we are gonna go out to *The Rock* or *Club Harbor* and dance the night away." Kristy shimmied her shoulders as she referred to the two dance clubs in Hopedale.

"You might need a babysitter first, Kristy." Alice O'Connor raised an eyebrow.

"That's not a problem. I've got the best mom in the world." Kristy winked at her mother.

"Maybe I want to dance the night away too." Alice winked at Bethany.

"Mom, your idea of dancing the night away is sitting on the couch with Dad and swaying to country music on the radio." Isabelle laughed.

"Fine, I'd rather spoil my grandson anyway." Alice smiled.

"That is the best part of being a grandmother." Kathleen laughed.

"You've got a few more than I do, Kathleen." Alice laughed.

Bethany sat back in her chair and listened to the lively conversation going on around her. She did feel like part of the family, and she hoped someday she would be, but until Slash was in jail, that would have to wait.

Chapter 26

Aaron sat in the back of John's car listening to his brother talk with Jordan. He wasn't paying attention to the conversation, and at that point, it just sounded like murmurs. All he could think about was if Quintin was okay and how long Bethany was going to be in danger.

They'd dropped by the pharmacy, but when Jordan came out, he said the staff said Larry hadn't shown up for work in two days. They hadn't been able to get in touch with him.

"That's not like Larry." Jordan was concerned.

"We'll head to his house and see if he's there." John made his way to the address Jordan gave him.

A few minutes, later they pulled up next to a narrow two-story house. It was grey with black shutters, and all the curtains closed. Since it was in downtown St. John's, the house was attached on both sides, and the only place to park was on the side of the road.

As Aaron, John, and Jordan got out of the vehicle, Jordan searched up and down the road for his cousin's car. It was evident to Aaron that the police officer was concerned about his cousin.

"His car is parked across the street." Jordan pointed to the green Toyota directly across from the house.

Jordan ran up the front steps and knocked on the door. After a few minutes and nobody answered, he knocked a second time. Aaron walked up to the end of the row of houses on one end, and John went the other way.

"This isn't like him." Jordan stood back and looked up at the windows on the second story.

"We could try around the back, but it looks like there's no way to get there unless one of the neighbors lets us go through their houses," Aaron heard his brother say as he came back to the front of Larry's house.

"Is he married or does anyone have a key to his place?" Aaron asked.

"No, he's a loner, and his parents are both gone. My siblings and I are the closest family he has, and he doesn't associate with us very often." Jordan sighed. "I can kick the door in."

"He could be hurt or sick." John looked up and down the street.

"Fuck it." Jordan ran up the steps and gave the flimsy door a couple of hard kicks.

It flew open, and without a thought, Aaron pulled his weapon out of its holster. He didn't have to look to know John and Jordan did the same as they slowly made their way into the house.

"Larry, it's me, Jordan." There was no response.

Aaron slowly made his way through the lower level of the house as Jordan continued to shout out his cousin's name. As they made their way up to the second story of the house, Aaron detected an odor that couldn't be mistaken.

"That smell isn't a good sign," John whispered.

"Jesus." Jordan gagged as he moved closer to the only closed door in the upstairs.

"You want one of us to do that?" John grabbed Jordan's arm before he opened the door.

"I got this." Jordan turned the knob while John and Aaron kept their weapons raised.

When Jordan shoved the door open, the putrid smell had Aaron choking. John covered his mouth and nose with his shirt and Aaron did the same. They stepped just inside the door and glanced around the room.

On the bed, something was covered with a dirty blanket, and Jordan stepped toward it. He lifted the corner and dropped it quickly turning away as he gaged.

"I'm pretty sure it's Larry." Jordan coughed.

"We need to call the coroner." John stepped out of the room and Aaron motioned for Jordan to go ahead of them as they stepped out of the room and made their way out of the house into the fresh air.

"I didn't see a whole lot, but he was wearing his lab coat." Jordan holstered his weapon.

"Something's weird about this," John said as he shoved his phone into his pocket.

"By that smell, he's been dead for a while. When was the last time you talked to him?" Aaron turned to Jordan.

"Last week. I'll check my phone." Jordan pulled his phone out and scrolled through his calls. "Ten days ago."

"They said he hasn't been at work in two days." John turned to Jordan.

"Yeah, but this is Wednesday, and he doesn't work on the weekends. The last time they would have seen him would have been Friday." Jordan turned and glanced at the open door. "Fuck."

"I'm sorry, Jordan." Aaron put his hand on the man's shoulder.

"I get the feeling all this is connected to this guy Slash. Don't ask me how I know but it's a gut feeling." Jordan turned to John.

"You think he's involved?" John glanced at Aaron.

"It's just too coincidental that A.J.'s girlfriend hears this ass Slash shoot someone who had fake invoices for the same pharmacy that Larry owns. Then there's Levi, who thinks he's sending me info on this gang but it's not my email." Jordan wasn't wrong.

It was as if there was a bunch of puzzle pieces, but they were missing the one part that joined them all. The good thing about it was Aaron loved puzzles.

"I don't believe in coincidences when it comes to this shit." Aaron shook his head.

"Me either and as much as I care about my cousin, I always found it odd that he knew when someone was illegally selling narcotics." Jordan sighed.

Two hours later, attendants from the coroner's office wheeled Larry's body to the transport vehicle. The corpse needed to go to the morgue for autopsy. John and Aaron borrowed masks to cover their mouths and noses to mask the smell that still lingered inside the room.

A team of forensic specialists collected evidence around the room. Aaron made his way into another room at the top of the stairs. It looked as if Larry used it as a home office and his laptop was opened up on the desk.

Aaron walked to the other side of the desk and glanced at the screen that was open to Larry's email program. Aaron pulled on a glove and leaned down to skim through the emails. Nothing seemed out of place, but *Jordan Foster NPD* was the name listed on the email in the sent folder.

"John," Aaron shouted as he opened one of the emails.

"What did you find?" John appeared in the doorway and Aaron motioned him to come around the desk.

"I found out who Levi was exchanging emails with." Aaron pointed to the listed of deleted emails still sitting in the folder.

"Jesus H. Christ," John growled. "Jordan's cousin is in this up to his fucking eyeballs."

"What?" Jordan's voice could only be described as an infuriated growl.

"Sandy said the emails were coming from an email service where you make up your own address. The problem is it's set up under your information," John explained.

"What the fuck was he doing? Was he trying to get me fired from the force?" By the expression on Jordan's face, Aaron was sure that the man was not involved.

"Jordan, I'm going to have to ask you to stay out of this investigation." John walked toward the distraught officer, but he held his hands up to stop John.

"I get it, John. I'll hand in my badge and weapon at the station." Jordan was about to walk off.

"I'm not suspending you, Jordan. I'm not your supervisor, but for this investigation, you need to step back," John explained as Aaron followed them out of the house.

"I understand, John. I can't believe he would do this to me. He's my fucking family." Jordan shook his head.

"Here's some advice. Tell your brothers and sisters about Larry and let yourself grieve for your family. Worry about the other stuff later. We know you had nothing to do with this." John and Aaron walked Jordan to his car.

"John's right, be with your family, Jordan." Aaron squeezed the man's shoulder and motioned for one of the guys to give Jordan a ride.

"Thanks A.J. Do me a favor?" Jordan grabbed Aaron by the shoulders.

"What?"

"Find the bastard who's the missing piece in this damn fucked-up shit." Jordan dropped his hands.

"We'll do everything we can. I want to get this fucker as much as you do." Aaron backed away to let the car drive off.

John was watching Aaron when he finally turned back to his brother. There was an expression on John's face that Aaron couldn't read and it concerned him. John never looked at a loss even when he was, but at that moment his brother looked utterly baffled.

"He's not involved in this, John." Aaron was completely confident in Jordan's innocence and he wanted to make sure John knew that.

"I know, A.J." John sighed. "I'm just worried about that kid."

"I know. I also wonder what exactly Quintin does know." Aaron followed John back to the car.

By the time Aaron arrived back at the safe house, Quintin was still missing, and Denise's family were beside themselves with worry. It was after midnight and Crunch had told him Bethany had gone to bed a couple of hours earlier.

He didn't want to wake her, so Aaron eased into the bed next to her, and as if she sensed him, she turned into him and wrapped her arms around his chest. She murmured she loved him and then she was sleeping again.

Just having her in his arms helped him relax and feel like everything would be okay. Bethany gave his life meaning, and he felt more focused on everything. For the first time in his life, he felt like his life was going somewhere. As soon as all the shit was over Aaron would ask Bethany the question he never got to ask her thirteen years ago.

Aaron woke up to something warm sliding down his stomach and slipping into his boxers. He smiled as a hand wrapped around his hardening cock, and he moaned at the slow stroking.

"This is an amazing way to wake up." Aaron opened his eyes and turned his head toward Bethany's smiling face.

"I have to agree." Bethany lifted her head and pressed her lips against his chest while she slowly stroked him.

"That feels so damn good." Aaron thrust his hips up in time with her strokes.

Aaron rolled onto his side and grinned when he noticed she was completely naked next to him. Aaron slipped his boxers down over his hips and kicked them off as best he could without pulling his dick away from the pleasure of her hand stroking him.

"I love waking up with you next to me." Aaron kissed his way across her jaw and down the side of her neck.

"Especially when you wake up with my hand around your little friend." Bethany giggled.

"That's a bonus, but the best part is my heart feels alive again." Aaron pulled her hand from his cock and pressed it against his chest. "You have always owned my heart. I could never give it to anyone else."

"Aaron, I love you so much. I can't wait until that guy gets caught and we can move on together." Bethany brushed her lips across his.

"And it will be together. I promise you that." With those words, he rolled her over on her back and covered her mouth with his.

He plunged his tongue into her mouth as he moved above her. The urgency to make love to her was overpowering, and he used his knee to separate her legs while Bethany's hand caressed his body. She met his kiss with a passion that matched his own.

Aaron pressed his throbbing erection between her wet folds and pushed inside. It took him less than a second to realize he'd forgotten something.

"Damn, Bethany. Fuck… Condom." Aaron moaned as he tried to stay still.

"I'm on the pill, remember." Bethany wrapped her legs around his hips and used her feet to push him deeper.

"I'm clean. I swear." Aaron was still afraid to move.

Being inside her with nothing between them put him in a state of euphoria he never felt before. He hadn't even come, and he already felt like he was having an out-of-body experience. The heat of pussy surrounding his dick felt intensified, and her wetness surrounded it.

"This feels so fucking good." Aaron groaned as he pulled his hips back and slowly slid back inside.

"Aaron, don't stop." Bethany panted as he increased his thrusts.

"Baby, I couldn't even if I tried." Aaron groaned as he felt her tighten around his dick and she trembled under him as an erotic moan escaped her lips.

It was enough to drive him over the edge, and he pumped into her once more. The pressure in the tip of his dick was almost painful as he slammed into her and exploded. Aaron didn't know if it was that he was completely bare inside her or if it was because it was Bethany, but the intensity of the orgasm caused every muscle in his body to contract, and he shook with pleasure.

"Baby, yeah." Aaron roared as he tried to hold himself up and keep himself from dropping his weight on top of her.

Aaron managed to muster the strength to roll over on his back and pull her on top of him. She was as boneless as he was and he chuckled when she let out a huge sigh.

"That's a satisfied sigh." Aaron kissed the top of her head.

"Uh huh." Bethany lifted her head, and the smile on her face probably mirrored his own.

"Can I tell you something?" Aaron grinned.

"You can tell me anything." She rested her cheek against his chest.

"I've been looking at a house on Beach Street. The one that's right on the beach." Her smile disappeared, and he faltered.

"That's your parents' house." Bethany's confusion made his anxiety ease a little.

"No, the one on the end of the beach up above our spot." Aaron grinned.

"That one's been abandoned since we were in high school?" Bethany wrinkled her nose.

"Yes, I've asked Keith and Billie's brother to have a look at it," Aaron explained. "I've been eyeing it for years, but when I'd think about taking that step, I'd back out because it was too hard to be that close to our cove."

"Aaron." Bethany cupped his cheek.

"Anyway, Keith said the house has a great foundation, and all I have to do is tear down the structure and rebuild." Aaron tried not to get excited about the prospect.

"You want to build a house there?" Bethany's voice didn't show any hint of her emotions.

"I want to build a house there. I want us to build a home there together" Aaron emphasized the word *us*.

"Me and you?" He could sense the slight tremor in her voice.

"Yes, you and me." Aaron smiled.

Bethany jumped out of bed and quickly pulled on the clothes she'd been sleeping in when he'd crawled into bed a few hours earlier. It was a little after six in the morning and his words caught in his throat as she practically ran out of the room.

Aaron sat up in the bed and dropped his head into his hands. It was too soon, or maybe she wasn't ready to take that step with him. Perhaps she wasn't even planning to stay in Hopedale.

"Fuck." Aaron blew out a breath.

"Aaron?" He lifted his head.

Bethany stood at the foot of the bed with her laptop and a bunch of papers in her arms. She walked around and crawled on the bed, and she was wearing a grin from ear to ear.

"What are you…" Aaron stopped speaking when she turned her laptop toward him.

The screen showed a picture of the run-down house on the beach and Aaron glanced at Bethany in confusion. She handed him the pile of papers she'd brought into the room as well. Aaron started to shuffle through them and realized what it was she was telling him.

"You were looking at the house too?" He lifted his eyes to meet hers.

"I fell in love with that area years ago. Almost as much as I loved you. As much as I still love you. I asked my dad to have a look to see if it was still there and what he thought about it." Bethany linked her arm into his. "He said it was a piece of shit and needed a complete renovation."

"Pretty much what Keith said too." Aaron laughed.

"I told him I didn't care and that I wanted him to look into who owned it and if they'd been willing to sell it. Dad said the town owned it because it was abandoned years ago. They'd be willing to sell it as long as the old house was torn down…" Aaron interrupted her rambling because he'd done the same thing.

"And a new house put there." Aaron finished.

"Yeah, they told me someone else asked about the property as well." Bethany laughed.

"Yeah, me." Aaron shook his head.

"Apparently." Bethany sighed.

"You'd really like to live there?" Aaron gazed into her eyes.

"I would." Bethany ran her thumb across his lower lip.

"I'll get Mike to look into getting this started and have Billie help him out with the real estate shit. She has her license now, and her friend Abbie can probably help us get this on the ball." Aaron jumped up on his knees and tossed the papers on the floor.

"I want our bedroom to have lots of windows so that we can look out at the ocean." Bethany jumped up to her knees as well.

"You can have whatever you want." Aaron pulled her into his arms.

"Can we call Billie's brother now? He's the architect, right?" Bethany grinned.

Her excitement was contagious, and he laughed as she excitedly clapped her hands. He'd waited thirteen years to be with the woman he loved, and it was better than he could ever imagine.

"I think it's a little early, but I've got a great idea to kill a little time until it's an acceptable time to call," Aaron smirked as he eased her back on the bed and stripped her out of the thin sleep shirt and shorts.

"I like your ideas." Bethany giggled as she pulled him down and killed some time.

Chapter 27

Bethany almost felt guilty about being so excited. She'd been so shocked that Aaron had been on her same train of thought with the house. That house had been rundown years ago, but she remembered imagining it as a place where she and Aaron would live.

Funny how that dream could become a reality. That was if the police could get Slash behind bars and find Quintin. Even in her excitement, she was sick with worry for the kid. She'd prayed that he was okay and would contact someone to let them know where he was.

If he'd been a typical teenager, they could have tracked him by his cell phone. Unfortunately, the family couldn't afford it. She'd called Denise earlier that day and told her if she needed anything to let Bethany know. It was hard to believe that one of the girls who used to make her miserable was in such a terrible situation.

Aaron sat with Sandy at the kitchen table while Bethany shuffled through some papers that Craig had sent her. They were more invoices that he'd found in Randy's office once the police allowed him to go in and clear it out.

With the news of what happened, Craig's business was in a tailspin, and he'd lost most of his customers. He'd basically given up and was in the process of dissolving the company. Bethany wasn't worried about finding another job, but she was concerned about his well-being.

"This guy had Levi fooled completely." Bethany heard Sandy say.

She'd been looking through Larry's computer all morning and most of the afternoon. There were more than a hundred emails between Larry and Levi talking about how the young man was doing a public service by bringing the drug dealers to justice and that he'd make sure he got into the right programs at the university.

"If this guy weren't dead, I'd want to kick the fucking shit out of him." Sandy was pissed that he'd put a kid in danger that was only trying to better himself by helping get criminals off the street.

They'd found out the money Levi had given his sister was the payment he got for being a *secure informant*. Larry told Levi only specific people attained the position. Of course, no such position in the police department existed, and when Aaron told Jordan what Larry did, Jordan had turned completely red with anger.

"I think you'd have to beat Jordan to that." Aaron snorted.

"I haven't known him that long, but he doesn't seem like the kind to lose his cool very often," Sandy said as she continued to click away on her laptop.

"He's not, but I think I'd be thrown for a loop if I found out one my cousins did something like this." Aaron raised an eyebrow.

"Me too," Sandy agreed.

Bethany glanced down at the invoices on her lap and stopped. She saw a name scrawled at the bottom of the page that didn't belong on the document. It was terrible writing, and she lifted it closer to see if she could see it better.

"Aaron, I think I have something here." She jumped up when she realized what she was reading.

"What?" He met her halfway across the room.

"Remember I said that woman called Slash by the name Melvin?" She glanced up.

"Yeah," Aaron looked down to where she was pointing.

"That says Melvin Archer. I'm pretty sure." Aaron took the paper from her and studied it.

"Sandy, look up this name." Aaron and Bethany stood behind his sister-in-law as she searched.

While they waited, Bethany and Aaron discussed what they wanted in their future home. Aaron's phone vibrated in his pocket, interrupting their conversation. From Aaron's expression, he didn't recognize the number but tapped the screen and put it to his ear.

"Hello?" Aaron put his finger in the other ear as if it was hard to hear the caller. "Can you speak up? I can't hear you."

Aaron listened for a moment and then his eyes widened. He put his hand on Sandy's hands to get her to stop typing as he tapped the speaker on his phone.

"Quintin, where are you?" Aaron spoke into the phone.

"I'm hiding behind Slash's hideout. He's on the phone talking to someone. Mr. O'Connor, he's going after your girlfriend's nephew to get her to come out of hiding. He said he was going to grab him at school." The whispered voice caused Bethany's blood to run cold.

"Quintin, how are you calling me?" Aaron asked.

"I can't tell you. You'll get mad." Quintin sighed.

"Buddy, I need you to tell me how to get in touch with you." Aaron's voice was calm, but his expression was showing anything but ease.

"I stole some money out of that bag and bought a prepaid phone." Quintin sounded so guilty.

"That's okay, pal. Text me the number and where you are. I'm coming to get you." Aaron wrote something on a piece of paper and handed it to Sandy, and she started to click on the computer keys frantically.

"I'm safe. Just get to Mia's friend. He's a good kid, and this asshole will hurt him until he gets his way." Quintin sounded too overconfident.

"Quintin, this is dangerous. Let the police handle this and get out of there." Aaron's jaw clenched.

"No. This guy killed my brother." Quintin raised his voice a little.

"Don't fuck up your life by doing something stupid. Send me the address, and we'll get this guy." Bethany could see the muscles in Aaron's arms flexing as he tried to stay calm.

"I'll send you the address. Wait." Quintin was quiet for what seemed like a long time.

"Quintin?" Aaron placed his hand on the top of his head and fisted his hair.

"Get to the school. He's on the way to get the kid." With that statement, the call ended.

"Fuck, fuck Fuck." Aaron tapped frantically into his phone and put it to his ear.

"I think I got his location narrowed down. He's somewhere near Pleasantville." Sandy glanced up at Aaron.

"I need you to find Cameron Sullivan and make sure he doesn't leave the school until a police officer shows there to escort him home." Aaron practically shouted into the phone.

"I'll call Ally." Bethany's hand shook as she tapped her sister's phone number.

After several rings, the phone went to voicemail, and Bethany realized her sister was probably still at work. She didn't answer her phone when she was in with patients.

"Thanks, Joey." Aaron sighed and made another call.

"Why would Joey be at Cameron's school?" Bethany had her arms wrapped around herself.

"He coaches kids' basketball, and he's there every day by two." Aaron was pulling on his jacket when his phone beeped.

"Aaron?" Bethany didn't like the look on Aaron's face.

"Joey just saw Cameron and Mia Watts getting into a car with a man," Aaron growled.

"Oh God." Bethany started to shake.

"Baby, I'll find him." Aaron pulled her into his arms and kissed the top of her head.

"Let's go." Sandy was next to the door.

"Where are you going?" Bethany asked.

"I'm a cop too, remember?" Sandy smiled. "And I really want to see this prick brought to his knees."

"Be careful, Aaron. Both of you." Bethany glanced at Sandy.

Crunch was walking into the house with Hulk behind him. They'd obviously been filled in because they didn't even question where Sandy and Aaron were running off too in such a hurry.

"Crash is gone to get your sister and Trunk is gone to get your dad. They're bringing them here." Hulk led her over to the armchair and helped her sit.

"He has Mia too." Bethany glanced up at Hulk.

"I know, Rick has someone going over with the family." Hulk crouched in front of her.

"They're just kids." Bethany couldn't stop the tears.

"I promise you, A.J. and the rest of the guys won't let anything happen to Cameron." Crunch handed her a box of tissues.

"He killed Levi and Randy without blinking an eye." Bethany sobbed.

"And A.J. and the police will make sure he gets what's coming to him." Hulk patted her knee.

Bethany leaned forward and wrapped her arms around her waist as she tried to stay positive and prayed that Aaron would bring Cameron and Mia back safe.

Twenty minutes later, she sat on the couch with her sister and father, waiting to hear from Aaron. It seemed like hours since he left and Bethany was sure Allyson would snap if anything happened to Cameron. Bethany wasn't sure she'd be able to handle it herself. The only way she knew to help her was to beg for his guardian angel.

Trent, your son is in danger. Please keep watch over him and the girl until Aaron gets to them.

As if her sister could read her mind she grabbed Bethany's hand and said her own prayer to her late husband.

"Trent, please help him be brave. He's got so much of your courage inside. Help him dig down and keep himself strong until the police get to him. Please, baby, help our son." Allyson's tears streamed down her cheeks, and it wasn't hard to see that her sister was not only tearing Bethany's heart out but Crash's as well.

Chapter 28

Aaron stood across the table from Darryl Lambe with rage flowing through his body. Quintin hadn't gotten back to Aaron with the address, and all they knew was Sandy was able to narrow it down to the old military base in St. John's, but Pleasantville was still a big area. So Aaron was working on the weakest link of the gang while Sandy tried to track Quintin.

"Darryl, if anything happens to those kids not only will you be going down as a co-conspirator to the murders of Randy Knight, Levi Watts, and Larry Foster, but the two kids as well. Trust me, the big bad guys in prison don't take kindly to people who hurt kids." Aaron stood with his hands fisted on the table as he leaned down over the scared looking man.

"I didn't kill nobody." Darryl spat with about as much aggression as a puppy.

"Don't matter if you did it yourself. You're part of the whole thing. You work for Slash, and he's killing people. He's got two twelve-year-old kids, Darryl. Do you want to be part of that?" Aaron slammed his hand on the table.

"No, but he's fucking crazy. He'll kill me if I rat him out." Darryl rubbed his cuffed hands over his head.

"I just need to know where he hides out." Aaron tried to calm his demeanor.

"You don't get it. The man slashed his own head to prove what a badass he is. His girlfriend stitched him up, and he didn't even have anything to numb it." Darryl sat back in the chair.

"I won't say where I got the information. Nobody knows you're here with me. Just give me an address." Aaron sat in the chair as to try not to be so intimidating to the man.

Darryl was only twenty years old. Practically a kid himself and probably got caught up in all the shit because of his brother. He had a few convictions on his record, but none were violent.

"Nobody will find out, right?" Darryl looked at Aaron with hope in his eyes.

"Not a fucking soul," Aaron promised.

"Fine, give me a piece of paper." Darryl shook his head as Aaron pushed a pad of paper and a pen across the table.

Aaron was almost to his car when he saw Bethany's cousin, Elijah, and two other men walking toward him. The men looked like the guys that worked for Keith. Tall, muscular but obviously military.

"We want to help," Elijah said as he stood next to Aaron.

"I know it's your family, but I can't let you in the middle of this," Aaron explained.

"We were already talking to John, and he said he was going to text you. This is Damon Blackwood and Adrian Hudson. They're retired military but Damon was one of the best snipers in the country." Elijah introduced the men but before Aaron could respond, his phone beeped.

The text from John told him to take Elijah and the other men to meet up with them a block from where they suspected Slash was holding Mia and Cameron.

"Are you coming with me or following?" Aaron asked.

"With." Elijah nodded as the three men jumped into Aaron's car.

"John said you just got the address," Elijah said from the passenger seat.

"Yeah, I just wish I knew where Quintin was at the moment." Aaron hoped that the kid wasn't about to make a huge mistake and get in the middle of a shootout.

The building Slash was using as a hideout was hidden back in the woods at the end of the base. Both Adrian and Damon said they used to use it when they first joined the army for practice. It was a concrete building that was crumbling because the military didn't use that part of the base anymore.

"How close do you think we can get before being detected by this guy?" John asked.

"Damon is heading around to that high point up there and see if there's any visibility inside the structure. He's got his equipment, and he has a radio." Adrian pointed to a hill behind the three concrete buildings stood at the bottom of it.

"I've got TAC moving into points as well," John said, referring to the Police tactical unit that most people would call SWAT.

"Do we even know if he's in there with the kids?" James asked as he secured his Kevlar vest.

Before anyone could respond, Aaron's phone vibrated and he pulled it out. The relief overwhelmed him at the sight of Quintin's number from earlier.

"Quintin?" Aaron tapped the speaker so everyone could hear.

"Mr. O'Connor, he has Mia. That bastard has my sister." Quintin sounded panicked.

"We know. Where are you, buddy?" Aaron glanced around at the group of men hunched over his phone.

"I'm behind the building. He has your girlfriend's nephew too," Quintin whispered.

"Buddy, you need to come up from the building. We have our team closing in, and we don't want you hurt if there's any gunfire." Aaron met Nick's eyes.

"I can't. My sister is hysterical, and Cameron's trying to keep her calm, but he looks pretty scared too," Quintin whispered.

"You can see them?" John cut in.

"Who's that?" Quintin's voice quivered.

"It's my brother, John. He's my supervisor," Aaron assured the kid.

"Okay, I can see Slash. He's pacing on the other side of the building. I'm in the middle building watching him through a crack between the two." Quintin seemed to be in a great spot.

"Would you be okay with one of my team coming in there with you?" John asked.

"As long as he doesn't let Slash hear him," Quintin whispered.

John smiled as he glanced around at the men. Aaron shook his head. If a teenager could get there without Slash hearing him, they were pretty sure a trained TAC officer could get there.

"Okay, great, Quintin. His name is Steve Parker, and he's making his way to you," John informed the kid.

"All right, but if Slash touches my sister, I'm going to shoot him," Quintin growled.

"I understand but until then just put your gun down and wait for Steve, okay?" Aaron couldn't blame the kid.

They waited for what seemed like forever for Steve to give the confirmation that he'd made it to Quintin and everything was okay. When John raised his hand to let everyone know that Steve was in place, Aaron breathed a sigh of relief.

"How is Slash not hearing Quintin talking to us?" Nick must not have realized that Aaron still had the kid on the phone.

"He's going around with his headset in talking to his girlfriend," Quintin responded.

"Can you hear what he's saying?" Nick asked.

"No, he's too far away." Quintin sighed.

"It's like he's waiting for something." Steve's voice came through the ear that all of them were now wearing.

As they waited for everyone to get into place, Aaron glanced down the hill. Sandy was watching the area with a drone and Cory was with her. Seconds later, Cory ran toward them holding his phone.

"Someone called Allyson's phone and threatening Cameron if Bethany didn't change her story and say she didn't see the shooter." Cory handed the phone to Aaron. "It's Crash."

"Crash?" Aaron put the phone to his ear.

"The voice was altered, but they told Allyson that she was to force Bethany to make a statement to the press saying she was wrong about the shooter. I mean, is this asshole stupid?" Crash sounded pissed.

"We got eyes on him now. Tell Allyson and Bethany not to worry." Aaron knew that was probably a stupid thing to say, but they were about to move in.

"He just took out his headphones." Steve's voice crackled in his ears. "Quintin just ended the call with you."

"Got ya," John said. "We're moving in."

Aaron followed behind the members of the TAC unit with his weapon ready. The door of the building had a piece of board placed against it. They waited for Steve to give the okay for them to go in. They wanted to wait until Slash was far enough from the kids they could become a wall if he just started shooting randomly.

"He's on the phone again. Go," Steve said.

The board was kicked down, and Aaron followed the unit as they flowed into the building in a smooth formation. Cory and James quickly made their way to Mia and Cameron. Slash had tied them to a wooden bench on the other side of the structure.

"What the fuck?" Slash shouted as he turned at the crash of the makeshift door.

"Drop your weapon, Archer," John shouted.

"The name is Slash, and I'm not droppin' nothin'." He pointed his gun directly at Mia and Cameron.

"Okay, Slash. How many guns are pointing at you right now?" John smirked.

"Only takes one to shoot one of those kids," Slash yelled.

"Those kids are surrounded by police with vests." John returned. "You don't want to add shooting a police officer on top of the charges already waiting for you, do you?" Aaron stepped next to his brother.

"I'd be a hero in the lock-up if I killed a fucking pig." Slash raised his gun and slowly moved it back and forth between Aaron and John.

"Drop it, asshole." Quintin's voice echoed through the building as he stood behind Slash with a rifle pointed at the criminal.

As if in slow motion, Slash turned his weapon toward Quintin. There was a swoosh and Slash's head snapped back. He fell backward, and his body hit the concrete floor sounded like the clap of a hand.

"I didn't shoot him. I didn't shoot him." Quintin dropped his rifle and held up his hands.

"I did." Damon's voice echoed through the earpiece.

Aaron handed his phone to Cameron to let him talk to his mother once the paramedics cleared him and Mia. Mia and Quintin spoke with their sister on the phone the kid bought.

Aaron leaned against the side of the ambulance and blew out a huge breath. It was over. Bethany was safe, and they could finally get on with their lives.

"Mr. O'Connor?" Quintin stepped in front of Aaron.

"Hey." Aaron smiled at the kid.

"I'm sorry." Quintin dropped his head.

"It's okay, buddy. I understand why you did what you did but it was dangerous, and you could have gotten yourself killed." Aaron dropped his hand on Quintin's shoulder.

"Yeah, but if it weren't for him, I wouldn't have gotten a clear shot at that prick." Damon walked up next to Aaron. "But don't ever put yourself in that situation again."

"I won't, apparently I'm grounded until I'm fifty." Quintin smirked. "Don't know how Denise is gonna do that but I wasn't arguing with her when she was so pissed and a little hysterical."

"Can't say I blame you there, buddy." Aaron laughed.

"Quintin, come on. I'm going to take you and Mia home." Cory stood with his arm wrapped around a shaking Mia.

"Thank you for helping to get justice for my family." Quintin held out his hand to Aaron.

"You're welcome. I'll see you at basketball next week." Aaron shook Quintin's hand.

"Thank you for shooting that asshole." Quintin turned to Damon.

"I don't like shooting anyone, but when there's a choice between them and an innocent person, they go down." Damon smiled. "Do me a favor?"

"What?" Quintin asked.

"Stay innocent for a while. Enjoy it while you can." Something in Damon's eyes told Aaron the man had a lot of pain behind them.

"I will." Quintin walked away leaving Aaron and Damon staring after him.

"I hear your brother is hiring for his security firm," Damon said quietly.

"I'm not sure but why don't you come back to The Compound and I'll introduce you." Aaron walked toward his car.

"If that includes a cold beer, I'm in." Damon grinned.

Two hours later, the safe house was full of most of his family, friends, and co-workers. Bethany had met him at the door when they arrived and practically launched herself into his arms.

Cameron was shaken, but when Ian showed up with Lily and Evie, he seemed to relax as he gave his version of what happened to

Aaron's two nieces. Aaron smirked when Cameron said he wasn't afraid and he had to make sure Mia was safe. Typical teenage boy bravery stories.

"Pam's picking Isabelle up, and they're going to bring some more beer." Jess handed Aaron a beer.

"I think we're going to need it." Aaron laughed.

"No shit. This family keeps getting bigger and bringing their friends." Jess waved her hand around the house.

"Why weren't you on the scene?" Aaron hadn't realized his cousin wasn't there until that moment.

"My damn car broke down again." She sighed. "I was on my way back from town, and it died. By the time I got a tow truck and got home, you guys were on the way home."

"You need to give that shit box a funeral." Aaron pulled away as she swung at him.

"Bite me," Jess returned.

"No thanks, but seriously it's a death trap." His cousin's car was ten years old, and Jess seemed to have some weird sentimental connection with it.

"No, it's not," Jess whined.

"Come on, the last time I had to bail your ass out when it broke down, there was smoke pouring out of it, and I'm pretty sure the fluid was supposed to be in the car." Aaron laughed.

"I don't know what to do with it." Jess leaned against the counter.

"I told you. Bury the fucking thing." Aaron chuckled.

Jess gave him the middle finger as she grabbed another beer and left Aaron in the kitchen. He would let her stew over her car for a little while before he'd introduce her to the mechanic that took care of the NPD's cars. Aaron wouldn't trust his car to anyone else. He'd also be able to find a good deal on a used car.

"I want to take you into the bedroom and lock the door." Bethany sidled up to him and whispered into his ear.

"Let's go." Aaron tugged her, and she giggled.

"No way. Too many people here." Bethany smiled.

"We can go to my bunkhouse." Aaron wiggled his eyebrows, he hadn't been there more than a few times since everything started and that was only to get clean clothes.

"Maybe later, I'm just enjoying that it's all over." Bethany wrapped her arms around his waist and stood up on her toes.

"Me too." Aaron bent his head and pressed his lips against hers.

"Move it," Isabelle grunted as she pushed Aaron and Bethany aside to place a large box on the counter.

"You know the house is full of men that could have helped with that." Aaron peeked in the box, and the smell of food had his stomach grumbling.

"There are three more boxes, and they are being carried in by them." Isabelle pointed to where Crash, Adrian, and Hulk were heading toward the kitchen.

"Let me guess, Nan?" Aaron laughed.

"Yep and Pam's pulling up with the booze." Isabelle grinned.

A few minutes later the floor was piled with cases of beer and Bethany was chatting with Pam, Isabelle, and Kristy. Aaron stood quietly with his arm around Bethany's waist with a cold beer in his hand. Heaven.

Aaron spotted Damon, Adrian, and Elijah chatting with Keith. Damon turned his head as if he sensed Aaron looking at him and nodded his head. He said something to Keith and strutted toward Aaron.

"Did you get the job?" Aaron chuckled.

"We're going to meet next week with all the details." Damon grinned.

"Since you're going to be staying, let me introduce you to some of my cousins and my beautiful lady." Aaron squeezed Bethany, and she turned to look up at him.

"Beautiful she is." Damon winked.

"Bethany this is ..." Before Aaron could continue, a soft gasp came from one of his cousins.

He turned to see Pam's face pale and eyes wide. Damon's face mirrored her surprise, but recognition in his eyes had Aaron curious.

"Trixie?" Damon drew out the unfamiliar name.

"Trixie?" Isabelle glanced between Pam and Damon much the same as Bethany, Kristy and he were doing.

"What ... what... are you doing here?" Pam stammered over her words and looked about ready to bolt.

"I could ask you the same thing." Damon raised an eyebrow.

"Pam? Do you know Damon?" Aaron started to feel a little protective over his cousin especially with the way she seemed to squirm under Damon's glare.

"Pam?" Damon's attention turned to Aaron.

It was enough for Pam to squeeze by Isabelle and practically run out of the house. Damon took a step to follow her, but Aaron grabbed him by the arm.

"What did you do to her?" Aaron growled.

"I didn't do anything, but I'm about to find out why she lied about who she was and why she took off without a word after I told her I loved her." Damon pulled his arm from Aaron's grasp and disappeared through the door.

"Well… that was interesting." Kristy raised an eyebrow.

Aaron glanced down at Bethany who seemed to be ready to fall asleep. He was prepared to fall into bed himself, and since the threat to her had ended, he could get a good night sleep and deal with the aftermath of the investigation in the morning.

Chapter 29

Bethany stood in her old bedroom and waited for Aaron to pick her up for their first date since she'd returned to Hopedale. It seemed like a step backward, but since their reunion had been out of the ordinary, that couldn't be helped.

Aaron made plans to take her to Isabelle's restaurant for a romantic dinner and then they were going to meet Matt Carter at the site of the property that she and Aaron had just bought.

Billie's older brother was an architect, and they were going to give Matt some ideas of what they wanted in their new house. She was beyond excited, but a voice in her head still needled at her that maybe they were moving way too fast.

She'd mentioned it to Aaron and in his sweet calming way, made her push that annoying voice to the back of her thoughts. Bethany didn't doubt she loved Aaron. She'd never been surer of anything in her life. It was still difficult to believe that she was finally with the only man she'd ever loved.

Over the past six days, Aaron, John, and James were clearing up the investigation into Randy's and Levi's murders. They found several firearms in the concrete structure where Slash hid. Aaron told her they matched both shootings as well as Randy's.

They'd also found a large hunting knife with traces of blood from Levi as well as Larry Foster. They closed the case on all three murders, and the other three men pleaded guilty to some charges that she didn't hear because she'd zoned out when Aaron and James were explaining it. Although they had not located the mystery woman, they still wanted to talk to her.

All she cared about was it was over, and she was about to have an enjoyable night with Aaron.

Bethany checked her makeup in the mirror once more when she heard the doorbell. Her stomach fluttered, and she rolled her eyes. How could she be so nervous about a date with the man she'd spent the last few weeks snuggled up in bed with and spending every moment they could together?

"Aunt Beth, A.J. is here." Cameron's voice echoed up the stairs.

Bethany walked slowly down the stairs. It had seemed like such a long time since she'd dressed up in a sexy dress and stilettos, but when she got to the bottom, the look of pure sexual desire in Aaron's eyes made every pinched toe she'd have later that night worth it.

"You look stunning." Aaron met her eyes and clasped her hands in his.

"You are looking pretty stunning yourself." Bethany blatantly allowed her eyes to take in his body from head to toe.

Dressed in black dress pants and a light-blue shirt, Aaron was gorgeous, and the color of the shirt made his eyes seem even bluer than usual. He wore a grey sports coat that highlighted his broad shoulders and for a moment she wanted to forget the date and drag him upstairs to strip him out of his sexy attire. At least until she heard her father behind her.

"Don't you two look spiffy." Her dad smiled.

"Thank you, but your beautiful daughter will outshine me every time." Aaron shook hands with her father.

"I don't disagree with you there, A.J." He grinned. "She's just like her mother."

After a quick chat with her dad, they made their way to Isabelle's restaurant, *A Taste of Hopedale*. On the way, they talked about their day and how she was in the process of looking for a new job. Aaron told her about the mystery that was Pam and one of the latest residents of Keith's Compound, Damon.

"Neither of them will say what happened, but they won't even stand in the same room together." Aaron opened her car door and helped her out of his Charger.

"I'm sure it will come out at some point." Bethany linked her hand into the crook of his arm.

"Right now I just want to concentrate on you and me and having a quiet romantic night." Aaron kissed her cheek and then moved his lips to her ear. "Then take you back to my place and remove that dress but leave the shoes."

"I like your style, sexy." Bethany winked.

Supper was incredible, and the conversation was even better. The sexual heat between them was making it difficult for her to remember they were in a public place.

"Isabelle's cooking is amazing, but she's looking for a new chef to help out." Aaron nodded as the waiter poured another glass of Merlot.

"The food is incredible. Who's she hiring? Bethany smiled as she slipped off her shoe and slowly slid the tip of her foot up Aaron's calf.

"He's a friend of Lora's brother." Aaron's voice quivered a little as her foot rose higher.

"That's great." Bethany giggled when he shifted his seat.

"You're truly an evil woman," Aaron growled as the waiter walked away.

"What time did you tell Matt to meet us?" She rubbed her foot against his erection straining against his zipper.

"In forty minutes." Aaron reached under the table and ran his hand over the top of her foot and as far as he could reach up her calf without looking obvious.

"Damn." Bethany sighed.

"You can say that again." Aaron licked his lips and groaned when she lowered her foot.

"I need to use the little girls' room." Bethany slipped her shoe back on and sashayed away from the table.

Bethany was smiling as she made her way through the beautiful restaurant. She almost didn't notice the woman that was waving to her from one of the tables.

"Beatrice. Beatrice." Bethany glanced to the side and wanted to run in the opposite direction.

"My name is Bethany, Raquel." Bethany tried not to sound annoyed, but she was.

"Oh, I'm such a scatterbrain. I see you're on a date with A.J." Raquel nodded toward Aaron.

"Yes, I was just on my way to the ladies' room." Bethany started to walk away.

"I feel I should warn you, as a woman with her ear on the pulse of Hopedale; he's got a playboy reputation," Raquel smirked at her supper companion.

Bethany stopped and slowly turned toward her old bully and smiled. The woman with her looked at her with the same smirk Raquel wore.

"Thank you so much for your concern about my well-being, but let me give you some advice, Raquel." Bethany bent over and kept her voice low enough that only the women at the table would hear. "I'm well aware of Aaron's past reputation. I'm also very familiar with yours and how nosey, vindictive bitches like you work. Just so you know, I'm not the same timid teenager you terrorized in high school. So yes, I know of his past reputation but trust me, I'll keep him very satisfied. My advice to you, keep comments and opinions to yourself, or you may need that surgically altered nose, altered a second time."

Raquel's eyes widened with what looked like fear. The other woman dropped her head and would not look up at as Bethany stood up. Before she left the table, Bethany smiled down at Raquel.

"It was so nice seeing you again. Try the strawberry cheesecake, it's incredible." Bethany turned on her heal and sauntered to the ladies' room feeling proud.

Bethany was inside the stall when the bathroom door opened and she heard a woman practically growling with anger. It was like Deja vu, and without thinking, she lifted her feet off the floor.

"I can't believe he has that bitch here. He's mine. Mine." The woman whined, and Bethany was sure she recognized the voice.

"Jocelyn, you need to get over this…" Bethany didn't hear the rest of the sentence because she knew who was outside the stall.

"He's mine, and if he thinks he can move on, I'll make him sorry he ever left me," Jocelyn shouted.

Bethany couldn't believe nobody could hear her outside the bathroom and she didn't know what to do at that point. Aaron told her that Jocelyn seemed unstable and probably used drugs. Bethany may have more confidence in herself, but she wasn't about to step out and be confronted by someone hyped up on drugs.

"Jocelyn, what are you doing with that?" The other woman sounded panicked.

"What? This?" Jocelyn giggled. "I'm going to show my man what I can do."

"Jocelyn, give me that." Bethany heard a struggle and the unmistakable sound of a gunshot.

What the fuck?

"Jocelyn… you…God…you… shot… me." A thud echoed through the room, and Bethany fumbled to pull her phone from her purse.

"You're next." Jocelyn's voice sounded deeper and crazed.

Bethany quickly texted Aaron and told him Jocelyn was in the bathroom with a gun, but before she finished it, the bathroom door swooshed as if it was pulled open and clicked closed again.

Bethany dialed nine-one-one as she bent over to glance under the door of the stall. The legs of the woman Jocelyn shot lay in front of the stall and not moving. After listening for several seconds, she turned the lock, pulled the door, and tapped call.

Bethany stared down at the motionless body on the floor. Blood was changing the color of her yellow blouse to a crimson red, and her chest wasn't moving. Bethany took a step toward the body and as she focused on the face, she shook her head in confusion. Jocelyn's glazed eyes appeared to stare back at her.

"Poor bitch didn't have a clue what I was talking about." Bethany's head snapped up as the woman she'd seen with Jocelyn at the diner that day stepped into view, a gun held confidently pointed at Bethany.

Bethany dropped her phone down to her side and kept the screen turned flat against her leg. Hopefully, the operator would be able to hear the conversation and the woman staring at her wouldn't notice the bright display.

"You killed your friend." Bethany forced the words out of her dry throat.

"You're really smart." Kylie nodded, the sarcasm in her voice evident as she grinned.

"Why would you do that?" Bethany stood a couple of steps from the door, but Kylie blocked her escape.

"Because I was sick of her constant whining over that cop. I mean, he's hot, but Jesus, move on with your life." Kylie looked down at Jocelyn's body as if she was talking to her.

"What do you want?" Bethany didn't know what else to say.

"I need to get out of this fucking town, and since you are the only person left that could tie me to Randy's murder, I had to take care of you first." Kylie took a step and nudged Jocelyn's head with her toe. "I've already gotten rid of this fucktard."

"You were the one with Slash?" Bethany recognized the insult that Kylie had used on Slash.

"Yes, I was." Kylie raised her eyes to meet Bethany.

"I didn't see you. I only saw him." Bethany shook her head when she made the connection and knew she was in deep trouble.

"You don't think he was smart enough to be running our operation, do you? I'm the brains behind it. I'm the one who got the whores for Randy to fuck in exchange for his drugs. I blackmailed Larry to bring the drugs into his pharmacy and keep it quiet. You see, Larry sold opioids out of his pharmacy, and I found out, so I negotiated a cut. I get a hundred percent of the profits, and I don't call his cousin the cop." Kylie took a step toward Bethany.

Bethany tried to take a step toward the door, but Kylie pointed the gun directly at her head. It wouldn't help her escape if she let the crazed woman shoot her.

"I begged Slash to take all the cash we had and move down south, but no he didn't want anyone left that could identify him as Randy's killer. Idiot. It was the only one he did kill. I did all the other cleaning up. I had to get rid of Levi because he figured out Larry was the one pretending to be the cop through emails and I had the stupid kid convinced I was his friend. The funny thing is it was my idea to get Larry to fuck with the kid. Then Larry got nervous. Slash couldn't even take those kids without my help, but that other kid screwed that up and got my man killed. We had everything we needed. Why did all of you have to fuck it up?" Kylie looked about ready to snap, and Bethany didn't want to be her next victim.

Bethany swallowed hard but didn't say a word because she was terrified she'd set Kylie off more than the girl was already off her rocker.

"Then I tell this twit she has to stay away from A.J. because he'll fuck up our business. Does she listen? No. She acts like a crazy stalker and follows him around like a starving dog. I mean I love the girl, but there's too much coke up her nose and not enough brains in her head." Kylie shrugged.

"What are you going to do?" Bethany trembled as Kylie stepped toward her.

"Well, I need to get out of Newfoundland, and since I just told you everything, I can't just leave you here. Now, you and I are going to walk out of the bathroom and out of this snooty place." Kylie lifted the gun and Bethany held her breath.

"Why don't you just leave? I'll stay here and to give you enough time to get out of town." Bethany prayed that there was still someone listening to her conversation. "You don't need to shoot me."

Kylie seemed to think hard as she stared down at Jocelyn. Bethany hoped she was mulling over the choice and deciding it sounded like a better plan than taking Bethany as a hostage.

"No, because you'll go running out to that pig boyfriend of yours as soon as I leave." Kylie moved the gun, motioning for Bethany to walk ahead of her.

"Kylie, people are going to see you leading me out like this." Bethany moved slowly toward the door.

"Yep, and they'll think twice when I shoot the first person that I see when I step into the dining area." Kylie snickered.

"Please, don't hurt anyone else." Bethany turned toward the woman pushing the barrel of the gun into her back.

"I could shoot that bitch you were talking to before you came in here." Kylie grinned. "She doesn't seem like a nice person."

"That doesn't mean she deserves to die." Bethany might dislike Raquel, but she wouldn't want to see the woman murdered in cold blood.

"As long as you behave yourself and A.J. doesn't try to be a hero, you and I will walk out of here without anyone getting shot."

Kylie rolled her eyes and motioned for Bethany to pull open the door.

The din of several conversations going on in the dining room made her stomach clench. The place was full, and although she didn't know much about guns, Bethany knew Kylie could probably kill several people before anyone could stop her.

Bethany dragged her feet as she made her way toward the main entrance, being careful not to make any mistakes that would set Kylie off on a shooting spree. Bethany glanced toward the table where she'd left Aaron, but he wasn't there, and she searched as much of the place as she could without looking obvious to Kylie.

She didn't see him anywhere. It was possible he'd gone to the men's room. Bethany hadn't realized she'd stopped moving until Kylie poked her in the back with the gun again. She took another step and reached for the door.

"Kylie, I need you to drop the gun." A voice she recognized came from behind them.

"I don't see that happening, what's your name again? Oh yeah. Jordan. Larry really fucked you over, didn't he?" Kylie grabbed Bethany around the neck and backed up, putting Bethany as a shield in front of her.

"Kylie, I don't want to hurt you, but if I feel like you're going to hurt anyone else, I'll take you down," Jordan warned.

"This is all her fault. If she'd kept her mouth shut, Slash and I could've been in Mexico by now." Kylie pushed the gun against the side of Bethany's face, but the woman's voice sounded calm as if she was having a normal conversation.

"Slash killed three people and kidnapped two kids. He was about to shoot another kid and had to be taken down." Aaron tried to reason with her.

"Slash only killed Randy, Jordan." Bethany winced when Kylie squeezed her arm tighter around Bethany's neck.

"Keep your fucking mouth shut," Kylie growled into Bethany's ear.

"Slash was about to shoot a kid." Aaron moved into view, and Bethany almost sighed in relief when she saw him wearing a Kevlar vest and holding a gun.

"He wouldn't have shot that kid." Kylie snorted.

"Kylie, you need to let Bethany go and put down your gun." Aaron's gaze met Bethany's and then flicked back to Kylie.

"You need to go fuck yourself." Kylie pushed the barrel of the gun painfully hard against Bethany's cheek.

Bethany winced, but it pissed her off that this woman thought she could use her as a shield. This woman had sent her life into a tailspin, and as terrified as she felt at that moment, anger started to bubble up over that fear.

Bethany kept her eyes focused on Aaron and waited for Kylie to drop her guard just a bit. She waited too long to find happiness and now that it was possible with the only man she'd ever loved, she wasn't about to let another bitch ruin her happiness.

As she tried to formulate a plan of escape in her head, she saw both Aaron's and Jordan's glance over her head and their eyes widened. Before she could do anything, she felt a heavy weight against her back. There was also a loud explosion to her right, and she felt a painful burn across her shoulder.

The weight on her back slowly slid down her body and disappeared. It took her a second to realize that she wasn't restrained anymore. Her ears rang, but the pain in her shoulder got worse, and she saw Aaron move toward her. His lips moved, but she couldn't hear over the loud roar in her ear.

Aaron grabbed her around the waist and pulled her away. Bethany still couldn't hear him, but when she turned, Kylie lay on the floor. That didn't seem to bother her, but the woman who stood over Kylie made Bethany's head spin.

"Ra ... Raquel?" Bethany gasped at the sight of her former bully holding a chair in her hands.

"She was going to shoot you." Raquel stared at Bethany with wide eyes. "I may have been a bitch to you, but I would never want to see you dead. Who is this nutcase?"

"She's killed three people that we know of and hurt a lot more. Thanks to you, we can make sure she gets put behind bars. That's if you didn't crush her brain." Jordan stepped toward Raquel and took the chair out of her hands as he helped her step over an unconscious Kylie.

Bethany didn't think twice as she pulled away from Aaron and wrapped her arms around Raquel. Never in a million years did she think she'd stand in the middle of a room and hug Raquel Evans for saving her life.

Bethany heard a muffled voice next to her ear but when Aaron appeared next to Raquel, he shouted, and she glanced down to where his eyes were focused.

"Bethany, you're bleeding," Aaron shouted

"My shoulder is burning. I think I got shot." Bethany stepped back from Raquel, and the room started to spin.

The last thing she saw was Aaron and Raquel reaching for her at the same time, then black.

Chapter 30

Aaron paced the hallway of the hospital as he waited for the doctor to tell him about Bethany's condition. He hadn't gotten a good look at her wound, but the enormous amount of blood covering her right shoulder looked awful.

He'd seen when Raquel stepped behind Kylie, but for a second he thought maybe they were working together, but the chair was raised over Kylie and brought down hard on the woman's head.

He heard the gunshot but saw it embedded into the post next to the entrance. Kylie dropped to the floor. His only concern after that was to make sure Bethany was out of danger, and the gun was secured.

His heart almost stopped when he got the text from Bethany and before he could move, Jordan entered the restaurant with the news that they'd found out the name of Slash's girlfriend. Jordan came to tell Aaron they were about to arrest her at her apartment.

Several officers stormed into the restaurant only minutes later. It was when Aaron found out about the call that had gone to an operator at dispatch. Someone was in the bathroom with a gun. Aaron's heart felt like it stopped.

Now the woman he loved was unconscious and bleeding. Aaron was scared to death. Blood covered her clothes, and he wasn't able to see where it came from. All he wanted was to know what the fuck was going on and if she was okay.

"A.J." Aaron turned to the sound of Allyson's voice.

Bethany's sister ran toward him with her father and Elijah behind her. Lewis looked white as a sheet and Elijah looked ready to kill someone.

"John told us what happened," Elijah snapped when they were next to him.

"Is she okay?" Allyson stepped in front of her cousin.

"I'm waiting for the doctor to tell me something." Aaron turned to the room where they'd wheeled Bethany a half hour earlier.

"You were there in the fucking room. How did she get shot?" Elijah glared at him.

"The gun went off when Raquel hit Kylie over the head." Aaron swallowed the lump that had been in his throat since the paramedics lifted her into the ambulance.

"Is that bitch dead?" Elijah growled.

"Elijah, that's enough." Lewis raised his voice.

"No, but she's in custody." Aaron turned back to the closed door.

"She's going to be okay, right?" Allyson linked her hand into Aaron's arm.

"Of course she is," Lewis assured them, but Aaron could hear the concern without even looking at the man.

Twenty minutes later, the majority of his family overflowed the waiting room, and Aaron still hadn't moved from in front of the door. He begged his father and Ian to see if they could find out anything and they did find out that they were still working on Bethany.

"What's the good of having a father and brother who are doctors if they can't find out what's happening?" Aaron murmured under his breath.

"A.J., she'll be okay." Aaron felt the weight of his father's hand on his shoulder.

"There was a lot of blood, Dad." Aaron sighed.

"Sometimes the smallest wounds can bleed the most." His dad always had to be a glass-half-full kind of person.

"I can't lose her." Aaron plowed his hand through his hair.

"You won't." His father turned Aaron so that he had to face him. "You can't think like that."

"I love her, Dad. So damn much and I can't lose her. She's my life." Aaron's eyes blurred with tears, and his father pulled him into a hug.

"A.J., my boy, that woman in there is so much stronger than you give her credit for. She's too much like the women in our family to let a little bullet take her out." His father chuckled.

"She can be stubborn." Aaron pulled back from his father and smiled. "But I love her, and all that feistiness more than I could ever put into words."

"You don't have to, my son. I know exactly how you feel." His father's gaze focused on Aaron's mother. "That woman right there is the reason I open my eyes every morning. Just a glimpse of her makes me happy to be alive and to have the love of a woman that I am damn lucky to have love me back."

"There's nothing like that feeling," Aaron whispered.

The door of the trauma room opened, and a familiar face appeared through the door. Dr. Adam Cramer seemed to always be on duty when one of Aaron's family got wheeled into the Emergency Department.

"I swear your family keeps me in the ER." Adam held out his hand to Aaron. "I understand you've been bitten by the love bug too."

"Fuck that shit, Adam. Is she okay?" Aaron growled.

"Oh, you definitely have." Adam chuckled. "To answer your question, she is fine. It looked like the bullet grazed her, but it was deep. She has about sixteen stitches, but she'll make a full recovery." Adam explained as Aaron and Bethany's families quickly surrounded him.

"Why did she pass out?" Lewis asked before Aaron could.

"The sound of the gun going off so close to her ear probably threw off her equilibrium. She said her ear is ringing and she can't hear out of it. Her hearing should return in a few days or so but if she has any other problems, she can see her doctor." Adam explained.

"So, she's okay?" Aaron asked.

"She's fine and asking for you." Adam smiled.

"Can I take her home?" Aaron was practically in the door before he finished his sentence.

"I'd like to keep her overnight just as a precaution, but she should be good to go in the morning." Adam turned to leave. "I'm sure I'll see you again sometime."

"Thanks, Adam." Aaron shook the doctor's hand and hurried into the room to see the love of his life.

Aaron pulled back the curtain and breathed a sigh of relief at the sight of her smile. White gauze covered her shoulder, but smears of blood still covered her arm and cheek.

Aaron spotted a cloth next to the sink and grabbed it. He poured some of the saline from an open bottle on the cloth and stepped next to her bed.

"You scared the fucking shit out of me," Aaron whispered as he gently cleaned the dried blood from her cheek.

"I can't hear on that side," Bethany spoke as if she was talking over a lot of noise.

"Shhh... you're yelling." Aaron chuckled as he stepped to the other side.

"Sorry." She blushed.

"How do you feel?" Aaron continued to clean as much blood off her neck and arm as he could without jostling her too much.

"I'm a little high, I think." She smiled.

"Adam gave you the good stuff, huh?" Aaron laughed and tossed the cloth into the sink.

"I guess, but I don't like it." Bethany furrowed her brow. "I feel like my bones are gone."

Bethany lifted her left arm and shook it in front of him. Aaron grasped her hand and pressed it against his lips.

"Was I dreaming or did Raquel Evans save my life?" Bethany tilted her head.

"She knocked Kylie out with a chair." Aaron chuckled.

"Wow. Before I went into the bathroom, I told her I'd alter her nose if she screwed with me again." Bethany snorted.

"That's my girl." Aaron bent his head and pressed his lips against her forehead.

"That's all I get after being shot." Bethany gasped.

"You'll get a lot more when you're healed, but I can give you this." Aaron brushed his lips against hers, but before he could pull back, she yanked her hand from his.

Bethany cupped the back of his head and plunged her tongue into his mouth. Aaron couldn't deny her what she wanted, at least some of it. He devoured her mouth, swirling his tongue with hers in a kiss filled with need.

"Jesus, she was just shot. Take a break." Cory's voice echoed through the room.

"Cory, you need a girlfriend." Bethany snickered when Aaron pulled back.

"I'm not going to argue with you there. Got any cute friends?" Cory winked.

"What are you doing here?" Aaron didn't mean to sound rude and cringed at the sound of his voice.

"I heard what happened. Why does all the exciting shit happen when I'm off?" Cory shook his head and sat in the chair beside the bed.

"Raquel clocked Kylie over the head with a chair." Bethany giggled. "She saved my life. Can you imagine?"

Bethany started to laugh harder, making Aaron and Cory laugh as well. It was clear the medication was having a strange effect on her, but thankfully she didn't appear to be in any pain.

"The gun…went off and I can't hear… I got a gash on my shoulder." Bethany held her stomach as she continued to laugh hysterically.

"What the hell did they give her?" Cory snickered.

"Laughing gas, I think." Aaron shook his head.

"Oh… oh my. My stomach." Bethany took a deep breath and blew it out. "I haven't laughed like that in a long time."

"I'm glad to see you're okay." Cory winked.

"What?" Bethany turned her head.

"She can't hear out of that ear right now," Aaron explained. "Cory said he's happy you're okay."

"Me too." Bethany yawned. "Am I going home now?"

"You need to stay overnight." Aaron smoothed his hand over her head.

"Probably a good idea. I don't think I could walk right now. I'm so…" Her eyes fluttered closed as she drifted off to sleep.

"Are you okay?" Cory whispered.

"I am now. Kylie didn't seem like a crazy drug lord, and I definitely wouldn't think she'd kill anyone. Especially, Jocelyn." Aaron kept his voice low.

"I only met her a handful of times, but I wouldn't suspect that either." Cory stood up. "I'm going to head home. Glad to see both of you are okay."

Aaron nodded and watched the door close behind Cory. He stared at Bethany's face, and his stomach clenched. He could have lost her earlier, and the thought was terrifying. His eyes blurred with tears and he swallowed hard at the thought of never seeing her again.

"I love you so fucking much, baby." Aaron brought her hand to his lips.

"She loves you too," Allyson whispered.

He hadn't heard Allyson or Lewis come into the room. They stood next to the bed, and the tears in their eyes probably mirrored his own.

"Mr. Donnelly, I know this is probably not the way to do this, but I want to marry her. I'd planned it thirteen years ago but … things didn't work out. I don't know how soon I'll be asking, but I want to make sure I've got your blessing. You too, Allyson." Aaron stared at Lewis and held his breath.

"I know you two have only been back together for a few weeks, but I've never seen her happier, and according to your Aunt

Cora, you two are meant to be. I only have one request, and then I'll give you my blessing." Lewis met Aaron's eyes.

"Anything." Aaron stood up but kept Bethany's hand in his.

"Keep putting that smile on her face that I see every time she sees you." Lewis held out his hand.

"I'll do everything I can to keep that smile there permanently." Aaron shook the hand of the man who would be his father-in-law.

"She's out like a light." Allyson chuckled.

"Yeah, she got some pretty heavy drugs in her right now." Aaron smiled.

"I'll go if you guys want to stay for a bit. I need to go talk to my family and let them know Bethany is okay." Aaron released Bethany's hand and placed it on the bed gently.

"I'll stay until you get back. Take your time." Lewis sat next to Bethany and Allyson sat in the chair.

Aaron spent almost thirty minutes explaining to his entire family and friends that Bethany would be fine and they could all go home. It didn't surprise him that they asked a million questions, but it was exhausting. Still, he loved every one of them because he knew they were there because they loved him and Bethany.

"As soon as da lassie is feelin' better we'll have a time." Aaron smiled because his grandmother always referred to a party as a *time.*

"Sounds great, Nan." Aaron wrapped his arm around her and kissed the top of her head.

"Come on, Tom. I'll need ta go ta da grocery store ta get some tings fer a scoff." Nanny Betty patted Aaron's cheek and linked into Tom's arm because a Newfoundland party wouldn't be complete without a ton of food.

"How are all of you still in such good shape with all the food that woman cooks?" Aaron turned around as Denise stood up.

"Denise, what are you doing here?" Aaron hugged her.

"My grandmother fell. I brought her here with my grandfather, and I ran into Cory. He told me what happened." Denise smiled. "Is she okay?"

"She's going to be fine. She has a few stitches and some temporary hearing loss, but she's alive." Aaron shoved his hands into his pockets.

"Good, give her my best. Maybe when things calm down, we can get together for supper." Denise's hopeful eyes broke his heart.

She seemed so lonely, and it was obvious her old friends were not there for her anymore. Aaron knew she'd been in a crummy situation with Raquel years earlier but people change, and he was willing to give her the benefit of the doubt.

"I'm sure she'd love that." Aaron smiled.

"I'll talk to you both soon." Denise left the waiting room, and Aaron blew out a breath.

"People change." Kristy wrapped her arm around his waist.

"Yes, they do." Aaron hugged his cousin.

"This looks good on you." Kristy grinned.

"It's full of blood." Aaron looked down at his soiled shirt.

"Not this." She swirled her finger in front of his shirt. "This." She pointed to his face.

"My face has been with me all my life." Aaron snorted.

"Oh my God, being in love, you idiot. Being in love looks good on you." Kristy slapped his chest.

"It feels pretty good too." Aaron grinned.

"That it does." Kristy glanced at Bull where he was bouncing little Decker on his lap while he chatted with Nick.

"Uncle A.J.?" Olivia tugged on his pants and Aaron crouched down in front of his three nieces.

Molly, Olivia, and Grace were all the same age and inseparable. It reminded him of Nick, Kristy, and himself when they were kids.

"Yes, Olivia?" Aaron smiled.

"Is Bethany okay?" She looked so worried.

"She's fine. She just got a little boo boo." Aaron took Olivia's hand in his.

"Did she get a Band-Aid?" Grace asked as she reached into the pocket of her dress. "I got one if she doesn't have one."

"They gave her lots of them." Aaron smiled and kissed the little girl on the head.

"Are you gonna marry her?" Molly asked.

"If she says yes when I ask her." Aaron grinned.

"Can we be flower girls like for Uncle Nick's wedding?" Olivia started to jump up and down.

"Definitely." Aaron laughed.

The three little girls ran to their mothers sitting next to each other in the waiting room. They excitedly told their mothers that they needed dresses for Aaron's wedding.

Stephanie looked up at him and smiled. She'd been with the family the longest and had been telling him when he found the love of his life, it would hit him like a ton of bricks. Of course, she didn't know he'd already met Bethany before Stephanie came into John's life, but she was right.

Chapter 31

Bethany stood outside the reception hall linked into Aaron and waving as Nick and Lora drove off with a just married banner stuck to the back of the truck.

The Hopedale Sailing club was right across the street from the beach, and with the warm July breeze blew across her face, she could smell the scent of the salty ocean. It was one of her favorite things and one of the reasons she couldn't wait for their house to get finished.

"That's a content smile." Aaron wrapped his arms around and rested his forehead against hers.

"I've never been more contented in my life." Bethany ran her hands over his chest and smoothed the lapels of his tuxedo.

"Me too." Aaron grinned and kissed the tip of her nose.

It had been three months since she'd returned to Newfoundland and although it had started out terrible, it turned into the best thing that ever happened to her. If someone had told her six months earlier that by mid-July she'd be back in Newfoundland and in the arms of the only man she'd ever loved, she would have told them they were insane.

"There's just one thing that would make me deliriously happy." Bethany tilted her head and gazed into Aaron's eyes.

"I can have us back to my place in ten minutes." Aaron grinned.

"As tempting as that sounds, I was actually talking about letting me see the progress on our house." Bethany fisted his lapels.

"You really aren't great at waiting, are you?" Aaron pulled her against him.

"No, I'm not." Bethany sighed.

"I promise you by the end of the month I'll bring you to see it. Then I'll let you decorate to your heart's content." Aaron smiled.

"All I can say is, it's a good thing you're hot." Bethany stood up on her toes and pressed her lips to his.

Aaron had told her after construction started on their house he wanted to surprise her with a few things he'd incorporated into the house. She wasn't sure what he did, but she impatiently waited.

Bethany started a job two weeks earlier with the hospital working in the pharmacy. Since she was a licensed pharmacist, they hired her from a recommendation from Craig. His sister-in-law was head of human resources and called her to offer her the position. Bethany was thrilled.

"Hey, you two, are you staying here tonight, or do you need a drive home?" Bethany turned at the sound of Crash's voice.

"I'm guessing things are dying down in there." Aaron wrapped his arm around Bethany's waist, and they walked to where Crash sat in the SUV.

"Yeah, there are only a few stragglers left," Crash replied.

"I'd like to walk back to Aaron's place, but I'm afraid my feet would hate me in the morning." Bethany looked down at the three-inch stilettos she wore.

"Why do women torture themselves with those things?" Crash looked down at her feet.

"Because they're sexy." Bethany grinned as she hopped into the vehicle.

"Good point." Crash laughed.

She'd gotten close to both Crash and Crunch over the last few months. They were great guys, and she had a feeling her sister was attracted to Crash. Bethany wouldn't push Allyson on it since she hadn't lost her husband that long ago, but who knew what could happen in the future.

"Take my beautiful lady and me back to my place, Mr. Crash." Aaron climbed in next to her and wrapped his arm around Bethany's shoulder.

"Yes, sir." Crash gave Aaron a mock salute.

Crash drove off back to the reception hall to pick up any stragglers that might be left and needed a way home. He'd apparently deemed himself the designated driver for the evening.

"Did I tell you how beautiful you looked tonight?" Aaron whispered against her ear as he wrapped his arms around her from behind.

"Mmm hmm." Bethany closed her eyes and soaked in the feel of his body pressed against her back, his arms embracing her and his lips brushing against the back of her ear.

"Did I tell you I want to rip off your dress and taste that delectable silky skin of yours?" Aaron licked slowly down the side of her neck as he moaned against her skin.

"As great as that sounds, this was an expensive dress, so maybe we can take it off without damaging it." Bethany tilted her head to the side to give him better access to her neck.

"We can do that, but maybe you should take it off for me and then I can watch how it's done." Aaron nipped her bare shoulder and growled.

Bethany pulled away from him and reached for the zipper under her arm. The strapless dress fit her like a glove, but at that moment, she was desperate to get out of it to see Aaron's eyes flame into pure desire.

"Are you going to remove your clothes too or am I going to be performing a striptease alone?" She held her hand against her chest keeping the dress in place as she slowly lowered the zipper.

"I'm liking the striptease." Aaron stalked slowly toward her, and she backed away until they were inside the bedroom.

"You know you'd make a great male stripper. You have great moves on the dance floor and that body, mmmm..." Bethany grinned as she let her dress fall to the floor.

She was wearing a peach strapless bra that pushed her breasts up and a matching pair of lace panties. She could tell when Aaron bit his lip that standing there in nothing but her underwear and stilettos that he enjoyed the outfit.

"You're trying to fucking kill me." Aaron stepped toward her, but she maneuvered away from him.

"No way, sexy. I want all those clothes off." Bethany sat on the foot of the bed and crossed her legs.

"You want a striptease, baby?" Aaron reached behind him and tapped the iPod behind him on the dresser.

"Show me what you got," Bethany smirked.

Aaron scrolled through the music and Bethany waited until he picked what he deemed to be the perfect song. He turned and grinned as he tapped the screen.

"Let's get it on." Aaron wiggled his eyebrows as that exact song played softly, and he gave her a strip show that would make Magic Mike look amateur.

Chapter 32

Aaron was about to lose his mind completely. He'd asked Allyson to find the engagement ring that he'd bought when he won the bet, but she'd searched Bethany's old room and couldn't find it. Aaron managed to check the things Bethany had left at the bunkhouse and even searched the safe house. Nothing.

He planned to propose to her and give her the ring along with a second ring he got for her earlier that week. The second ring was a gold infinity ring with a diamond in the center of the loop. Aaron wanted her to know that his love was forever.

"A.J., I've searched everywhere. I can't find it." Allyson sighed into the phone.

"I know she took it with her the day your house was shot up, but that was the last time I saw her with it." Aaron sat back in his chair and stared out through the door of his office.

"I'm sorry, but I'm sure she has it somewhere. She'll still be ecstatic when you propose even if you can't find the ring," Allyson assured him.

"Maybe she'll tell me after I propose." Aaron snorted.

"Probably." Allyson laughed. "So, I just left the house, and Kristy has all the lights set up down the stairway to the beach. Isabelle had the wine and glasses set up on the back deck when I left."

"I don't know what I'd do without you guys. I'm picking her up at work at seven. I told her we were going to dinner and she took an outfit with her to change into." Aaron's heart pounded in his chest as he fixed his tie.

"Do you have the blindfold?" Allyson asked.

"Yeah, Kristy said it was the same one Bull used when he proposed. Might be good luck." Aaron laughed.

"I bet I'll hear her say yes all the way from the beach to our house." Allyson chuckled.

Aaron certainly hoped so.

The late August breeze blew across his face as he opened the car door for her to get in. Aaron smiled as she narrowed her eyes when he handed her the blindfold.

"What kind of kink are you trying to get me into?" Bethany picked up the black mask and shook it in front of him.

"I just want you to be surprised when you see the house for the first time." Aaron sort of told the truth.

"I don't like not being able to see where I'm going." Bethany sighed.

"Do you think I would let you fall?" Aaron laughed.

"No but... argh," she grumbled.

"Trust me, okay?" Aaron reached across the seat and grasped her hand in his.

"I do." Bethany smiled, and Aaron prayed she was ready to say those two words at the altar.

Before Aaron pulled into the long driveway leading to their new house, he helped her with the blindfold. She whined for a moment and then held his hand as he slowly pulled in front of their new home.

It took three months for his brother's crew to rebuild the house. The only things not finished were the three extra bedrooms. Aaron figured they could finish them after they'd moved in and decided to have a family.

It was a two-story with a covered front and back porch. A white railing closed in the front porch, but the back one was left open to enjoy the view of the ocean. The house was about ten feet up on a hill, and they'd built a staircase leading down to the private area where he and Bethany would go to be alone as teenagers.

The landscape of the backyard had only been finished the day before. Aaron had two flower beds placed in front of the house on both sides of the steps because she wanted to do it but thought she would have to wait until next summer.

"Aaron, if I fall, I'm going to smack you." Bethany clung to his arm as if she would fall over a cliff if he let her go.

"Then I don't have to worry because I'll never let you fall." Aaron kissed the side of her head as they stopped in front of the house.

Aaron removed the blindfold and smiled at Bethany's gasp. He had to admit the sight of the sun setting behind the house and shining through the windows, making the house look like it was lit up, looked breathtaking.

"Aaron, it looks amazing." Bethany slowly stepped toward the steps. "Oh my, look at the flowers."

Aaron grinned as she crouched to touch them. He held out his hand as he stepped beside her. She placed her hand in his, and they walked up the steps and walked into the house.

"I can't believe it's done." Bethany slowly spun inside the large living room and continued into the rest of the lower level.

She stopped at the patio door and stared out on the back porch. She seemed confused at first and then slid the door open.

"Is that a staircase?" Bethany pointed to where the soft lights were glowing on the railing of the top step.

"Yes, it is." Aaron walked down the steps and held out his hand to her again. "I want to show you something."

Bethany didn't hesitate as she grasped his hand and walked with him down the steps to the beach. Her smile was huge as she saw the bench placed on the beach.

"You did this?" She grinned and ran her hand across the back of the bench.

"I had lots of help." Aaron walked around to the front of the bench and motioned for her to join him.

She sat down and gazed out at the ocean. The look of contentment on her face made his heart swell with pride. It had always been a place for him to get his thoughts together and it was obvious it did the same thing for her.

"Bethany, this spot has always reminded me of you. Even when I didn't want it to but whenever I felt like I was lost or needed to get my head on straight, which was a lot, I'd come here and sit on the beach." Aaron stood up and turned to face her.

"We spent a lot of time here in high school." She smiled and started to stand with him.

"Stay there." Aaron bent over and kissed her cheek then turned and went to the spot where he'd asked Kristy to place what he needed.

When he'd retrieved them, he returned and stood in front of her. He handed her a square box wrapped in purple ribbon. Bethany raised an eyebrow and glanced up at him as she tentatively accepted the gift.

"It's a gift for our new home and something I want to attach to this bench." Aaron tried to keep his face expressionless.

"Okay?" Bethany slowly tugged on the ribbon and opened the box slowly.

She stared at the contents for a few minutes before she looked up at him. Bethany glanced down at it again, and when she finally looked at him, Aaron was down on his knee.

"Aaron." Bethany covered her mouth with her hands.

"Bethany, thirteen years ago I wanted to do this exact thing, right here in this spot. It didn't happen, and that was probably for the best because thinking back, I don't know if either of us would have been ready for what getting married meant. Right now, I know I'm more than ready, and I don't want to spend another day without you in my life." Aaron swallowed as he tried to keep the tears in his eyes from falling. "I've loved you since I was eighteen years old. No matter how much I tried to forget you, I never could, and the reason is that we're meant to be together. You're my heart, my soul, my life and nothing would make me happier than to have you as my wife. Bethany, will you marry me?"

Aaron opened the black box he'd had in his hand and held it out to her. Bethany didn't look at the ring; she just stared at him, nodding her head with tears streaming down her cheeks.

"I'm hoping the nodding means yes." Aaron smiled as he took her left hand and slipped the ring on her finger.

"Yes, hell yes. I'll marry you." Bethany wrapped her arms around his neck.

Aaron stood up and pulled her into his arms. He covered her mouth with his and kissed her with everything he had. A loud cheer from above made both of them turn around and look up at their family and friends at the top of the steps.

"I love these nameplates." Bethany giggled as she pointed to the box sat on the bench.

"Me too, do you like the ring?" Aaron smiled.

"Of course, I loved it the first time I saw it." Bethany glanced down at her hand and then back up to him. "That's not the ring."

"No, I wanted to give you both, but we couldn't find where you put it." Aaron smiled.

"Aaron, give me your wallet." Bethany held out her hand.

"Why?" Aaron slipped his wallet out of his back pocket and handed it to her.

Bethany unsnapped the small coin pouch and reached inside. She pulled out the ring and held it up in front of him. Aaron stared at it for a few minutes before looking back at her.

"I put it in your wallet the first night at the safe house. You left it on the counter. I thought I'd told you." Bethany giggled.

"I've been carrying the damn thing around all this time." Aaron laughed.

"I love this new ring, but I love this one too. I want this to be my wedding ring." Bethany put it into his hand and closed his fist.

"Whatever you want, baby." Aaron pulled her against him and kissed her hard.

"Come on, we want to party." Mike shouted from the top of the hill and Aaron glared at him.

"Oh, and we're planning your bachelor party." John wiggled his eyebrows.

"I'm fucking dead." Aaron groaned.

"Should I tell them that you are a great stripper?" Bethany winked.

"I'm sure my brothers would appreciate me stripping at my bachelor party." Aaron laughed as they made their way up the steps to be swarmed by his amazing family.

Chapter 33

Aaron stood at the mirror and stared at himself. He was about to marry the love of his life. He listened to the idle chatter of his groomsmen standing around the room waiting for the time to head out to the altar.

All his brothers would be by his side like he had for them. Next, to his father and uncles, the six men stood around the room were the men he looked up to the most.

"Nervous, little brother?" John reached around Aaron from behind and fixed the twisted bow tie Aaron struggled to tie.

"Not even a little." Aaron grinned.

"Can you believe after today, we'll all be old married men?" Mike sat in an armchair in the corner of the room with his ankle resting on his knee.

"Speak for yourself. I'm not old." Nick kicked Mike's foot off his knee.

"Yeah, I'm not old, just ask my wife." Keith wiggled his eyebrows.

"We don't need to ask Ian's wife. Sandy lets us all know about their sex life." James nudged Ian's shoulder.

"I love every minute of it. Why do you think I work out? I need to keep up with her." Ian chuckled.

The door to the sacristy opened, and his father walked in and closed the door behind him. He stood and glanced around the room and Aaron didn't need to look at his brothers to know they all wore similar smiles.

"I know your mother will kill me for doing this, but no O'Connor man gets married without a shot of Screech." His dad pulled a flask out of his pocket and eight shot glasses out of the other.

"How did Mom not see that bulge in your pocket?" James laughed.

"She probably thought it was something else." His father wiggled his eyebrows.

"Then Mom wonders where we get the dirty minds." Nick snickered.

His father placed all the glasses on the small table and poured equal amounts into each glass. He handed one to Aaron and then each of his brothers, picking up the last one for himself. Before he could say anything, the door opened again, and Kurt stepped in.

"Sean, you don't have a shot without me." Kurt pulled a glass out of his pocket.

Aaron and his brothers laughed as his dad rolled his eyes and filled Kurt's glass. It was an O'Connor tradition, and Aaron had expected it.

"My father started this the day I got married and we continued it with Kurt, John, James, Ian, Keith, Mike, Nick, and now A.J. I've always been proud of every one of you and watching you take that next step in each of your lives is the best thing I've ever seen. The beautiful ladies you've married, or are about to marry in A.J.'s case, are some of the strongest women I've known. They'd have to be to deal with an O'Connor, but I see the look in your eyes when you look at them, and it's the same look I have when I see your mother. It's love, and it's forever. There's an old Irish Blessing you all know well so let's say it together." His father held up his glass

Aaron, his brothers, and Kurt held theirs up as well, and as if it was a prayer to God they repeated the phrase that they'd heard all their lives.

"May joy and peace surround you, contentment latch your door, and happiness be with you now and bless you evermore. Cheers." Aaron recited together with everyone.

Aaron slammed back the shot and winced as the burning liquid of the Newfoundland rum slipped down his throat. He didn't drink it very often, but his grandfather used to say a shot of Screech was good for what ails you.

"Are you ready, A.J.?" Nick wrapped his arm around Aaron's shoulder.

"More than ready." Aaron grinned.

"Jesus, I never thought I'd see the day Aaron Jacob O'Connor would be happy to be tied down to one woman." Mike laughed.

"We thought that about you once too." John shoved Mike playfully.

"Let's get you married." James winked as they made their way out of the sacristy and filed in at the front of the altar.

Allyson fixed Bethany's veil as they waited for the knock that it was time to go. The large bride room was filled with her six bridesmaids and three flower girls.

Bethany chose her sister to be her matron of honor for obvious reasons but mostly because her sister was her best friend. Aaron's three nieces Olivia, Molly, and Grace wore dresses similar to her own and were utterly adorable. She'd chosen Kristy, Jess, Sandy, Emily, and Lora to be her bridesmaids although she'd wanted to have all of Aaron's sisters-in-law and cousins, he'd asked her to keep it to six. Although, she did convince him to include many of his older and younger nieces and nephews.

Alexander and Colin were excited to be ring bearers. Cameron, Danny, and Mason were proud to be junior ushers, and Evie and Lily were thrilled to be junior bridesmaids. Bethany also asked Billie's niece, Chloe. The young girl spent a lot of time with Aaron's older nieces. Chloe was Matt's daughter and had been born deaf, and Bethany was amazed every time she watched Aaron's older nieces and nephews speak fluently in sign language.

"You look really pretty." Grace stared up at Bethany.

"Thank you, Gracie. You look very beautiful too." Bethany crouched down in front of the little girl.

"I know." She sighed.

Bethany burst out laughing, and Grace looked at her as if she was crazy. She hoped Grace continued in life with the confidence she had in herself. It would take her a long way, and she wouldn't have to struggle with self-doubt the way Bethany did in her teen years.

The door to the bride room opened, and her father stepped through looking very handsome in his tuxedo. He had a smile that lit up his face, but it didn't hide the tears in his eyes.

"Ladies, they want you to line up next to the entrance." Her father held open the door for her attendants to leave.

"We'll see you outside." Allyson kissed her cheek and left Bethany alone with her dad.

"You're stunning." Her father folded his hands in front of him and stared at her.

"Thanks, Dad." Bethany took a deep breath and tried to calm her beating heart.

She wasn't nervous about marrying Aaron, she was excited and couldn't wait to see him. They'd been apart for a full day, and she missed him like crazy.

"You're sure you want to marry that punk out there?" The serious look on her father's face made her heart plummet.

"Dad, I love him, and I thought you liked Aaron." Bethany was about to burst into tears.

"I'm kidding, honey." Her father laughed and pulled her into his arms.

"Okay, that was so not funny." She breathed but giggled as he kissed the top of her head.

"I wanted to know you were sure about this." He gazed down at her with a broad smile that took years off his handsome face.

"I've never been more sure of anything. I know I've denied it for years, but I've always loved him. We were meant to be together." Bethany smiled at her dad.

"Cora has mentioned that once or twice." Her dad chuckled.

There was a light knock on the door, and Bethany turned to pull her veil down over her face. She picked up her flowers and linked into her father's arm as she walked toward her future.

Epilogue

Jess dropped down on her bed and sighed. She'd worked four twelve-hour shifts straight, and she was ready to fall into her comfy bed and sleep for twelve hours.

It was the first day of her two-week holidays, and she was about to enjoy them. After she slept, of course. She stripped off and climbed into her bed, letting out a huge sigh.

She closed her eyes and snuggled into her pillow. Jess was dozing off when her telephone buzzed on her nightstand. Wanting to ignore it but knowing she'd never sleep if she did, she sat up and snatched it off the nightstand.

Isabelle's number appeared on the screen, and Jess groaned as she tapped the screen. Her sister was in need of another chef for her restaurant, but she kept putting it off. Her sister had trust issues with letting anyone take over the kitchen at her fine dining business. The last one had left, and it had taken her almost two years to hire him finally.

"Hello," Jess answered and lay back on the bed.

"I'm going to do it." Isabelle groaned.

"Do what?" Jess closed her eyes and lay her arm across her eyes.

"Hire Lora's friend. Well, her brother's friend but I'm going to hire him. He's coming by today, and I'm trying hard not to be negative because his references are amazing and Lora says he's a great guy but ..." Isabelle rambled.

"But you have control issues and hate to give anyone else the reins." Jess cut off her sister with a snicker.

"I do not... okay, maybe I do, but this is my baby. I worked hard to get the reputation I have, and I don't want to screw it up." Isabelle sighed.

"Do you trust Lora?" Jess asked.

"Yes," Isabelle responded.

"Do you trust the references?" Jess knew the only way to make her sister calm was to get her to have confidence in her decision.

"Yes, he's worked at several great places, and I know two of the managers very well," Isabelle returned.

"It's been over two years since Lora told you about this guy and you've been busting your ass trying to keep up with how busy the place is. If you don't get help, your business is going to suffer because you'll be too exhausted to make sure things get done right." Jess yawned.

"How am I the oldest and you give the best advice?" Isabelle chuckled.

"Because I've always been the smartest." Jess laughed.

"Bitch." Isabelle snorted

"Yep, now I'm going to sleep, or I will be a bitch." Jess turned on her side and ended the call before her sister could respond.

Before she put her phone down, it vibrated in her hand. She cursed and glanced at the screen. Pam sent her a text that she needed to come by right away.

"Are you fucking kidding me?" Jess growled and called Pam.

"I'm out by your door. Come let me in." was the way her cousin answered the phone.

"Fine," Jess tossed her phone on the bed and scuffed out of her room to the front door of her loft apartment.

"I need a place to stay for a few days." Pam looked completely panicked.

"What's wrong?" Jess lost all her exhaustion at the sight of her cousin's expression.

"Mom." Pam plopped down on the couch.

"What's Aunt Cora done?" Jess sat next to her cousin.

"She keeps inviting Damon to the house for supper and not telling me." Pam pouted.

"What is it about that guy you dislike and why does he call you Trixie?" Nobody had been able to get the information out of Pam or Damon since he'd come to town more than a year earlier.

"I don't want to talk about him. I need a place to stay until the apartment over my store is ready." Pam turned to Jess and put her hands together as if she was praying.

"You'll have to sleep on the couch. I only have one bed, and I remember sleeping with you in a bed when we were kids. You kick. A lot." Jess shoved her cousin.

"Thank you, thank you." Pam hugged her tightly.

"But you're going to have to deal with whatever crap is going on with that guy and to be honest, why the hell would you not want to jump him. He's freaking hot." Jess laughed.

"Not talking about it." Pam sighed.

"Fine. How's the store going?" Jess stood up and stretched.

Pam had recently opened a clothing boutique. She'd designed all the clothes in the store as well as the purses, belts, and scarves. Pam was very talented, and it was the reason she'd gone away in the first place. She'd done well for herself because she'd bought a piece of land next to Emily's beauty salon and built a cute little store. It was opened on October first, and she'd named it Cupid's Closet.

Her mother was elated when Pam named the store after Cora. Pam had a place in the back of her store for creating her clothing and had an apartment for herself put over the shop.

"Now, as much as I love you, I need to get some sleep." Jess waved to her cousin as she made her way into her bedroom and flopped down on her bed.

The only thing she had to worry about now was sleeping and in the morning picking up her car from the garage where Aaron had brought it after it broke down. Again.

Jess woke to the phone ringing again, and she wanted to toss it through the window, but when she opened her eyes, she realized it was morning and later than she intended to sleep.

"Shit." She jumped out of bed and picked up her phone.

"It's about fucking time you answered," Aaron grumbled.

"Sorry, I must have died last night. I'll be ready in five minutes." Jess tossed her phone on the bed.

Aaron was taking her to get her car, and she'd told him she would be ready at nine in the morning. It was now after ten. Jess pulled on a pair of jeans, a t-shirt and pulled her hair back into a ponytail. After she shoved on her sneakers, she grabbed her keys and headed out the door, almost tripping over her own feet as she ran down the steps from her apartment over her parent's garage.

"Sorry," Jess huffed as she got into Aaron's car.

"Late night?" Aaron chuckled.

"No, just four long shifts, a sister that is in panic mode and a cousin who is running away from her problems." Jess snorted.

"Sounds fun." Aaron drove onto the highway.

"How's married life?" Jess poked him.

"Incredibly satisfying." Aaron wiggled his eyebrows and Jess made a gagging sound as Aaron pulled into *Wade's Auto Service.*

"I don't take my car to this place." She sighed because the place was not cheap.

"Which is why the fucking thing was falling apart." Aaron motioned for her to follow him.

"This place costs a small fortune." Jess groaned

"This is the same guy that fixes the department's vehicles, and I wouldn't trust my car to anyone but Wade." Aaron opened the door for her to go ahead of him. "Come on; I'll introduce you."

Jess reluctantly stepped inside and the reception area. A man behind the counter handed a set of keys to a woman who looked like she just walked off an issue of *Cosmopolitan.* Jess glanced down at her jeans and wanted the floor to open up and swallow her.

"Run for the hills, the cops are here." The man behind the counter held up his hands as Aaron approached him.

"You couldn't run the length of yourself, Kennedy." Aaron held out his hand to the grinning man.

"Remember who beat your ass in basketball last week." He poked Aaron in the shoulder.

"Only because you cheated, you fucker." Aaron gave the man a playful shove.

"That's real nice language to be using in front of this beautiful lady." The man winked at Jess as he rested his large arms on the counter.

Aaron glanced at her. Her cousin was sure to see the annoyance at the blatant flirtation. She wasn't the typical girlie girl. None of the sisters were, and even Pam could be a bit of a tomboy.

"How the hell do you always end up with the hot women?" Everett glanced at Aaron then his eyes moved back to Jess.

"Gross." Jess gagged.

"Kennedy, you're a fucking idiot. This is my cousin Jess O'Connor. Jess, this dick is Everett Kennedy. By the way, I'm a married man now." Aaron laughed.

"She obviously got all the looks in the family, and I know a guy who sells seeing eye dogs because the only way a woman would marry someone with a face like yours O'Connor is if she was blind." Everett stepped back as Aaron made a swing at him.

"My wife is not blind, but she's damn hot, and Jess is Uncle Kurt's daughter." Aaron grinned.

"Rivers, the cops are out here," Everett shouted through the opening behind him as he held up his hands.

"Chicken shit." Aaron chuckled.

"I'll see you this weekend at practice." Everett disappeared into the back of the garage.

"Well, he's interesting." Jess stepped next to Aaron.

"He's a good egg." Aaron nudged her with his hip.

"I don't know if I can afford this place, A.J.," Jess whispered as she looked around the pristine place.

It wasn't that she didn't have any money saved if she really needed it for her car, but she saved every cent she made from her job and her flower shop, so she could buy her own house. It was also the only reason she hadn't bought a new car because she wanted to get out of her parents' garage.

"Trust me. Wade's a good guy, and you work for N.P.D. which means he'll give you a good price." Aaron rested his elbows on the counter and mirrored his stance.

It took a few minutes before she heard heavy footsteps behind her. From the sound of the steps, the person walked with a limp. Jess turned around just as a gorgeous man appeared.

"Hey, Wade." Aaron held out his hand to the large man.

"A.J., what brings you to this neck of the woods?" Wade asked, but his eyes kept flicking back and forth between Jess and Aaron.

He was tall. Probably about the same height as Bull or even a little taller. His hair was thick and dark, and her fingers suddenly itched to run through it to see if it was a soft as it looked. Long dark eyelashes surrounded hazel eyes, and all she could think was how women would kill for lashes like his. His face showed at least a two-day growth of facial hair that only made him look that much sexier.

"Jess, are you okay?" Aaron poked her, making her jump.

"What? Yeah." Jess glanced behind her and then back to her cousin.

"I need to know if you can fix a vehicle for me," Aaron said to the man.

"I told you those Chargers were shit." Wade grinned as he wiped his hands with a rag.

"Not my car, fucker. My cousin Jess has a piece of shit that broke down yesterday, and I got it towed here." Aaron winced when she elbowed him in the ribs.

"My car is not a piece of shit," Jess grumbled.

"I see by the key it's a Honda." Wade raised an eyebrow, and the corner of his mouth twitched.

"Yeah, so?" Jess turned and looked up at Wade.

"I'm afraid I'll have to agree with A.J. on the car being a piece of shit." Wade chuckled.

"Hmm, and here I thought A.J. brought me to a place where they knew how to fix vehicles, but I guess not." Jess turned and started to walk out. "Come on, cuz. I'm pretty sure that place down the street knows how to fix my car."

"She's Kurt's daughter, isn't she?" Wade laughed.

"One of three and the one that can kick your fucking ass." Aaron snickered.

"I don't doubt it, and she's got her father's attitude." Wade tapped his hand against the thigh of his left leg.

"I'm still here, you know." Jess turned around and fisted her hands on her hips.

"I'm well aware you're here." Wade's voice rumbled and her stomach clenched.

Jess was pissed because she hated when anyone insulted her car but the heat in her cheeks had to be visible and she narrowed her eyes when she saw Aaron smirk out of the corner of her eyes.

"When you're able to stop hitting on my cousin, could you go have a look at her car and find out what the hell is wrong with it now?" Aaron waved his hand in front of Wade's face, and the man shook his head as if he was hypnotized.

"I don't hit on women. Especially when I know I wouldn't have a snowball's chance in hell. Maybe if I had a pretty boy face like you and your brothers, instead of this ugly mug." Wade winked at Jess as he disappeared into the small office off the reception area.

"Is that guy serious?" Jess said as she followed Aaron.

"About what?" Aaron asked.

"Ugly mug? That man is far from ugly," Jess whispered.

"You want a date, cuz?" She knew he was teasing her.

"You'll get the hard part of my knee in your favorite appendage if you open that big mouth, A.J." Jess narrowed her eyes at him, and he crossed his legs, making her laugh.

"You'll never get a date with that attitude." Aaron cringed.

"I get dates when I want them." Jess punched his arm.

"That's good to know." Wade appeared at the counter again, and she saw Aaron press his lips together to keep from laughing at her gasp of embarrassment.

"Yeah, I'll be outside." Jess turned and practically ran out of the building.

"Jesus, Wade. You always scare them away like that?" She heard Aaron laugh at Everett as she pushed through the door.

"Just go pull the fucking car inside," Wade shouted as Everett followed Jess outside.

Jess sat shooting daggers at Aaron with her glare as he sauntered toward her. The bastard smiled at her probably because she didn't usually get so flustered around men. There was just something about Wade Rivers that had her heart pounding and her body aching with need. Something that drew her to him and she so didn't need that right now.

About the Author

What does someone say to describe themselves? You could start with giving what others say about you. Scratch that. It doesn't really matter what others think about you. It matters what you think of yourself. So here we go.

First of all, I'm a wife and mother. I'm also a grandmother. That alone would fulfil any woman's life and to be honest it does. But.....

I'm also a writer. Someone who loves to tell stories of love, suspense, heartache and of course happily ever after. For most of my life, I've written those stories for myself. A type of therapy, I suppose. I love the characters I create. They become part of who I am because there's part of me in them.

So.... Now that you know this about me. I hope when you read my books, you fall in love with them.

You should also know that I'm a Newfoundlander. What is that you ask? Well we're a proud people who live on an island, off the east coast of Canada. Some people believe Canada ends with Nova Scotia. It doesn't. If you keep going east, there is a beautiful island full of amazing people and magnificent scenery. That is where my stories are set because let's face it. The best stories always come from the places you know and love.

If there is anything else you would like to know about me. Ask me!

Coming in 2019

O'Connor Girls

Book 2 – Hidden Enemy

Book 3 – Hidden Menace

Book 4 – Hidden Target

O'Connor Brother Series

Read about the sexy O'Connor Brothers

In Books 1, 2, 3, 4, 5 & 6

Available on

Amazon and

Kindle Unlimited.

Also Available

Dangerous Therapy

Book 1

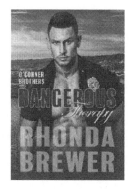

Officer John O'Connor is giving up on life after a terrible accident. His family are at their wits end when he refuses any kind of therapy. The only thing keeping him sane is his dreams of a beautiful woman he pulled in for a traffic violation months before.

Physical Therapist Stephanie Kelly is healing from a broken heart. When she is hired by Nightingale's personal care and physical therapy, she's ecstatic, but she's shocked when her boss asks her to take on a new patient. Shocked because the patient is her boss's nephew and he's not exactly keen on therapy. He's also the cop who's been heating up her dreams.

As Stephanie helps John get back on his feet, they grow closer, but someone is out to hurt Stephanie, or worse. After multiple attempts on her life, John's family tries to figure out who's after the woman he loves and stop them before it's too late.

Dangerous Abduction

Book 2

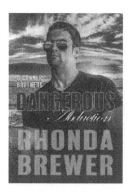

Widower James O'Connor has been fighting his growing attraction to his brother's sister-in-law for four long years, but when someone breaks into her home, destroying everything she owns, James takes her and her young son into his home. The break-in wasn't random. Marina and her son are in danger, and James swears to protect them, but can he keep them safe?

Marina Kelly dedicates her life to caring for her sweet little boy, Danny. Since she broke free from her abusive husband, she's sworn off men, but when James O'Connor keeps entering her thoughts and her dreams, it takes everything she has to keep her feelings hidden. Now, her sister and parents are out of the province, and she's in danger, Marina has no choice but to accept James's help and try to hide her attraction and growing feelings.

The attraction between them impossible to resist. Only her ex's family secret may tear it all apart. Can Marina and James unravel the family's hidden mystery without losing each other?

Dangerous Secrets

Book 3

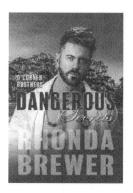

Ian O'Connor has everything going for him. He's got the O'Connor drop dead good looks, an incredible body and to top it off he's a doctor. Why wouldn't anyone want the man but none of that was the reason Sandy Churchill was head over heels in love with the man. After he had stood her up for their first official date, she was weary of taking another chance. When she ends up in the hospital because she turned her back on a criminal determined to get away from her, Ian admits that he loves her and wants another chance. A secret from his past throws Sandy into a tailspin, but she has a secret that she's hiding from everyone.

Ian's on cloud nine when he finally takes a leap of faith and tells the woman he's loved for four years how he feels and wants a chance to make up for his screw up. They have two weeks of bliss, but a murder and secrets come back to haunt him. Sandy's reaction tells him there's another reason why she's avoiding him. She's hiding something, but he has no idea what and to make matters worse there's danger coming from her past that could hurt the people he loves the most.

Dangerous Beauty

Book 4

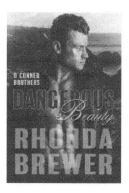

When you come from a privileged family, you're expected to follow a particular path in life. Unless you're Emily Bradshaw. Defying her father, Emily turned down a full scholarship to Dalhousie University. Instead, she followed her dream and opened her own salon in the small town of Hopedale with her friend. She's happy. Then her mother vanishes. Her father receives threatening messages and hires Newfoundland Security Services to protect his children. Emily doesn't like the idea, especially when the man that walks into her salon dressed in a black leather jacket makes her weak in the knees. Emily knows she's in danger but not the kind her father is worried about.

Keith O'Connor isn't expecting his newest security job to be anything out of the ordinary. Then he walks into Snippy Gals, a beauty salon in Hopedale. Keith gets the shock of his life when an auburn haired beauty turns to face him. Emily is defiant, sassy, and her sexy curves have him in a complete spin. Fighting his feelings for her becomes almost impossible, but when Emily's mother is found, a family secret is revealed turning Emily's life upside down. Can Keith help her cope and keep her out of the clutches of a vengeful stranger?

Dangerous Silence

Book 5

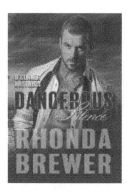

Mike O'Connor's reputation earned him the name Mr. Homerun, but after two hours with Billie, he's ready to change all that. There's one problem. She disappears before he can find out her last name.

Billie Carter had little choice but to leave when she received a desperate text from her friend. Peggy and her daughter have no family, both are deaf, and Billie wants to protect them from an abusive man.

When Peggy is brutally murdered, Billie is determined to protect Chloe. Like a dream come true, Mike walks through her door to help. They soon learn that the little girl is not the only one in danger, and it may take more than Mike to keep them safe.

Dangerous Delusion

Book 6

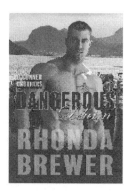

Lora Norris quits a great job and moved to Hopedale to escape an unknown stalker. Little did she know that finding employment at Jack's Place would lead her to some of the best friends she would ever have. Of course, there is also one man she wanted to be a lot more than a friend, but can't take a chance and put him in danger.

Nick O'Connor never thought the pretty waitress working at his Aunt's diner would give him a second glance. Especially with his playboy reputation. She's friendly toward him but doesn't seem the least bit interested.

When women show up dead and bearing a striking resemblance to Lora, Nick and his family do everything to protect her and her little girl. As they admit their feelings for each other, the danger moves closer than they even realize.

O'Connor Girls

Book 1

Available on

Amazon and

Kindle Unlimited

Hidden Betrayal

Book 1

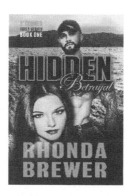

Kristy O'Connor never hid the fact that she wanted Dean 'Bull' Nash. He's kept her at arm's length since they met but he's pushed her away for the last time.

Dean loves Kristy more than he could ever tell her. He wants her desperately, but his family secrets could destroy them both.

When he can't stay away from her any longer, murder and a shocking betrayal shake them to their core. Can their new relationship survive?

Rhonda Brewer

Keep up to date on all things new.

Follow me on

Facebook

Twitter

Instagram

Sign up for my newsletter and never miss another release!